Here's what critics are saying about
The High Heels Mysteries:

"A saucy combination of romance and suspense that is simply irresistible."
—*Chicago Tribune*

"Stylish…nonstop action…guaranteed to keep chick lit and mystery fans happy!"
—*Publishers' Weekly*, starred review

"Smart, funny and snappy…the perfect beach read!"
—*Fresh Fiction*

"The High Heels Series is amongst one of the best mystery series currently in publication. If you have not read these books, then you are really missing out on a fantastic experience, chock full of nail-biting adventure, plenty of hi-jinks, and hot, sizzling romance. Can it get any better than that?"
—*Romance Reviews Today*

"(A) breezy, fast-paced style, interesting characters and story meant for the keeper shelf. 4 ½!"
—*RT Book Reviews*

"Maddie Springer is like a cross between Paris Hilton and Stephanie Plum, only better. This is one HIGH HEEL you'll want to try on again and again."
—*Romance Junkies*

BOOKS BY GEMMA HALLIDAY

Anna Smith & Nick Dade Thrillers
Play Dead

Marty Hudson Mysteries
Sherlock Homes and the Case of the Brash Blonde

High Heels Mysteries
Spying in High Heels
Killer in High Heels
Undercover in High Heels
Christmas in High Heels
(short story)
Alibi in High Heels
Mayhem in High Heels
Honeymoon in High Heels
(short story)
Sweetheart in High Heels
(short story)
Fearless in High Heels
Danger in High Heels
Homicide in High Heels
Deadly in High Heels
Suspect in High Heels

Tahoe Tessie Mysteries
Luck Be A Lady
Hey Big Spender
Baby It's Cold Outside
(holiday short story)

Hollywood Headlines Mysteries
Hollywood Scandals
Hollywood Secrets
Hollywood Confessions
Hollywood Holiday
(short story)
Hollywood Deception
Hollywood Homicide

Jamie Bond Mysteries
Unbreakable Bond
Secret Bond
Bond Bombshell
(short story)
Lethal Bond
Bond Ambition (short story)

Young Adult Books
Deadly Cool
Social Suicide

Other Works
Viva Las Vegas
A High Heels Haunting
Watching You (short story)
Confessions of a Bombshell
Bandit (short story)

HOMICIDE IN HIGH HEELS

a High Heels Mystery

GEMMA HALLIDAY

For Gemma's Gems. I love you ladies!

CHAPTER ONE

——

Babies are rough on romance. Have you ever tried to seduce a man while wearing spit-up, mashed sweet potatoes, and a fine dusting of baby powder? It gives sexy a whole new meaning. Which is why, after almost a year of being the parents of twin babies—Olivia and Max—my husband and I realized that if we were ever going to have an adult conversation again, we had to make some "us" time. Twice a month we vowed to leave the twins with my mom and spend an entire day together, just the two of us.

At first it was like we were prisoners on furlough from our teeny-tiny wardens, giddy with the freedom. We found no shortage of adult activities to engage in. Dinner at a restaurant with actual cloth napkins. Movies that didn't involve animation or talking animals. Wine tastings where not a soul under twenty-one was in sight. But once we'd exhausted the options of alcoholic outings and R-rated movies, my husband and I realized that we had a distinct conflict of interests.

My husband, Jack Ramirez, is an LAPD homicide detective with a big gun, a big tattoo of a panther on his left bicep, and a big scar running through his left eyebrow from an altercation with a perp. Other alpha males look girly next to him. I, on the other hand, am a 5' 1 ½" blonde who designs high heeled shoes for a living and am never, under any circumstances, without a tube of Raspberry Perfection lip gloss somewhere on my person. When someone calls me girly, I take it as a compliment.

But you can see where our interests might not always coincide.

So instead of trying in vain to find things that we both enjoyed doing, we decided that we would trade off picking our "us" outings. Two weeks ago we spent our "us" day shopping—

starting at the Farmer's Market on 3rd street and ending at the Beverly Center. (Which I suspect that Ramirez secretly enjoyed when he realized the mall had a Ferrari Store.) Today we were at the L.A. Stars baseball game, courtesy of two tickets my step-father had scored for me at the last minute from one of his semi-celebrity clients who was dating a player.

And if the frozen margaritas continued flowing, I might admit that a baseball game wasn't altogether bad.

"So, why is the thrower tossing the ball so far away from the guy with the bat?" I asked, slipping a straw into my mouth as I squinted down at the action, several tiers of bleachers below us.

"The *pitcher*," Ramirez responded, "is throwing outside the *batter*'s strike zone in order to walk him."

"Huh. And why do they want him to take a walk?"

"It's a higher percentage play. They're putting a man on first in order to get the opposing pitcher at the plate."

"Ah," I responded, nodding. "And why do they want that?"

"Because he can't hit if his life depends on it. We have a better chance of striking him out, which we need to do with their man on third in scoring position."

"Right. He's about to score a touch down."

Ramirez turned to me and grinned. "Score a *run*. Wrong sport, babe."

"Hey, I had a sport."

"True. You get points for that," he agreed.

"Thank you," I said, grinning back as I sipped contentedly. The truth was, all I knew about baseball was that on the reality show *Baseball Wives*, the players looked hot shirtless, the wives were deliciously catty to one another, and the drama peaked whenever the team was on the road.

The higher percentage play must have worked, because the crowd cheered, my husband included, and some guys moved around the bases. Two more hitters later, the inning ended with our rivals, the Oakland A's, not scoring a *run*. Our team mascots ran out onto the field: a Charlie Chaplin and Marilyn Monroe with huge, oversized heads that looked like they might topple at any second. They danced around, threw some T-shirts into the crowd, then waddled back to the dugout as the A's took the field and our team came up to bat.

The announcers called the name of our first player over the loudspeaker, and the crowd went nuts.

"Number twenty-four, Bucky Davis!"

I'll admit, I leaned forward in my seat to get a better look. Even a sports-illiterate gal like me knew Bucky's name. He was the top player on the Stars, the face of the team, and for the last two months the face of L.A., showing up everywhere from movie premiers to toothpaste commercials. It was his girlfriend who'd scored us the tickets, and while I didn't know her personally, I'd seen her petite, model-thin frame hanging on his arm in several *Fashion Police* episodes.

I watched the jumbo screen zoom in on Bucky's face as he waved back at the crowd. He was blond, tanned, and had a boy-next-door look about him that had both teenage girls and baby boomer women cheering his name. I heard a group of twenty-something girls a few rows over screaming a marriage proposal.

"This guy's amazing," Ramirez said, looking a little starry-eyed himself. "He was a rookie last year, but his batting average is three-thirty with seventy-two RBIs."

"Uh-huh." I stared at the guy on the field, watching him approach the plate. "And is that good?"

Ramirez grinned at me again. "It's great. He's looking at MVP this year." He paused. "Most valuable player."

"I know what MVP stands for," I said, punching him in the shoulder. "I'm not a total ditz."

"Of course you're not," he wisely agreed.

"Hey, you didn't know the difference between a slingback and a wedge at Nordstrom last month. Cut me some slack. You have your lingo. I have mine."

"Fair enough," he agreed, flinging an arm around my shoulders and kissing the top of my head.

I snuggled into the crook of his arm, as much as I could in the confines of the plastic seats, as I watched the action down below.

Bucky swung at a pitch and missed, causing the crowd to let out a groan of disappointment. He did a repeat of the miss.

Then a couple of balls went foul, flying into the grateful hands of the crowd on the second tier. Then finally Bucky connected with a ball, the crack echoing in the bowl-shaped stadium, followed by a roar from the crowd as it sailed high over the field, landing in the stands on the other side of the wall.

Ramirez jumped to his feet, throwing both hands in the air and yelling. As did ninety percent of the people around me. I followed suit. I was pretty sure that was a home run, but I didn't say anything until I saw the jumbo screen confirm it in huge, animated letters.

"Damn, Davis is on fire," Ramirez remarked, sitting back down in his seat.

"Who's next?" I asked, getting into the excitement of the game.

"Ratski," Ramirez informed me.

I watched a tall, broad-shouldered guy take the plate. He had a week's worth of stubble covering his chin, a small beer belly straining against his uniform, and he spit on the ground before taking his batting stance.

"Is he good?" I asked.

Ramirez shrugged. "He's hit-and-miss. Last year he had a decent hitting average, but he's faltering this season."

Ratski hit the tip of the ball, sending it flying wild into the stands. The next pitch went past him completely. Ramirez made some disgusted sounds, taking a long swig of his beer.

"You're killing me, Ratski," he mumbled.

I'll admit I didn't really get the difference between fouls, strikes, and fair balls. But I tried my best to follow the pitch count as the player swung again. This time he caught the end of the ball, sending it high up in the air behind him. I watched the catcher throw his mask to the ground, trying to position himself under the ball.

But instead of coming down on the well padded catcher, I watched as the ball came hurtling into the stands.

Right toward me.

"Eep!" On instinct, I ducked, throwing both hands up to cover my head. I felt something hard crack against my right hand, then a frenzy of movement in the seats around me as people dove for the ball.

"Got it!" I heard my husband yell.

I opened my eyes to find him grinning like a kid on Christmas morning, holding a smudged baseball high above his head in a victory pose.

"Ahem," I said, still in my crouched position.

To his credit, he quickly turned to me, his expression morphing to concern. "You okay, babe?" He held out a hand, pulling me from the cement floor.

I nodded, looking down at my hand. The ball had snapped a nail, but as I flexed my fingers I could tell that my manicure had taken the brunt of the damage. "Maybe a bruise, but I'll be fine."

Ramirez grabbed my hand and kissed it. "Better?"

I couldn't help grinning back. "Getting there."

He leaned in and kissed me just below the ear. "Tell you what? When we get home, I'll *really* kiss that boo-boo away."

I felt my cheeks heat as I snuggled into the crook of his arm again. Apparently being lucky enough to get smacked by a foul ball just might get me *lucky* later, too.

* * *

In deference to my hurt manicure, my first move the next morning was to call up Fernando's Salon. "Fernando" was actually my stepfather, Ralph, who, upon hitting Beverly Hills via the Midwest, indulged in faux tans, a European-sounding faux name, and a faux Spanish ancestry to go along with it. The real housewives of Beverly Hills had eaten it up, flocking to Faux Dad's salon to soak up his manufactured exotic flair ever since.

Luckily, they'd had a cancelation that morning and said they could fit me in ASAP. I dropped the kids at my cousin, Molly's, place, then hightailed it to Rodeo and Wilshire.

The first thing I saw when I pushed through the glass doors was Faux Dad's receptionist Marco.

"No, no, no. I asked for daffodils, not dahlias," he said into a Bluetooth while pacing behind a large, chrome and glass desk. Marco was slim, Hispanic, and wore enough dark eyeliner to single-handedly keep Sephora in business. His complexion was flawless, his lashes enviously long, and his accent much more San Francisco than south of the border. He was dressed today in metallic silver pleather pants, a skin-tight baby-doll T-shirt in hot pink, and a pair of white loafers sans socks. He looked up just long enough to give me a little wave, before continuing his conversation. "That's right. Two dozen. One dozen wrapped in pink ribbon and one in blue." He paused. "This is going to run how much?" Another pause. "Ouch. Maybe make it half a dozen of each. But keep the calla lilies! They *make* the centerpieces, am I right?" He paused again, listening to someone on the other end. "Perfect. I'll have someone pick them up this weekend. Ta!"

Then without missing a beat, he spun and launched himself at me with air kisses. "Maddie, my dahling, how are you this morning?"

"Fabulous, thanks for asking." Which, after my night celebrating the Stars' seven-to-four win with my husband, was the truth. "Planning another party?" I asked, gesturing to his Bluetooth. In addition to manning the phones and schedules at Faux Dad's salon, Marco had started a part-time business party-planning to the stars. Or at least the D-listers. So far he'd done Britney Spears' sister's son's birthday party, the afterparty for the warm-up band at Daughtry's last concert, and a charity event for the Rihanna Look-alikes of West Hollywood.

Marco nodded vigorously. "I am. And it's going to be to-die-for."

"Who's the client?" I asked as I browsed the rack of colored nail polish along the wall.

"You!"

I almost dropped a bottle of Ravenous Red. "Me?"

Marco bobbed his head up and down, his spiky black hair not moving an inch. "Surprise!"

"Uh, but it's not my birthday…" I hedged, not sure I was in the market for a surprise where the flowers ran into the "ouch" realm.

"Of course it's not, silly," he said, waving me off. "It's for the twins. You didn't think I'd let their first birthday go by without a signature Auntie Marco party, did you?"

Honestly? I'd kinda hoped. "Oh, wow. That's… really nice of you. But they're just babies. They don't need anything big."

"Nonsense. It's their *first* birthday."

"Right. Which means they won't remember it anyway. Really, just some cake and they'll be happy."

"Oh, honey, I have cake! Three tiered, fondant covered, from Duff's Celebrity bakery!"

I blinked at him. "You know they have a combined total of six teeth, right?"

But Marco was on a roll, completely ignoring me. "I also have a waterslide, a pony, a candy bar, and I'm working on booking an ice skating rink where I'll have Johnny Weir do a personalized ice dance for the twins!" he said, ticking off items on his fingers.

"You're joking right?"

Marco frowned. "Babydoll, I never joke about figure skating."

"Exactly how much is all of this going to cost?" I asked, a headache brewing at my temples from the conversation that I now realized was with *my* florist.

Marco pursed his lip and shook his head. "Oh, Maddie. You can't put a price on something as precious as your babies' birthday."

I was pretty sure their father would disagree.

"I'm not sure—" I hedged.

But that was as far as I got before Faux Dad came bustling up from the back of the salon.

"Maddie, love, how are you?"

"Good," I told him, giving him a hug. "Better once I get this fixed." I held up my cracked nail.

Faux Dad gasped. "Oh, honey. Tragic!"

While I'd had my doubts about Faux Dad's heterosexuality before he and my mom had married a few years ago, I had to admit that it was nice to have a man in the family who understood.

"I know, right?" I agreed.

He clucked his tongue. "We'll get you fixed up in a jiffy. Come on to the back. I've got Petra waiting for you."

I followed him through the salon, currently decorated in a Greco-chic motif with large, ornate chandeliers hanging above cut and color stations, a gilded mirror and dainty vanities at the blow dry bar, and flocked wallpaper in a rich burgundy covering the walls.

"So, how did the tragedy occur?" Faux Dad asked, gesturing to my ruined manicure.

"Ball game," I responded. "I caught a foul ball."

Faux Dad shook his head and did more tsking. "Sports and shellac do not mix."

"Amen," I agreed. "But thanks, by the way, for the tickets. Ramirez had a blast."

"Happy to help," he told me. "When Lacey gave them to me, I didn't know what I was going to do with them. It's not as if I was going to the game myself," he said, chuckling as if that were the most absurd thing he'd ever thought of.

"Well, be sure to thank Lacey for me the next time you see her."

Faux Dad nodded. "I can do one better. She's in the back getting spray-tanned now. You can thank her yourself."

"Oh, I don't want to bother her..." I started.

But Faux Dad waved me off with a swift flick of his tanned wrist. "No bother at all. She's just drying now. She's a hoot. You'll want to meet her."

Actually, I'll admit that her semi-celebrity status had me curious. I did kinda want to meet her.

I followed Faux Dad through a door at the back which led to private tanning booths. Each room was equipped with a stall that looked a lot like my shower at home. Only these had several nozzles where tanning solution was sprayed out in a fine mist to evenly cover all the exposed skin. Usually patrons would hit a button, spin slowly in the tanning cloud, then allow themselves to air-dry for a few minutes before clothing and reemerging from the room.

Faux Dad stopped at the second door on the right and did a small knock. "Lacey, doll? It's Fernando."

No answer.

"Are you decent?" he asked.

Again, nothing.

Faux Dad frowned. "That's odd. I know she's in there."

"Maybe she can't hear you over the spray?" I offered.

Faux Dad put his ear to the door. "No, the jets are off. Lacey, honey, everything okay in there?" he asked, knocking again. He tried the handle, but the door was locked.

I could see the frown increasing.

"Wait here," he instructed me. "I'm going to get the key from Marco. Be back in a jiffy."

I did, standing awkwardly outside the door, checking my watch. As much as meeting Lacey sounded fun, I only had an hour before I had to relieve my cousin of the twins. I needed to get to Petra and that manicure, stat.

Luckily Faux Dad was true to his word, and one jiffy later he was back, a small, brass key in hand. He did one more repeat of the knock-and-call before slipping it into the handle and turning the lock.

"Lacey, love?" he asked, gingerly pushing the door open.

Then he froze, and I heard him suck in a big breath of air.

I craned to see around him, pushing my way into the small room.

Then I did a repeat of his gasp.

Lying on the floor of the tanning stall was a young woman with thick brunette hair wearing a pair of teeny tiny bikini bottoms and nothing else. Her skin was streaked in uneven brown and pale lines, her body twisted inward on itself at an awkward angle, and her eyes dilated, staring straight up at the ceiling in a glazed, unblinking stare that could only be achieved by one type of body.

A dead one.

CHAPTER TWO

———

There are some people who have all the luck. When I was eight years old it bugged me to no end that my arch nemesis, Melinda Masters, seemed to be one of those people. Not only did she always have her name picked from the second grade good-behavior ticket jar, she was always the rock-paper-scissor elected dodge ball team captain, and the "randomly chosen" line leader at recess. But as I've grown into adulthood, I have come to realize that I have a certain kind of luck all my own. Dead body luck.

I'm ashamed to admit that Lacey was not the first dead body I had ever encountered. In fact, my friends have started to joke that I'm kind of a dead body magnet. Not that I actually *cause* anyone to die, but I seem to have an uncanny knack for finding the recently deceased. Some people would say it's a fortunate thing that my husband is a homicide detective.

Those people have never faced the business end of my husband's Bad Cop glare.

I sat in a plastic chair in the lobby of Fernando's, where the responding officers had corralled the entire staff as they scoured the salon with fingerprint dust, luminal spray, and a bunch of other chemicals that I feared would cause a fire bomb reaction when mixed with the dyes, straighteners, and other hair products already hanging heavily in the salon air.

When Faux Dad and I had run from the back room and told Marco what we'd found, the ensuing screamfest had pretty much alerted the entire patronage of the salon that something was up. And as soon as they'd figured out just what that something was, they'd bolted, some still mid-color in their foil wraps. I feared there would be over-bleached hair-dos all over Beverly Hills this week.

Faux Dad was pacing the lobby floor, muttering to himself and shaking his head. The three stylists on shift today where huddled together, whispering in hushed tones. My two favorite nail ladies were in the corner, talking in rapid Vietnamese. Marco sat on the plastic chair beside me, patting my shoulder, and murmuring, "there, there," at comforting intervals. And I was taking deep breaths, as if the act of pulling air in and out of my lungs could somehow erase what I'd just seen.

Marco shook his head, clucking his tongue. "It's just tragic."

"Did you know her?" I asked, trying to block the image of her crumpled body from my brain.

Marco nodded. "Only in passing. She was a new client, but she came in regularly for tanning, nails, hair, the works."

I glanced toward the back of the salon where crime scene techs were pulling bottles of every chemical under the sun out of the storeroom. It was sadly ironic that she'd put so much care into her appearance then had ended up a spray-streaked mess.

"Uh-oh, here comes trouble," Marco mumbled.

I looked up, and froze. Marco was right.

Ramirez walked through the glass front doors, gaze cool and assessing, posture stiff and intimidating, jaw set in a tight line. His eyes scanned the assembled group, and even before they honed in on me, I could feel him seeking me out. He knew Fernando's was my stepfather's place. He'd probably had the entire car ride over to seethe about the fact that I was once again at his crime scene.

I thought about ducking behind Marco, but the fact that he underweighed me by about twenty pounds wasn't going to afford me much shelter from the brewing husband storm.

Instead I took a deep breath, reminded myself that luck—whether it's over being a second grade line leader or finding dead people—is never a person's fault, and stood to face the music.

Ramirez's eyes hit me immediately.

"Hi, honey," I said, bravely marching up to him on legs that felt like Jell-O.

"Hi." It was his deadpan cop voice, one that gave zero hint of emotion.

I cleared my throat. "So, we've had a little incident," I told him, doing my best to downplay the obvious.

His expression didn't change, but I'd swear I saw amusement flit across his eyes. "'Little' incident?"

I nodded. "In the back. Tanning accident."

His eyes cut to the crime scene techs. "Hmph," he grunted.

"You can take my statement now, or I can give it to Charlie," I said, gesturing to one of the uniforms. "Blake's already taken my fingerprints," I waved to the CSU guy near the reception desk, "and Alex took a hair sample."

Ramirez paused. "Wow. You really know the drill. It's like you've done this before."

"Ha, ha. Very funny."

"Oh, I'm not laughing," he said, back to the deadpan. "In fact, I don't see anything remotely funny about my wife being in the same vicinity as a dead body. Again."

I swallowed hard. "Hey, it's not as if I wanted to see her like that, you know."

He paused, his eyes softened a touch, and he cocked his head at me. "I know. You okay?"

I felt tears back up behind my eyes as the image of Lacey's crumpled body came flooding back to me. But I bravely sniffed them back, nodding vigorously to convince myself as much as my husband. "Yep. I'm fine."

He shot me a look. "Really?"

"No. But I will be."

He reached a hand out and gave me a little squeeze on the shoulder. "Tell me what happened," he said.

I took a deep breath and did, giving him the sparse details I had.

"Did you know Lacey?" he asked when I'd finished.

I shook my head. "No. But she's the one Faux Dad got our baseball tickets from. She was dating Bucky Davis."

That got his attention, both of his eyebrows heading north. "That should make things interesting with the press. Okay, you wait here. I'm going to go talk to the responding officer."

I nodded, happy to be out of Bad Cop's clutches with only the minimum of interrogation.

I watched as he spoke to a guy in uniform, then made the rounds, talking to various CSU, slipping into the back to see the victim, then slowly making his way back out to the lobby to see me.

"So?" I asked. "What killed her?"

He paused, his eyes going over the assembled group of Fernando's employees as he answered. "We're not sure. We're waiting for the ME to arrive and weigh in."

I bit my lip. "But if you had to guess…natural causes?" I asked hopefully.

Ramirez sighed. "I wish. But if I had to guess? No. The body didn't show any obvious signs that would point to a natural cause. She also didn't display any signs of outward trauma."

I felt a frown pull between my brows. "Which means?"

"If I had to hazard a guess, I'd say death was due to some kind of poisonous substance."

I glanced up at the CSU taking bottles from the supply closet and realized that they were all jugs of tanning solution.

"Oh, no," I said. "Don't tell me it was something in the tanning spray?"

"We'll know more when CSU gets their collections back to the lab," he said, dodging a direct answer.

But the unreadable Cop Face he'd so neatly slid into place again told me he already had his own suspicion.

Death by tanning. I suddenly felt infinitely glad I'd decided to go with the "pale is the new tan" motto this summer.

"Oh, Jack, thank God you're here," Faux Dad said, rushing up to us. Completely obliviously to Bad Cop mode, he threw his arms around my husband's neck, giving him a big bear hug.

Ramirez lifted one eyebrow at me and awkwardly patted Faux Dad on the back. "Uh, hi, Ral—er, Fernando."

"This is a tragedy," Faux Dad said, breaking the embrace. "A travesty. A horror! How could this have happened in *my* salon?"

"That's what I'm here to find out," Ramirez assured him. "Can I ask you a few questions about the victim?"

Faux Dad paled. "Victim. Does that mean…?"

Ramirez cleared his throat. "At the moment, we're treating this as a homicide investigation."

Faux Dad put one hand on his heart, the other on my shoulder, swaying slightly on his feet. "Oh, no. Oh, heavens. Oh, this can't be. This is Beverly Hills," he said, shaking his head. "This sort of thing just does *not* happen here."

"What can you tell me about Lacey…" Ramirez looked down, checking his notes.

"Desta," Faux Dad supplied. "Lacey Desta. She was a new customer, but a good one. Came in every Monday for her tan, every Saturday for her mani-pedi, and every other Tuesday to touch up her highlights. Waxing on Friday and facials on Thursday."

I felt my own eyebrows rise. I knew as well as anyone what went into a high-maintenance beauty regimen, but Lacey sounded like she took it to the extreme. Even I went two weeks between pedicures.

"Did she always come in alone?" Ramirez asked.

Faux Dad nodded. "Yes, as far as I saw."

"Did she have any family, friends, anyone close to her that you know of?"

He shook his head. "She mentioned some family back east, but I didn't get the feeling they were close. She really just talked about Bucky. She was dating that ballplayer," Faux Dad explained.

"Right. I'm familiar with Davis," Ramirez answered. "What about your staff?"

"What about them?" Faux Dad responded, shooting a nervous glance to the crew still assembled in the lobby.

"Which one added the solution to Lacey's tanning booth?"

I watched Faux Dad's Adam's apple bob up and down as he wiped his palms against the legs of his white trousers. "I did," he squeaked out. "Why? Was there something wrong with it?"

But instead of answering, Ramirez fired another question at him. "Who had access to the solution prior to its use?"

"Well," Faux Dad glanced behind him again. "Anyone, I suppose. I mean, the storage cupboards aren't locked."

"What time did you add the solution to Lacey's booth?"

Faux Dad licked his lips. "Around 10:00. I knew Lacey was scheduled at 11:30, but I had another client coming in for a cut and color at 10:30, so I wanted to get the booth ready early."

"So, between 10:00 and 11:30, the booth was not monitored?"

Faux Dad nodded. "That's right." He paused. "You think someone tampered with the spray?"

"We're just trying to establish a timeline at the moment," Ramirez said.

I resisted the urge to translate into real person speak for Faux Dad that, yes, someone did tamper and, yes, you were the last person to put fingerprints on the murder weapon. Mostly because I wasn't sure I could catch him if he fainted.

"Who knew Lacey would be in today?" Ramirez went on.

Faux Dad wrinkled his forehead in concentration. "Well, I...I don't know. I mean, it was written on the schedule."

"And the schedule is?"

"At the reception desk."

"Marco's desk?" Ramirez asked.

"Yes," Faux Dad agreed. "But anyone can see it. It's not like it's hidden."

"Was Marco away from his desk at any time this morning?"

"I...uh...I don't know," Faux Dad sputtered.

"It's okay," I reassured him, putting a hand on his shoulder.

Ramirez must have realized that his Bad Cop routine was making Faux Dad sweat, because he quickly eased off. "I'll ask Marco about his movements," he said. "And I'd like to get a list of all the other stylists and staff you have. We're going to need to get statements from everyone."

Faux Dad nodded, his face about three shades paler than when I'd entered the salon this morning. "Of course."

"Ramirez!" one of the guys in uniform shouted, hailing him to the back room again.

He nodded an exit to Faux Dad and me and went off into cop mode again.

"That's it," Faux Dad said, watching him go. "I'm ruined. Word will get out that you tan at Fernando's and end up dead. I'll be finished in this town."

"Don't worry," I told him, patting his shoulder again. "Ramirez is great at his job. He'll find whoever did this. Everything will be back to normal around here in no time."

Unfortunately, it was a statement I only half believed. Crime scene veteran that I was becoming, I knew that "normal" was a relative term after a murder had occurred.

After I'd given an official statement to Charlie and another uniformed officer (who I didn't know—he must have been new), I rushed to my cousin's house where I gave her all the gory deets on the case while making profuse apologies for being late. She made the appropriate "ohmigod" sounds, and then I took the twins home and called my best friend, Dana.

Dana was an actress and, unfortunately, currently on location in San Francisco, shooting a scene for the cable drama *Lady Justice*, and didn't pick up. I left her a quick voicemail telling her to call me back ASAP.

Then I put *Dora the Explorer* on TV (for the twins) and pulled up the *L.A. Informer*'s celebrity news website (for me), following the latest posts and tweets as news of Lacey's death broke all over the tabloid universe. Speculation was rampant, but the facts were sparse, limited to those I'd already learned from Ramirez. I noticed that someone had leaked the method of death despite the absence of an ME's report, the case already being referred to in the press as the "Tanning Salon Murder."

I hated to admit it, but as much as I'd tried to reassure Faux Dad earlier, I had to agree with him. This murder had the potential to be death to his salon.

* * *

The next morning Ramirez was predictably gone before dawn. I was awakened by my human alarm clocks an hour later. Their dual cries, clamoring for their morning bottles, broke through the baby monitor static on my nightstand as soon as the sun peeked through the yellow curtains in their nursery. I stumbled to do their bidding, feeding, changing, and cleaning Livvie and Max. Then I plopped them into their walkers with a handful of cheerios each and I shuffled into the kitchen to get some much needed caffeine while they watched Elmo. God bless that furry little monster. He was the only way I was ever able to get a full cup of coffee in the morning.

Half an hour later I had showered, dressed, and even managed to apply a little mascara and lip gloss before *Sesame Street* ended.

The twins were just starting to fuss when the doorbell rang.

"Knock, knock," Marco said, not waiting for me to answer before poking his head into the house.

"Come on in," I told him, waving him into the living room as I surfed the on-demand channels for another episode of toddler faves.

As he stepped through the doorway, I noticed that today he was adorned in a pair of hot pink biker shorts, matching jellies sandals, and a black tank top with mesh down the sides. He'd topped it off with a neon green ascot with tiny hot-pink Chihuahua's on it. The outfit was so loud I almost didn't notice the petite, Asian woman who slipped into the house behind him.

"Hey, you got a pretty nice place here," she said, eyeing her surroundings. "It's small but homey. Cozy. You know, kinda like one of those sitcom sets but without all the expensive furniture and nice artwork and stuff."

Ling was 4'11", eighty pounds, and had the kind of smooth complexion and glossy hair that made it totally impossible to tell her age. She worked at the Glitter Galaxy, a strip club out in Industry, which meant her fashion sense tended toward the short, low cut, or pasted on. At first I'd felt sorry for her and her limited career options. Then I'd learned she made six figures a year dancing and felt sorry I didn't have the rhythm to join her.

"Um, thanks," I said, choosing to take Ling's words as a compliment.

"So how are my favorite almost-one-year-olds?" Marco ask, doing little air kisses at Livvie and Max. They both greeted him with squeals of delight and outstretched chubby arms. Auntie Marco had been gun-shy about the idea of "short, sticky people" at first, but as the twins had gotten older, and less likely to spit up on his designer clothing, they'd bonded like glue.

"They're good," I answered for them. "You want coffee?"

"Black, lots of sugar," Marco said nodding.

"Ditto," Ling added, leaning down to shake a rattle at Max.

"You're not working at Fernando's today?" I asked Marco, ducking into the kitchen and grabbing two mugs.

Marco shook his head as I returned. "Nope. It's closed up tight. The police had crime scene tape all over the doors."

I cringed, feeling a pang of sympathy again for Faux Dad.

"Which is why we're here..." Marco trailed off, shooting a meaningful look at Ling. She nodded and winked back at him.

A "hair-brained scheme" alarm immediately started going off in my brain, an uneasy feeling in my stomach mixing uncomfortably with the strong coffee.

"*What* is why you're here?" I prompted.

"Well, just that we need to help Fernando."

"Why do I get the feeling you don't mean by sending him a sympathy muffin basket?"

Marco rolled his eyes so far I feared they'd pop out of their sockets. "No, silly goose, I mean with the *investigation*."

I narrowed my eyes. "What investigation?"

"Well, duh!" Ling jumped in. "That tan chick's murder!"

"You mean the death that the *police* are looking into?" I clarified.

Marco crossed his arms over his chest and shook his head at me. "Maddie Springer, you don't really mean to tell me that a murder practically falls into your lap, and you're not going to investigate?"

I shook my head from side to side, feeling my blonde hair whip my cheeks. "No, I am not. My husband is perfectly capable of figuring this one out on his own."

More eye rolling. "But your stepfather is counting on you!"

I shook my head again. "Oh, no. Don't you play the family card with me."

"But what about the salon?" he went on. "The press is kiiilling him." He drew the word out with a dramatic flair that could have won him a role on Broadway.

"I think he'll live."

"But will his business?"

I paused. I hated to admit that I'd worried about the very same thing.

"Here's the thing," Ling said, jumping in. "I got inside connections that the police don't have."

I paused. There was that uneasy feeling in my stomach again.

"Okay, I'll bite," I said, sipping at my coffee. "What kind of connections?"

"I happen to be good friends with one of the other players on the Stars."

"Define friends?" I said.

"He gets half priced lap dances."

I had to ask.

"Okay, so you have an…in with a player," I conceded. "I'm not sure that really helps us."

"Of course it does!" Marco said. "We can pump him for information."

"'Pump for information?' You have to stop watching Mark Wahlberg movies, Marco."

Marco grinned. "But he's so hot."

"John Ratski is the player," Ling continued. "He comes into the Galaxy all the time. I'm sure I can get all sorts of info from this guy."

I bit my lip. I knew that name. Ramirez had pointed him out to me at the ballgame the other day. He had a shaky RBI or

BMI or BMX or something like that. But I was pretty sure it wasn't good.

"So what kind of info do we think Ratski has?"

"Ratski and Bucky are tight," Ling said. "Like thick Bromance tight. If Bucky confided in anyone about killing his girlfriend, it's Ratski."

"Whoa." I held a hand up. "Who said Bucky killed Lacey?"

Again I got the duh look from the double trouble. "Come on, you know it's *always* the boyfriend who kills the girl. Don't you watch CNN?" Marco asked.

My turn to roll my eyes. "Okay, even ignoring your complete lack of evidence other than television sensationalism, what makes you think that Ratski will talk to us?"

"Leave it to me," Ling said, sending me a wink. "I can soften him up."

I bit my lip. Knowing how Ling made her living, I wasn't sure *soften* was the right verb. On the other hand…Marco had a point. While normally all press is good press, the idea that Fernando's tanning booths were killing clients wasn't going to do much for his business. The salon was Faux Dad's life. I couldn't let the speculation take it down. While I had complete faith in Ramirez to get to the bottom of things, it couldn't hurt to just go talk to Ratski, could it?

"Okay. Let's go talk to the ball player," I conceded.

Marco let out a high-pitched squeal.

"But just *talk*," I emphasized. "No 'info pumping.'"

"Right." Marco nodded. "Just talk."

"He'll be in at four," Ling informed me.

I paused. "Be in…"

"The Glitter Galaxy."

Mental forehead thunk. "We're talking to him at the *strip club*?"

"Well it's not like he'd give me his home address," Ling said, rolling her eyes. "Duh! How would that look to his wife?"

Oh, boy. Why did I have a feeling I'd just aligned myself with Tweedle Diva and Tweedle Devious?

CHAPTER THREE

———

Once Marco and Ling left, I still had a few hours to kill before my strip club appearance and felt obligated to play domestic goddess. I did a round of dishes, loaded the washing machine, and even pulled the vacuum out of the closet. Luckily I was saved from actually using it when my cell rang, displaying my best friend, Dana's, number.

"Ohmigod, Maddie," she yelled in my ear as soon as I picked up. "I just saw it on the news. What happened?"

I quickly filled her in on all I knew, ending with my plans to question Ratski at the Glitter Galaxy later that afternoon.

"So you think the boyfriend did it?" she asked when I'd finished.

"I don't know," I told her honestly. "But there are only two possibilities. One—it's a total random killing."

Dana sucked in a breath.

"Or, two—someone close to her wanted her dead. Someone who knew her tanning schedule."

"Too creepy. I'm never going to look at a spray booth the same."

I'd ditto that. I just hoped Fernando's clients didn't feel the same way.

"Well, I wish I could go with you," Dana continued, "but I'm shooting until three."

"How's it going?" I asked, tucking my phone in the crook of my neck as I intervened between the twins. Livvie had grabbed Max's toy duck, causing tiny screams of protest. I picked up my little thief, hoisting her onto my hip.

"It's flippin' freezing here. They have me in a bathing suit on the Golden Gate Bridge. Can you believe? It's fog city."

"How many more days do you have?"

"Hopefully this is it. If we can get the sun to peek out enough to get the shots today."

"Well, good luck," I told her.

"Thanks. Hey, by the way, I got the invitation."

"What invitation?" I asked, switching the phone to the other ear as I deposited Livvie into her high chair along with another handful of Cheerios.

"To the twins' birthday party. It was adorable. Where did you get it?"

I groaned. "I haven't actually seen them. This is all Marco's doing."

"Oh, they're beautiful. Linen and gold embossed, with a light tissue overlay. Cute but super classy."

I felt myself mentally adding up the cost of that classiness as the guest of honor tried to stick a Cheerio up her nose.

"Anyway, I'll be there for sure," Dana told me.

I didn't have the heart to tell her I was still a maybe.

* * *

After I had fed, changed, burped, then re-changed the twins, I packed them and their diaper bag into my minivan and drove them to my mom's house. Mom had graciously agreed to watch them while I "took care of some business." I let her believe it had to do with my shoe designing business and not investigating business. I didn't want to get her, or Faux Dad's, hopes up that this trek to the strip club was going to yield any results. Personally, I still thought it was a leap to assume the boyfriend was guilty, and an even bigger leap to assume he might have purged his guilty conscience to his best friend.

"How are my babies?" Mom squealed as soon as I walked in the front door, attacking Livvie and Max in a round of perfume scented hugs.

"Fed and mostly clean," I answered for them.

"Oh, wait until you see what Grammy bought for you-oooo," Mom sing-songed.

I tried to hide my dread. While I loved my mother with all my heart, her sense of fashion had peaked somewhere around

1985 and stalled there like a Volvo with a car phone. She was the only person in the entire L.A. basin who still wore acid washed jeans with high-top sneakers. Today she'd paired them with a sweater featuring a koala in a shade of purple that exactly matched the heavy eye shadow extending from her eyelids clear up to her plucked brows.

"Oh, gee, Mom, you shouldn't have," I said, fully meaning it as she grabbed a bag from her kitchen counter.

"Oh, now, you know I love to spoil my babies," she protested. I watched as she pulled out two little rompers: one in blue, the other in pink. She held them up to her chest so I could see the silk-screen design on the front. They both said "I'm 1," with a spotted giraffe contorting himself into the shape of the number.

While they weren't haute couture, it could have been worse. "Cute," I said, nodding my approval.

"Aren't they? They'll be perfect for the party."

I heard myself groan before I could rein it in. "Marco sent you an invitation, too?"

Mom nodded. "They were gorgeous, honey, but don't you think they were a bit much for a *child's* party? I mean, you can't just go throwing money around like that, Mads."

I opened my mouth to protest that it was *someone else* throwing *my* money, but before I could get it out, the front door opened again.

"Yoo-hoo? Anyone home?" a voice called. A beat later the woman who went with it appeared in the doorway, Mom's best friend, Mrs. Rosenblatt.

Mrs. Rosenblatt was a three-hundred pound Jewish psychic who looked like the Pillsbury dough boy had a love child with Lady Gaga. Her make-up was loud, her muumuus bright, and her ex-husbands numbering almost as high as her cholesterol count. She and my mother had become fast friends after a particularly enlightening reading Mrs. R had given my mom on the Venice Boardwalk one afternoon, saying she would meet a tall, dark stranger soon. Two days later, a chocolate lab had wagged his tail into Mom's life, and she'd been a believer ever since.

"Oy, *bubbee*," Mrs. R said, her eyes immediately going to me. "Come here."

I took a step closer as she squinted at me. "You got something right there," she said, waving her hand in the region of my forehead.

"Where?" I went crossed-eyed trying to see.

"There." She pointed.

"What is it?" I asked, swiping with my hand. "Baby food? Spit up? Smudged mascara?"

Mrs. R shook her head. "Nope. Aura flares."

Mental face palm. "Aura flares?"

"Maddie, your aura is a hot mess. You got any stress in your life?"

I thought of the pole dancer and the queen waiting for me at a strip club to interrogate a murder suspect. "Nope. None I can think of."

"Well, you gotta relax. Get some fresh air. Maybe a long, meditative walk."

A long walk sounded like heaven. It also sounded like someone else's life. The last time I had time for a walk, it was from my refrigerator to the babies' crib in the middle of the night with two fresh bottles.

"Listen, I'll be back at six by the latest," I told my mom. Then I planted a kiss on each of the twins' heads and slipped out the door before Mom and Mrs. R had a chance to interrogate me about my interrogation.

* * *

Glitter Galaxy was located in the City of Industry on Main, sandwiched between a John Deere wholesaler and a warehouse with the words "China-Co" printed on the sign. By six on a payday, it would be packed. Right now, the parking lot was mostly empty, only a smattering of late model sedans near the entrance. The building itself was a squat, one story affair that looked like any of the other warehouses in this part of town. Only this one had a ten foot tall naked woman rimmed in neon standing on its roof.

I spotted Ling and Marco in Marco's Fiat at the far side of the lot, and I pulled into the slot beside them. Marco scrunched his nose up as he got out of the car, studiously avoiding looking at the giant yellow nipples flashing above us. "This place always gives me the creeps."

Ling punched him in the arm. "Toughen up, Nancy."

"Ow," Marco said, rubbing his bicep.

"Look, let's just get in, get the interview, and get out," I said, not a huge fan of the place myself. While I was no prude about the human form in all its naked glory, something about men sitting with their hands under the tables threw my squick radar to a ten.

Ling led the way inside, pausing to wave to a girl on stage in alien antennae, pointy flashing neon ears, and nothing else. She had her leg wrapped around the top of the pole, hanging upside down and arching her back in a pose that clearly screamed "double jointed." Very impressive. I had a hard time tearing my eyes off her as I followed Ling through the club, which was dark, smelled like stale beer, and perpetually felt like last call. No windows, lots of walled off areas for private dances, and music so loud my feet were getting a massage through my slingbacks.

"He's not here yet," Ling shouted to me. She pointed to a booth near the back of the club which was currently empty. "That's his favorite spot."

"So what do we do?"

Ling shrugged. "I'm gonna make some tips while we wait. You do whatever you want."

Knowing what Ling cleared, I was tempted to join her. But instead Marco and I opted to take a seat at a table near the door. As soon as we did, a Princess Leia in Jabba servant clothes came up and asked if we'd like a drink. What the heck? It was almost five, and the kids were elsewhere. Marco and I ordered a pair of cosmos.

As soon as she arrived with them, I turned to Marco. "I heard that you sent out invitations to the twins' birthday?"

Marco nodded, beaming. "I did. And they were fab!"

"Fab as in expensive?"

Marco shook his head at me. "Maddie, how can you put a price—"

"—on my kids. I know, I know. Humor me for a moment and say I can. Would that price have one zero after it or two?"

Marco made a tsking sound between his lips. "Honey, those were custom designer label invitations."

"Which means?"

"Three zeros."

I grabbed my cosmo, taking a long swig as I pictured just how many pairs of shoes I'd have to design to pay for this "priceless" party.

"Trust me, everyone has loved them so far," Marco assured me. "I've had tons of RSVPs already."

I paused. "Tons? Exactly how many people have you invited to this party?"

"Now that number only has two zeros."

I downed the rest of my drink, thinking what bad form it would be to wring his neck and spend my children's first birthday in jail.

Luckily for Marco's safety, the front door opened, blasting the interior with a bright light. Once it subsided again, I caught a tall, dark haired guy in jeans and a polo shirt standing near it. He wore at least a day's worth of growth on his chin, a six pack worth of beer belly hanging over his belt, and a ball cap pulled low over his ears as if hoping no one recognized him. Just like Ling said, he took a seat at the booth in the back, sliding low in his seat and signaling Princess Leia for a drink.

Ling must have spotted him too, as she quickly left the group of guys in cheap suits she'd been working and made her way to the back booth.

Ratski's eyes lit up as she approached, and I watched Ling lean in, whisper something in his ear, then giggle flirtatiously as the waitress returned with his draft beer.

"What did she say to him?" Marco asked, leaning in.

I shrugged. "Got me."

"Come on. We're missing the interrogation."

"*Talk*. We're just here to talk," I hissed back. Even though I knew it was a lost cause. Marco loved to play Nancy Drew like I loved a good sale at DSW.

I followed him as he slipped from our table, taking a spot instead at the booth next to Ratski. The backs were high enough that he couldn't see us, but we were close enough to overhear every word.

I put my finger to my lips as I heard Ling's voice float over the top of the booth to us.

"You must be so tense. I heard all about that dead girl on the news last night."

A grunt was the only response she got.

"You know her?" Ling pressed. "Lacey something?"

"Desta," Ratski responded, his voice low and raspy. "Lacey Desta."

"Yeah, that the one! She died terrible, no?"

Ling was laying the accent on thick. I figured it was her version of "playing blonde," a trick I'd admit to using myself once or twice. The less a person thought you knew, the more apt they were to tell you everything *they* knew.

"Terrible," Ratski agreed, and I heard him pause for a sip of beer.

"That boyfriend of hers must be pretty upset."

"Yeah."

"They close? The boyfriend and the dead girl?"

I cringed. It wasn't the most finessed questioning.

"Of course," Ratski responded, a defensive edge to his voice now.

"No fighting?"

"No."

"They weren't having any relationship problems?"

"No!"

"You sure?"

"Look what is this?" he asked, and I heard him get up from the booth.

What it was, was a very poorly conducted *talk* on our part.

I slid out of my own seat just in time to see Ling pop up in front of him, her barely-taller-than-a-third-grader frame barring his way.

"You know what this is," she said, hands on her hips, eyes narrowed. "The boyfriend always guilty. So, fess up. He do it?"

"What the hell?" Ratski said, pushing past her.

I sighed. So much for her and Ratski being "good friends." This was going downhill fast.

And then it went into downhill in speed-skater mode.

Out of the corner of my eye, I saw the door to the Glitter Galaxy open, blinding sunlight reflecting off a gold badge as a cop held it up to the doorman.

Oh, no.

The light faded, and as my eyes re-adjusted to the dark, I saw my husband and two other plainclothes detectives enter the Galaxy.

I immediately turned, putting my back to the door and grabbing Ling by the arm. "Uh, look. We're very sorry to have bothered you."

"Who are you?" Ratski asked, his gaze pinging from me to Marco and back to Ling.

"I'm no one. No one, who will be on her way now."

"I don't know what this is," he said, addressing me. "But you can tell your whore friend here to leave me the hell alone."

Ling sucked in a breath, her jaw tensing. "I am a *dancer*. Not a whore," she ground out.

Ratski shook his head. "Whatever."

"You have no right to call me that! That is big disrespect!"

I glanced at the door. Our altercation was causing unwanted attention. Namely from the tall, dark, and coming-dangerously-close-to-identifying-me-in-the-dimly-lit-strip-club husband.

"Look, I'm sure he didn't mean it. Now let's get out of here," I said, tugging on Ling's arm again.

But she was taking a stand. "You apologize right now or else!"

Ratski scoffed, shaking his head. "You have got to be kidding. I'm outta here."

"I no kidding!" Ling shouted, bouncing on her toes to bar his way.

"Move it, chick," he warned.

I tugged on Ling's arm. But for a small girl, she had crazy lower body strength, her legs planted firmly in a stance that was not budging. I mentally made a note to try some of those pole dancing exercises later.

"You say you're sorry," Ling demanded again.

"Look," I jumped in, "I'm sure we can handle this in a rational, speedy, fashion if we just—"

But that was as far as I got before Ratski grabbed Ling's other arm, shoving her backwards. Ling let out a yip like a terrier, stumbling back against the next table and falling flat on her butt on the hard, linoleum floor.

"Hey, that was uncalled for," I said, stepping toward Ratski as Marco rushed forward to help Ling up.

Ratski turned on me. "Listen, bitch," he yelled, his voice getting louder now. "I don't know who you think you are, but no whore is gonna tell me what to do." Then he grabbed my arm, ready to do a repeat of the shove and run routine.

But before either of us could react further, a large fist went flying through my field of vision, connecting squarely with Ratski's nose, sending him reeling backward and crashing hard into the booth behind him.

I looked up.

And realized the fist was connected to my husband.

CHAPTER FOUR

———

Ratski stumbled backward, his head smacking against the edge of the table and bouncing off. But it only phased him for a second before he was on his feet, turning toward Ramirez. I watched as events seemed to play out in slow motion. Ramirez cocked his fist back again. Ratski lunged at Ramirez. Marco squealed and covered his eyes. Ling jumped on Ratski's back, and I put all 110 pounds of myself behind the effort of holding my husband's arm back. I might have been successful too, if I hadn't been wearing adorable slingback heels which slipped on the slick linoleum giving me the traction of a pony on an ice skating rink.

"Stop! No! Don't hit him!" I yelled in vain, appealing to both men at once.

Luckily, one thing the Glitter Galaxy did not skimp on was security. A bouncer in a black shirt appeared from nowhere, inserting himself between Ratski and Ramirez just as Ratski managed to shake Ling off.

"Take it outside," the bouncer yelled, his voice a deep rumble.

"LAPD," Ramirez spat back.

"I don't care who you are. There is no fighting in the Glitter Galaxy."

While Ramirez could have argued with him, I could see the fire dulling in his eyes, sanity returning. Clearly beating up a ball player in a strip club was not going to get him anywhere.

He turned, his eyes falling on me instead. "You," he said stabbing a finger my way.

I did a dry gulp. "Me?"

"Outside. Now."

I nodded agreement, dread building in my stomach as I made a beeline for the door. I felt Ramirez's breath hot on my neck as he followed me, but it wasn't until we were outside in the bright sunshine again that he spoke.

"What the hell were you doing in there?"

I bit my lip. "Having a drink." Which was the truth. I had thoroughly enjoyed my one cosmo.

His eyes narrowed, and a vein in his neck started to bulge. "Nice try, Springer. What were you really doing there?"

"What? I can't enjoy a strip club in the afternoon like any other L.A. housewife?"

His eyes turned into fine slits. "And Marco?"

I swallowed hard. "He was…enjoying the strip club too?"

Ramirez closed his eyes. His nostrils flared with the effort of taking deep breaths. I could feel him mentally counting to ten. When he opened them again I couldn't see much difference in his expression, but the vein in his neck had stopped pulsing.

"Please tell me why I just punched a guy for calling my wife names in the middle of a strip club?" he said, his voice treading that fine line between controlled calm and explosive anger.

"Sorry," I said.

"For?"

"Look it was Marco's idea."

He sighed. "Go on."

"I didn't even want to come. But Ling said that she knew Ratski, and that the boyfriend is always guilty, and that Bucky is best friends with Ratski, so maybe Ratski had some inside info about Lacey's death. Which, I know, seemed like a long shot but…" I trailed off as a teeny tiny light bulb went off in the back of my mind. "Hey, exactly why are *you* here?"

Ramirez sighed again. "Turns out there were rumors that Bucky and Lacey *were* having some issues."

"Shut the front door! Ling was right? Bucky killed his girlfriend?"

Ramirez held up a hand. "I wouldn't go that far. But they'd been heard arguing lately. Bucky said he was with Ratski and another player when Lacey was killed, so I was checking up on his alibi."

I glanced at the door of the club. "I don't suppose Ratski's gonna be in the mood to talk to you now."

Ramirez sighed again, expelling the last of his air, and ran a hand through his dark hair, making it stand up in little tufts. "No. He's not."

"Sorry," I said, as much for my part in the scuffle as his. "But, if it makes you feel any better, that whole defending my honor thing? Kinda sexy."

The ghost of a grin tugged at the corner of his mouth. "A *little* better."

"Tell you what," I said, taking a step toward him, "the kids are at my mom's for another hour, and I just picked up this move in there where you hang upside down from the pole and arch your back, and..." I trailed off seductively.

A full-fledged grin took hold of his features. "Now that might make me feel a *lot* better."

* * *

Ramirez was up before the sun again, muttering about doing some "damage control" in a sleep-filled voice as he rolled out of bed. I vaguely registered the shower turning on, smelled fresh aftershave and coffee, then heard the front door slam shut. I rolled over and went back to sleep until Max let out a cry over the baby monitor.

Two bottles, one shower, and three diaper changes later, I was in my kitchen contemplating my breakfast options when Dana walked in, a Starbucks cup in each hand.

"Location shoots are ridiculous. You know how much easier it would have been to pop a poster of the Golden Gate behind me and shoot here in L.A. than trying to wait for the sun to peek through the frickin' permanent fog layer at the actual Golden Gate?"

"Hi," I said. "Good to see you."

"It would have been so much easier," she continued, answering her own question. "I swear they were just looking for excuses to blow their budget." She paused and handed me a cup. "Hi. Good to see you too."

I grinned, taking a sip. Mocha latte with extra whip. She knew me so well.

"So the shoot was a total bust?" I asked.

Dana shook her head, downing her own drink. "No, we got the shots. I just nearly got pneumonia in the process. I mean, it's spring for heaven's sake. Doesn't San Francisco know that?"

"Maybe it didn't get the memo?"

She shot me a look that said it was too soon for levity about her ordeal. "Anyway, I'm so glad to be home. And...you owe me some deets. How did the interrogation go yesterday?" she asked, taking another long sip from her cup. Filled with a non-fat, soy, decaf latte, if I knew her as well as she knew me.

I groaned. "Worse than your shoot," I said, filling her in on all of the gory details, including my husband decking a sports celebrity.

"Ouch," she said when I was done. "Sounds like that lead is a dead end now."

I nodded. "No kidding. I feel terrible."

She took another sip. "Hey, it's not like *you* punched the guy."

I nodded. "I know. But I didn't help the situation any. And now Ratski is about as hostile a witness as they come. I think the words 'sue' and 'your ass' were even shouted as the bouncers dragged Ramirez off of him."

"Sucks," Dana agreed. She paused to sip. "Well, maybe we can help him get the dirt on Bucky another way."

While part of me was pretty sure I'd *helped* my husband enough already, there was a teeny tiny part of me that perked up at the idea of making it up to him.

"What did you have in mind?"

"Well, Ramirez said there were rumors that Lacey and Bucky were having problems. I happen to know where all good baseball rumors start."

"I'll bite. Where?" I asked

"*Baseball Wives!*"

I cocked my head to the side. "Right. The show is gossip central. And...?"

"And maybe we can get the 411 on the rocky relationship for Ramirez. The show airs on the same network as *Lady Justice*, and I did a promotional spot with some of the ladies in the cast a couple of months ago." Dana pulled out her cell and started scrolling through her contacts. "I think I still have Kendra's number."

"That would be Kendra Blanco?" I asked, recalling from the show a tall blonde with a serious shopping addiction.

Dana nodded. "Her husband is Gabriel Blanco. The pitcher. Ah! Got it." She held up her phone, displaying a local number.

"You think Kendra can help?" I asked.

Dana shrugged. "It's worth a try. If the couple was having issues, maybe Bucky talked to Kendra's husband or one of the other players. Kendra is in the know for anything that happens on that team."

"I don't know…" I hedged.

"Come on, Maddie. You know you want to help. Besides, you really think that Kendra, or anyone associated with that team, is going to gossip to a cop the way she would over a mimosa with us at lunch?" Dana reasoned.

She had a good point. "I could really use a mimosa," I agreed.

* * *

Kendra Blanco was as beautiful in person as she was on the show. Tall, blonde, and slim, with skin that had been exfoliated, waxed, and Botoxed within an inch of its life. She was dressed in a white, linen pant suit that on anyone else would have shown off every teeny ripple of cellulite. Of course, cellulite didn't dare deposit itself on Kendra's thighs, so she didn't have to worry. She'd paired the suit with a hot pink cami and a pair of pink, pointy-toed, leather pumps that somehow screamed kick-ass and total girly-girl all at the same time.

She was seated at a table on the patio of Bando Café on Sunset, a pitcher of the promised mimosas already in front of her. To her right sat a shorter, more curly-haired version of her blonde fabulousness, and to the left a brunette with her hair sleeked back into a tight ponytail. I easily recognized both from the TV show. Elizabeth Ratski and Elizabeth DeCicco—the two "E"s.

"Dana!" Kendra called, hailing us from her table as we approached. I noticed that her manicure matched her heels in a beyond put-together look. I was suddenly glad I'd opted to change into a slim, a-line skirt and loose blouse before dropping the kids at my mom's again. I prayed both items of clothing were still baby food free.

"Kendra, it's so good to see you again," Dana said, doing an air-kiss greeting before introducing me. "This is my good friend, Maddie Springer, the shoe designer."

Kendra nodded my way and introduced the two E's.

"Beth Ratski," the curly-haired blonde said, sticking her hand out. "My husband plays first base."

I shook her hand, glossing over the fact that I knew very well who her husband was and how he'd gotten a black eye yesterday afternoon, quickly moving on to the brunette who did a repeat of the hand shake.

"Liz," she told me. "Right field."

"I know," I admitted this time. "I watch the show."

Turns out I could not have come in with a better intro as all three beamed at me as if the cameras were on them right then.

"Oh, I'm so embarrassed," Kendra said. "They completely take things out of context in the editing room, don't they?" she asked the two E's.

Both women nodded in vigorous agreement. "Completely," they said in unison.

"I mean, they make it look as if we're 24/7 drama queens," Kendra went on.

"Speaking of drama," Dana said, lowering her voice. "I couldn't believe it when I heard about Bucky's girlfriend."

An instant pall came over the wives, their expressions shifting to appropriately morose. "A terrible tragedy," Kendra agreed, sipping her drink.

The E's did a repeat of their nodding routine. "Terrible," they said in freaky unison again.

"Did you ladies know her well?" I asked.

Liz snorted, then quickly tried to cover it in a cough.

"We knew her," Kendra said, carefully. "But she was not one of us."

"Meaning?" Dana asked.

"She wasn't on the show," Beth said. She paused. "At least not yet."

Kendra shot Beth a look that clearly said to keep her commentary to nods.

"Yet? Was she joining the show?" I asked.

"With Bucky's batting average so high, the producers were talking about including her next season," Kendra conceded. "But I doubt it would have actually happened."

"Why is that?" Dana asked, pouring a mimosa for each of us.

"Well, for one thing, she wasn't a baseball *wife* now was she?" Kendra said, smirking at the exclusivity of her club.

"Plus, she didn't fit in," Liz offered.

"How so?" I asked.

Liz cleared her throat, then shot a glance Kendra's way as if asking for permission to continue. "Well, Lacey worked for me. At my clothing boutique, Bellissima?" she said, her voice going up in a question at the end.

I nodded my encouragement. "I've heard of it." And I had. While it wasn't rivaling Kitson, thanks to the TV show, it had gained some popularity among the celebrity shopping set.

"Anyway, that's how Bucky met her. He and my husband came in the boutique to take me to lunch one day, Lacey was there, and, well…trust me, I never thought Bucky'd get involved with an *employee*."

I tried not to roll my eyes. I was pretty sure these three women weren't born with silver baseball mitts on their hands, but they were clearly drawing social lines in the sand now.

"I tried to discourage him from getting serious with Lacey," Liz continued.

"We all did," Beth jumped in, nodding.

"I take it you weren't friends?" Dana asked.

"God, no. She was such a gold digger and a total poser," Beth blurted out. Then she yipped, and I could have sworn Kendra kicked her under the table.

"Posing how?" I prodded, turning my attention to the brunette at the table.

"Well," Liz answered, shooting a glance at Kendra again. "We called her the 'knock-off' queen. Once she stopped working for me, she'd come to the ballpark in a Juicy cap, with Dolce jeans, a Michael Kors top, and a Coach bag. Everything was label with her."

"But it was all fake," Beth added.

"Cheap knock-offs," Kendra clarified. "I mean, I don't know who she thought she was fooling. We all knew she didn't have the kind of money for that stuff."

"She couldn't have gotten it from Bucky?" I asked.

Liz snorted again. "Honey, Bucky doesn't have any money."

"Wait, isn't he looking at MVP this year?" I asked, sure that celebrity ball players made *some* money.

"*Possible* MVP. My husband is doing very well this year, too," Kendra clarified.

"Bucky was a rookie last year," Liz explained. "He signed a five year contract at league minimum. If he keeps playing the way he is, he might be able to renegotiate next year, but as it stands, he's making about as much as my son's kindergarten teacher."

"Ouch. He must not be too thrilled about that," I said.

But Kendra shrugged. "It's the way things work. All of us went through it with our husbands when they were rookies, too. Of course, not all of us resorted to garish knock-offs like Lacey did…" she said, trailing off as if that sin was reason enough for her demise.

"I felt so sorry for Bucky," Beth said. "He deserved someone with some class, you know."

"We heard they were having problems?" Dana jumped in. "Lacey and Bucky?"

"Bucky is all Midwestern charm, but the kid's naïve," Kendra told us. "He fell for her façade."

"But he's no idiot," Beth piped up. "I mean, she was only dating him for the status, you know? And he caught onto Lacey's celebrity seeking."

Liz shot her a look.

"What? He did," she said. Clearly Beth didn't catch the subtle undercurrent of guilt she was casting on Bucky.

"How do you know he caught on?" I pressed before Kendra could kick her into silence again.

"I heard them arguing. It was after a game last week."

"What were they arguing about?"

Beth's eyes cut to Kendra and Liz, both giving her hard stares. She licked her lips. "Well, I don't know for sure. I mean, they were arguing, but I couldn't hear what they were saying. Bucky just looked…upset. Sorta…" she trailed off, grabbing her mimosa to cover the heat creeping into her cheeks.

While these women had no problem airing the dirtiest of their laundry on TV, it seemed they were reluctant to let it out in person. I wondered if it was because they were saving the drama for the camera or if they had something to hide.

Either way, it was looking more and more like Ling and Marco's CNN-fueled theory might be right. The boyfriend really was the most likely suspect.

* * *

I swung by Mom's place to pick up the twins before heading home, and when I pulled into my driveway, I was surprised to see Ramirez's black SUV already there. A foreboding hit the pit of my stomach. Ramirez home in the middle of the day was a rare occurrence even when he *didn't* have a celebrity murder on his hands. And the foreboding only grew as soon as I opened the front door and heard banging in the kitchen.

"Jack?" I asked tentatively, setting the twins down in their play yard in the living room.

No answer. Just more banging.

I poked my head around the doorframe into the kitchen. Ramirez had a jar of pickles, a can of olives, and a sliced ham on the counter. He grabbed mustard from the fridge and squirted it on a hunk of ham, which he then stuffed into his mouth.

"Hey?" I asked. "Home for lunch?"

He grunted, shoved more ham into his mouth, then chewed violently.

"How did the damage control go?" I asked.

Ramirez pinned me with a look that said he was not in the mood to talk about it.

"You okay?" I asked, taking a careful step into the room.

"No. I am far from okay," he said, swallowing. "I'm not home for lunch. I'm just home."

I bit my lip. "Just home as in…"

"I'm suspended."

I froze, letting that information sink in. "You're joking?"

He shot me a hard look. "Do I look like I'm joking?" he asked. Though he didn't wait for an answer. Instead he turned to the refrigerator, reached in, grabbed a beer, and popped the top before downing half of it in one gulp.

"Wait, what do you mean suspended? They can't just do that, can they?"

He nodded. "Oh, yeah. They can. Apparently Ratski complained about my 'excessive force' to the manager of the team, who complained to the mayor, who complained to the captain. The entire chain of command is gunning for my head now. I'm off the case."

"That's ridiculous," I said, shaking my head. "The whole thing was Ratski's fault anyway."

Ramirez just grunted. "It doesn't matter. I'm out of it." He paused to swig more beer.

"That's so not fair," I said, feeling a little niggle of guilt that maybe I was as much at fault as Ratski.

"So where have you been?" Ramirez asked.

"Huh?"

He shot me a suspicious look, his brows forming a "V" over his dark eyes. "Maddie, please tell me you were shopping?"

I bit my lip. "Sorta."

"Sort meaning…?"

"Meaning not at all. I was out with Dana having lunch," I confessed

He shrugged, his expression relaxing. "Oh."

"With the Baseball Wives."

The eyebrows fell back down. "The Baseball Wives?"

"The wives of the Stars players. You know they have that reality show?"

He gave me a blank look. Not that I expected him to have seen it. If it wasn't on the Discovery Channel or ESPN, it wasn't on his radar.

"Anyway, we…Dana and I…we thought maybe it would be helpful if we heard what kind of gossip they had on Bucky and Lacey. You know. If they had any."

He paused. "And did they?"

"Some. Beth said she'd seen Bucky and Lacey arguing, but she didn't know why. Mostly they just hated Lacey."

"Any particular reason?"

"The usual. She was younger, prettier, her boyfriend was hitting more balls."

Ramirez sighed, running a hand through his hair. "Sadly, you've still gotten further today than I have."

I crossed the room and rubbed his back. "I'm sorry. I feel so bad about this"

He shook his head. "No. It's not your fault. *I* hit the guy."

"Well, don't take too much blame," I told him. "After a couple of mimosas, Beth let out that Ratski has a really short temper. Liz, the right fielder's wife, said he even got into a fist-fight with another player last year when they wanted to bench him before the playoffs."

"Wow, you really got those ladies to talk," Ramirez said.

I shrugged. "Dana had a lot do with it. But you know, we're good at girl talk. It's kind of our thing." I sent him a grin.

"Huh." He took a deep breath, running his hand through his hair again. "Look, I know this might be asking a lot, but there's something I need you to do for me," he said, a look I couldn't read suddenly running through his eyes.

"Of course," I agreed.

Then my husband turned to me and uttered the words I never thought I would hear him say.

"Maddie, I need you to investigate a murder for me."

CHAPTER FIVE

———

I blinked, not quite sure I'd heard him right. "I'm sorry, you want what?"

Ramirez took a long swig of beer, his features pinched as if it pained him to say it. "I want your help."

I couldn't suppress the goofy grin spreading across my face. Since we'd met, I'd had the misfortune to get involved in several of Ramirez's cases. While it had always been through no fault of my own, Ramirez had fought me every step of the way—asking me to back off, demanding I back off, even pleading once or twice that I leave his cases alone. So to hear him actually asking for my help was like I'd entered a parallel universe.

One I was going to enjoy as long as it lasted.

"Wipe that goofy grin off your face, Springer," he told me.

"Sorry." I tried, suppressing it to a mild smirk.

"Look, while I'm on suspension, I've been warned away from any contact with anyone who even remotely has ties to the Stars ball club."

"But I'm sure the captain has other detectives on the case, right?" I asked.

Ramirez sighed again, doing more hair mussing. "Right. Laurel and Hardy."

"Oh, they can't be that bad."

"No, those are their names. Laurel McMartin and John Hardy."

"Oh," I said suppressing that grin again.

"And the trouble is they *are* that bad. They're lazy, and they're total yes-men." He paused. "Or a yes-man and yes-woman. But the point is the Stars want this to be a random killing of some sort, quickly swept under the rug and stuck in a cold case file somewhere and forgotten. The city depends on Stars income, and the police depend on the city. Everyone is looking to make this swift, sweet, and tidy."

"But you don't think it's that simple."

He shot me a hard look. "No. I don't."

I nodded. "I don't either. People don't randomly poison other people by spray tan." I paused. "Especially at Fernando's." While a random killing might be good for the Stars, it would be the worst for Faux Dad's salon. No one would ever feel safe going into his tanning booths again, for fear the Tanning Salon Killer would strike again. It would ruin him.

"Exactly," Ramirez agreed. "Which is why I can't just sit here looking like a jackass while Laurel and Hardy let the perp slip through their fingers."

"So…what exactly are you proposing?" I hedged.

"I need you to be my eyes and ears. I need you to do the legwork I can't."

I bit my lip. While I'd helped Ramirez on cases before, I was the first to admit I wasn't exactly LAPD detective material. Truth be told, I accidentally stumbled on the truth as often as I happened to stumble on dead bodies. "Like, what kind of legwork?" I asked.

"Like the lunch you just had with the players' wives. Look, you and Dana have an in that Laurel and Hardy don't. I trust that they'll process any evidence that presents itself, but I also trust they'll avoid asking any hard questions that may lead to ruffled feathers. Or paperwork," he added.

"What about the babies?" I asked, gesturing to the twins, currently playing with colorful foam blocks.

"I'll watch them."

I froze. "Really? *You're* going to play stay-at-home-dad while *I* go investigate a murder?" The universe really had turned on its head.

Ramirez shrugged. "It'll be fun. I haven't gotten to spend enough time with them lately, anyway. We need some bonding."

"You sure? I mean, they can be a handful…"

Ramirez shot me a look. "I think I can manage watching my own kids, Maddie."

I was sure he could, too. For about an hour. Which was the absolute longest he'd been alone with both babies at once since they were born. It wasn't that Ramirez was a bad father by any stretch. But I was 100% sure he had no idea what he was in for.

On the other hand, it might not be a bad thing if he found out.

"Okay," I said, shrugging my shoulders. "When do I start, boss?"

The tension in Ramirez's jaw relaxed for the first time since I'd walked into the kitchen. "Tonight. The team management is throwing a memorial event for Lacey at the Marchmont Hotel. All the players should be attending. I need you to get Gabriel Blanco alone."

"The pitcher?" I asked. "Kendra's husband?"

Ramirez nodded. "Bucky says he was with Ratski and Blanco the morning Lacey was killed. But Bucky and these guys are tight."

"So you're thinking they might be lying for him?"

Ramirez shrugged. "It's a distinct possibility. Ratski isn't saying anything, so I'd like to know what Blanco says." He paused. "And more importantly, how he says it. If it's a rehearsed sounding story, we'll know he's full of it"

"On it," I promised.

I watched out of the corner of my eye as Livvie threw a block at Max's head, causing a chain reaction of block tossing and crying. I moved to intervene, but Ramirez stopped me with a hand on my arm.

"I'll take this one."

I cocked an eyebrow at him.

"Hey, they might as well get used to me being in charge around here," he reasoned.

I stepped back, letting him step between the babies. I was more than happy to pass the referee baton to him.

Besides, if I was going to be playing detective tonight, I was going to need to call in backup.

I grabbed my cell, scrolled through my numbers, and waited while it rang on the other end. Two rings in, Dana picked up.

"Hey," I told her. "Want to crash a memorial service with me tonight?"

* * *

The Marchmont Hotel was located in the heart of Orange County. While Hollywood is the glamour capital of the west coast, the money to finance that glamour comes from Orange County. Originally a suburb for commuters, it had quickly grown to be known as the ritzier, cleaner, swankier cousin to L.A. Even the freeways here were clean. If you took the 5 south, the second you entered Orange County the graffiti and battered medians immediately gave way to wide, smooth pavement, art deco carvings on the walls, and litter-free emergency lanes.

Dana and I valeted my mini-van and stepped into the hotel lobby, where we were greeted immediately by the scent of fresh flowers and the low hum of tasteful jazz music being pumped in through hidden speakers. We took the gold elevator to the third floor, where the Pacific Blue Ballroom was located, opening up into a room that looked more decked out for a wedding reception than a memorial service. A large bar extended down one side of the room, a small stage area of sorts on the other end, where posters of the team and the Stars insignia mingled with flower arrangements and photos of Lacey. Though I noticed that all of the photos looked recent, and all had been taken at the ballpark. There didn't seem to be any hint of Lacey's life outside the Stars franchise.

The room was filled with players, managers, and behind the scenes guys in suits and women in cocktail dresses in tasteful muted colors. I fit right in, even if I did say so myself, in a simple grey shift dress, embellished with a ruby, teardrop pendant and a pair of black pumps in a snakeskin pattern. Dana had gone with a black, floor length dress with an Angelina Jolie worthy slit up one side that already had a couple of the guys at the bar leering.

"So, which one is Blanco?" Dana asked, grabbing a glass of white wine from a passing tray.

I followed her lead, grabbing one as well as I let my eyes scan the room. Before I'd left the house, Ramirez had pulled up the team's website, making me memorize the faces of all the key players. Though, out of their uniforms, I was having a hard time matching them up. I guess I could only be thankful he hadn't made me memorize their stats, too.

"Dark hair in a buzz cut," I said, calling up the picture in my mind. "Six-foot-two, slim. He's from Argentina."

Dana nodded, craning her neck to scan the crowd.

"Dana?" a voice sounded behind us.

We spun as one to find Kendra, a small frown pulling at her cherry-red mouth. (Though I noticed that the Botox prevented it from actually extending to her forehead.) "I didn't know you were attending tonight?"

Dana and I did the appropriate air-kiss greetings before pulling back.

"We felt it only right," Dana said, quickly covering. "You know, here to represent the network and all."

Kendra nodded, as if she perfectly understood the etiquette. "Of course. Well, I'm so glad you could make it. I'm sure Bucky will be touched."

"Is he here?" I asked. While Ramirez had sent me on a mission to get the alibi from Blanco, I figured it wouldn't hurt to take the initiative and have a few words with Suspect Number One.

Kendra nodded. "By the bar. He hasn't detached himself from the tequila all night. Poor kid."

I glanced in the direction she indicated, seeing a fair-haired guy in his twenties hunched over a glass. While I could clearly tell it was Bucky, he had lost all of the swagger I'd seen from him on the field. It was as if in this setting he looked just like what he was—a young guy from the Midwest completely out of his element in a glamorous OC ballroom. And, at the moment, he was either completely grief stricken or doing a very good job of acting it.

"Would you mind if I excused myself to give my condolences?" I asked.

"Of course," Kendra agreed, grabbing Dana by the arm and steering her toward the two E's, parked at a table near the windows.

I threaded my way through the growing crowd toward Bucky. I was a couple of barstools away when I saw a tall, pot-bellied frame coming toward the bar, empty glass in hand. Ratski.

Immediately I ducked my head, turning my back to him. While the Glitter Galaxy had been dark, I was pretty sure he'd have no trouble recognizing me here. And not be overly thrilled to see me. I feigned interest in a potted palm while Ratski ordered a scotch, neat, downed it, and then had the bartender pour him another before weaving his way back into the crowd.

Unfortunately, by the time I thought it was safe to turn around again, Bucky's seat was empty.

I frantically scanned the room for him and felt my heart sink as I saw him taking the stage, chatting with a couple of white haired guys in expensive suits. From their age, I could only guess they represented the team's management, not players.

Damn. So much for my initiative.

I was just about to concede that my skills in no way measured up to Ramirez's faith in them, when I spotted a dark haired, tanned guy with a buzz cut standing near the French doors to the balcony. Bingo. Gabriel Blanco.

As I made my way toward him, a voice came over the PA system. "Everyone, may I have your attention please?"

All eyes shot to the front of the room, where a paunchy, white haired man was talking into a microphone.

"I'd like to thank you all for coming tonight. It is heartwarming to see all of the support for our Bucky. I can only imagine how hard this is for him," the man said, glancing toward his star player.

Bucky's face was a blank slate, though his eyes held dark circles beneath them, his skin a shade paler than when I'd last seen it on the Jumbotron.

"But I'm sure that seeing all of your friendly faces will help him get through these trying times."

I only vaguely paid attention as the guy went on about how special Lacey was, keeping my eyes instead on Blanco. I made it to his side just as Bucky stepped up to the mike to say a few words.

"Thank you all for coming," he said, his voice tight. "It means more than you know." Then he stepped back again, relinquishing the mike to the white haired guy. Clearly Bucky was not one for long speeches.

"Thank you all, again," the older man said. "We will be donating a portion of the proceeds of the next home game to the pediatric wing of Cedar-Sinai Hospital in Lacey's name. If you'd like to add a contribution, please see Kendra Blanco for more information."

With that, the crowd immediately went back to murmuring amongst themselves and mingling, as if to cover the awkwardness of thinking about a dead girl who none of them had really known well.

I watched as Blanco looked down at his glass, noticed that it was empty, and started to turn toward the bar.

I jumped before he could. "Gabriel Blanco?"

He turned my way, a pair of startling blue eyes peering out at me from his tanned face. "Yes?"

"Hi. I'm Maddie," I said, sticking a hand his way. "I, ah, I'm a friend of your wife's," I added, stretching the truth just a little.

He nodded, shaking my hand. "Nice to meet you."

"I'm so sorry about the loss. Were you and Lacey close?" I asked.

He shrugged. "Bucky and I are."

"This must be very difficult for him."

He shrugged again. "It's not easy, that's for sure."

"Were you with him?" I asked. "When he found out about Lacey?"

Blanco shook his head. "No. We were at the gym together earlier that day, but I'd gone home by then."

"Oh, how horrible," I said, putting a hand to my mouth. "You mean you were actually together while she was…being killed?" I did a stage whisper for effect.

Blanco shifted from foot to foot, looking down at his empty glass again as if he really wished something would materialize there. "Yeah. I guess."

"Then you're his alibi?"

"Bucky doesn't need an alibi," he quickly shot back. "He'd never hurt anyone."

"Oh, right, of course," I backpedaled. "I didn't mean to imply he would. Obviously he wouldn't hurt her. I mean, he couldn't have. He was with you the whole time."

Blanco nodded vigorously. "Right."

"At the gym, you said?"

"That's right," he agreed again.

"So, you two worked out together the whole time. Like, side by side?"

His dark eyebrows drew together. "Well, no, not the whole time. I mean, he didn't follow me to the john or anything. It's not like we were joined at the hip."

"So, you didn't have eyes on him the whole time?" I pounced, wondering just how far from the salon this gym was.

He spun on me, frowning again. "Look, we arrived together, we worked out, we left together. That was good enough for the cops, so I'm not sure what you're implying."

I bit my lip. Ramirez was right about Laurel and Hardy. They obviously hadn't dug too deeply into Bucky's alibi. "I'm not implying a thing," I said, pulling out my most charming smile. "Except that Bucky is lucky to have friends like you at such a trying time."

Blanco grunted a noncommittal response, but the frown eased some. "I need a drink," he said, pushing past me toward the bar.

I watched him slip away and sipped at my own glass, mingling through the crowd, trying to catch any little snippets of conversation I could that pertained to Bucky, Lacey, or her death. Though mostly I just heard people murmuring polite condolences, admitting they hadn't known the deceased very well and expressing sympathy for Bucky.

I wandered over to the display of photos near the stage. Bucky and Lacey at the ballpark, at charity events, hand in hand as he received some award. The wives had been right about Lacey's designer label fetish. In every one Lacey was wearing an obvious designer piece. A Channel logo bracelet, a Gucci branded jacket. I had to admit, they might have been knock-offs, but she knew the hot labels.

I sipped at my drink, honing in on another photo of Lacey, this time cheering for Bucky from the stands at a Stars game. She had her feet up on the empty seats in front of her, doing a diva pose for the cameras with a sassy smile.

But it wasn't the playful smirk on her face that caught my eye. It was her shoes. They were black ankle straps with a gold clasp on the side fashioned into the familiar "BR" logo of one of my fave designers, Berto Raul. I knew those shoes. I knew them because I had an order in for a pair, but they weren't out yet until next month. Meaning there was no way a made-in-China knock-off could have been put into production yet. The only way Lacey could have gotten a pair of those shoes was by purchasing at a runway show directly from the designer.

My eyes quickly scanned the rest of the photos, squinting at the details of her other outfits as I realized the Baseball Wives were wrong. Lacey was not wearing knock-offs. This wardrobe was the real deal.

So where had Lacey gotten the money for it?

CHAPTER SIX

I knew something was wrong as soon as I got home. The house was quiet. And it smelled like…I paused, sniffing the air in my foyer…Windex? Alarm bells immediately went off in my head.

"Jack? You guys okay?" I called out.

Ramirez popped his head in from the kitchen, putting a finger to his lips. "Shhh. The little ones are down."

I glanced at the clock above the mantel. "Already?"

He grinned. "We had a lot of playtime. They were tuckered out."

"Huh," I said, wandering into the living room, expecting to see the toy explosion that normally accompanied playtime. Only I felt my feet freeze as I scanned the room. The play yard was spotless, the toys all tucked neatly into the toy box in the corner. The floors were crumb-free, and even the babies' blankets had been folded into tidy little squares on the sofa.

"You…cleaned?" I asked, choking out the last word.

I felt Ramirez come up behind me, his arms wrapping around my waist. "Well, don't sound so surprised."

I swallowed. "I'm not," I lied. "I'm just…how did you manage the time to do this?"

He turned me around and blinked at me as if not understanding the question. "I told you the twins went to sleep."

I tried to shove down a tiny feeling of suddenly being outshined in the parenting department. Most nights that Ramirez worked late, I barely survived the twin's two-pronged assault of play time, dinner time, and trying-to-get-two-crying-babies-to-sleep time. I couldn't think of a single night I'd had them down early and had energy left to fold blankets, let alone Windex.

"How was the party?" Ramirez asked, pulling my thoughts away from Mr. Mom's surprising performance as he led me to the sofa.

"Good." I sank down in the cushions, slipping my heels off one at a time.

"You talked to Blanco?"

I nodded. "I did. And the alibi is shaky." I told him what I'd learned about their trip to the gym as well as my findings about Lacey's wardrobe choices.

Ramirez frowned when I'd finished. "So, she wears nice stuff. What kind of money we talking here?"

"You're cute. *Nice* stuff? You want to know how much these *nice* shoes cost me?" I asked, gesturing to my snakeskin pumps.

"Something tells me I don't."

I grinned. "Smart man. Let's just say in those pictures at the memorial alone, Lacey was probably wearing at least two grand per outfit."

Ramirez's eyes went round, then shot down to my shoes. "Those are why we're a two income household aren't they?"

I gave him a playful punch on the arm. "My *point* is that Lacey was spending a lot more than people thought she was. It could be the reason she and Bucky were fighting. Maybe she was trading on his credit or his celebrity status, looking to milk him once the contract negotiations went through next year. Maybe he found out and wasn't too happy."

Ramirez raised an eyebrow at me. "Wow. Look at you, all coming up with theories and stuff."

I couldn't help a small lift of pride. "Well, hey, it's not like I Windexed or anything."

Ramirez frowned as if not understanding the reference.

"Anyway," I went on, "I know one person who would know how Lacey was paying for her extravagant lifestyle."

"Who?"

"Faux Dad. He said she was in the salon all the time. If she was paying on credit, he'd know about it. Who knows, Lacey might have even confided some of her relationship woes to him. He is her stylist after all."

The corner of Ramirez's mouth lifted. "As long as we're not asking him to break his stylist-client privilege."

I swatted him again. "Very funny. Hey, I thought I did a darn good job tonight."

"You did." He pulled me closer, his arms going around my waist again. "Now how about we take the rest of this conversation into the bedroom?"

Now that was an offer I couldn't refuse.

* * *

The next morning I got up early, showered, dressed in a pair of skinny jeans, hot pink ballet flats, and a loose kimono style silk top. Then I grabbed a cup of coffee, kissed my husband on the cheek, and wished him well with Operation Mr. Mom as I headed out the door. Half an hour later I pushed through the glass front doors of Fernando's. The crime scene tape was gone now, the residue of fingerprint dust cleanly washed away. The only thing that betrayed that any sort of tragedy had occurred here was the fact that half of the styling stations were empty.

As soon as I walked in I noticed two people at the reception desk standing next to Marco who were clearly not clients. The first was a short, portly guy with a trendy-two-years-ago soul patch on his chin and shoes that were shined within an inch of their lives. The second was a woman with short, dark hair wearing a utilitarian pant-suit and low-healed loafers. Even if she hadn't been standing next to Marco—who was a vision in a white leather jumpsuit with lilac accents today—she would have looked drab enough to blend into any background.

"So you were the one who scheduled Lacey for her tan?" the woman asked Marco, looking down at an electronic tablet in her hands.

"Y-yes. I schedule everyone."

"Including the deceased?" the guy pressed.

Marco swallowed hard, then nodded. "Yes, Officer Hardy."

"Detective," he corrected.

"Sorry," Marco mumbled.

"This scheduling book was in your possession the entire morning?" the woman, who I deduced to be the Laurel in the duo, asked.

"Yes."

The two detectives gave each other a meaningful look.

"Wait—no!" Marco amended. "I mean, yes, it was here at my desk, but anyone could have seen it."

"Did they?" Laurel asked.

"I-I don't know. Maybe. I mean, they must have because someone killed her, and it wasn't me," Marco squeaked out.

More meaningful looks were exchanged, then Laurel jotted something on her tablet.

"What are you writing?" Marco asked.

"Back to the book," Hardy said. "Where did you keep it?"

"Here," Marco said, slapping his hand on the reception desk for emphasis.

"So you're saying anyone who came through those doors," Hardy said, pointing to the ones I'd just entered through, "could have seen this book."

Marco nodded vigorously.

"Okay, who came in that day?" Laurel asked.

Marco swallowed again. "I don't know. The other clients. The staff. I think I saw the UPS guy."

"You *think* or you *did*?" Hardy pressed.

"I-I don't know. I mean, I wasn't watching the doors like a hawk. I had to grab Mrs. Johnson a smock, and Jennie needed more acetone in her kit, and I did use the little boys' room a couple of times."

"Hmph," Hardy said, nodding to Laurel, who jotted down more notes.

Marco paled. "What? What is she writing now?"

"Thank you for your time," Laurel said, slamming the cover on her tablet shut instead of answering. "We'll be in touch if we need anything more."

"And don't go anywhere," Hardy told him, stabbing a chubby finger his way as the two left the salon, Laurel's heels shuffling on the floor and Hardy leaving a wake of cheap cologne behind him.

"Ohmigod, Mads," Marco cried as soon as they left. "Did you see the way they were looking at me? They think I had something to do with Lacey's death!"

"I'm sure that's not true," I said, patting him on the shoulder. "Those were just routine questions."

"This is an absolute nightmare. We're all living under a cloud of suspicion here."

"I'm sure it will blow over soon," I said, doing more patting.

"You know we had three cancelations this morning alone?"

I glanced behind him to the nearly empty salon. Two women were getting pedis and just one lone woman sat in the styling chairs, Faux Dad hard at work coloring her long locks.

"One of our stylists quit this morning, Maddie," he went on. "She said she couldn't come back to the scene of such carnage. Carnage, Maddie!" He threw his hands in the air for emphasis, his leather outfit squeaking in protest.

I bit my lip. I had to admit, things were not looking rosy for Fernando's at the moment.

"Listen, you think you could fix this for me?" I asked, holding up my still chipped nail. In all that had happened in the last two days, I'd yet to get it fixed.

Marco nodded. "Sure. It's not like we're busy," he said glumly, leading me to a nail station in the center of the salon. Twenty minutes later I was buffed, trimmed, and shellacked, letting my nails dry under UV light as Faux Dad finished with his client.

He shuffled toward me, much the same glum look on his face that I'd seen on Marco's. Only on Faux Dad the bad mood made everything sag from his fleshy cheeks to the bags growing under his eyes.

"You don't look so hot," I said honestly.

"I don't feel so hot. I was up all night reading the *L.A. Informer*'s sensational take on our salon."

I cringed. I could just imagine the field day the tabloid was having with the Tanning Salon Murder.

"Maybe you should close the salon for a bit and take some time off?" I suggested.

But he shook his head violently. "No way. We need to show the world a brave face and carry on."

While I wasn't sure just how much bravery was involved in doing cut and colors, I nodded. "I understand."

"Is Ramirez making any headway on the case?" he asked, sitting at the empty table next to me.

"We're, uh, working on it," I hedged. I didn't have the heart to tell him that Ramirez was out, and I was now his best chance at clearing the salon's image. Instead, I changed the subject. "Actually, I wanted to ask you a couple of questions about Lacey."

"Sure, though I'm not sure what I can tell you that I didn't tell the police."

"Did Lacey talk about Bucky much?"

Faux Dad pursed his lips, his eyes narrowing as he contemplated the question. "Some. I mean, everyone chats a little while they're getting foiled and highlighted. But nothing out of the ordinary."

"What about any arguments or disagreements between them? Any trouble in paradise lately?"

But Faux Dad shook his head. "Nothing she confided in me." He paused. "Why? Do you think Bucky killed her?"

"It's possible. Someone said she saw them fighting a few days before Lacey was killed."

Faux Dad perked up.

"But," I added, trying not to get his hopes up too high, "Bucky may have an alibi."

"Oh." His jowls sagged back into a frown.

"Ralph, Lacey seems to have been spending an awful lot lately," I said, switching gears. "Can you tell me what kind of credit she was using here?"

Faux Dad shook his head. "Marco handles payments." He hailed the receptionist in question over, repeating my question to him.

"Oh, Lacey didn't pay with credit," Marco told us. "It was cash."

I paused. I'll admit, that was the last thing I'd been expecting to hear. "Wait—she paid cash. Like, actual greenbacks?"

He nodded. "I know. No one does that anymore, right?"

"Exactly how much cash was she throwing around here?" I asked them.

Faux Dad shrugged. "A lot."

"I guess I just assumed it was Bucky's," Marco added.

I bit my lip. I could see shop owners all over Beverly Hills assuming the same thing. Only, they'd all be wrong.

"Bucky didn't have that kind of money yet. Did she give any indication of where else she might have gotten it?" I grasped.

"I didn't ask," Marco admitted.

"I know she did work at a clothing boutique," Faux Dad piped up.

"Right. Liz DeCicco's place, Bellissima." I bit my lip. But I knew from my brunch with the Baseball Wives that Lacey hadn't been making bank at the boutique as a mere *employee*. So where had she gotten the money?

"Who has that much *cash*?" I mused out loud. I'd be hard pressed to find more than a twenty in my own wallet. Anything above-board and legal was all credit, debit, or direct deposit these days.

Marco raised his hand in the air like a kid in the back of the classroom. "Ooo, ooo, I know! A stripper! Ling always has stacks of twenties."

I pause. "*Stacks* of twenties?" I was seriously in the wrong profession.

"Maybe Lacey was working the pole, Bucky found out about it, and killed her," Marco said, running with his theory.

I scrunched up my nose. "I don't know. I doubt that she'd be so public about being Bucky's girlfriend if she had some secret life like that. I mean, it would take all of five seconds for someone at the tabloids to follow her around for a day and figure out she was a dancer, right?"

Marco's shoulders slumped. "Good point."

"Okay, so she wasn't stripping. What was she doing?"

"Do you think the *Baseball Wives* show gave her an advance?" Faux Dad asked. "I mean, she talked about the show all the time. She said the producers were thinking about putting her on next season. Maybe they fronted her some money?"

I nodded. While the other wives had made it sound like the show was far from a sure thing, it was certainly possible that Lacey had made some quiet deal with the producers behind their backs.

Unfortunately, finding out the details of her contract was beyond my snooping scope. I pulled my cell out, dialing home.

"Hey," Ramirez answered on the first ring. I could hear the sounds of *Mickey Mouse Clubhouse*, two crying kids, and some toy that played the "Farmer in the Dell" in the background.

"Hey. You guys doing okay?" I asked.

"Yeah, sure. Great. Why wouldn't we be?"

"I don't know, it sounds a little—" I started.

But Ramirez cut me off by yelling, "Livvie, don't touch that! That is not food!"

"Um, what's not food?" I asked.

"Nothing. It's fine. What were you saying?"

"You sure you don't need me to come home and—"

"Nope," he said, quickly cutting me off again. "I'm fine. I got this." Then I heard him cover the mouthpiece, yelling again. "*Do not* put that in your mouth, Livvie."

"Uh, okay. Look, I was just wondering if you could do something for me, but I can call back later."

"Nope, we're fine. Shoot," he said. I had to admit, for how chaotic it sounded there, his voice was perfectly calm.

"I need some financial info on Lacey."

"You find something?" he asked.

"Maybe. She seems to have had more cash than we can account for," I said, filling him in on what Marco and Faux Dad had told me. "We're wondering if the show paid her an advance or something. Any way you can get that info?"

I heard him nodding on the other end. "I'm sure I can get someone at the station to float it to me. I'll call you as soon as I have something—Livvie, spit it out. Spit!"

"You sure you don't need me to—"

"Hey, I gotta go, babe. Call if you find out anything new."

And before I could stop him, he hung up. My hands itched to hit redial. But if Ramirez said he had it under control, I had to trust him. Hey, he was trusting me with the investigation.

It was a two way street, right? Besides, I was sure Livvie couldn't have put anything *too* bad in her mouth.

I hoped.

CHAPTER SEVEN

———

With Lacey's mysterious cash in Ramirez's capable hands, I decided to focus on the argument Beth had said she overheard between Lacey and Bucky. Let's face it, CNN was sometimes right—it usually was the boyfriend whodunit. Bucky was still my number one suspect, and the truth was I'd yet to talk to him.

As I left the salon, I pulled out my phone, dialing the number for Kendra's cell.

Four rings in, it was answered with a sing-song, "Hello?"

"Hi Kendra, it's Maddie Springer. We met the other day?"

"Of course. Dana's friend."

"Yes. Listen, I was wondering if you know where I could find Bucky Davis today?"

She paused, and I could hear mental wheels turning. "May I ask why?" she asked.

"I, uh, never got to give him my condolences at the memorial yesterday," I said lamely.

But it must have been good enough for her, because she answered, "Well, he's at practice today. The whole team is."

"Oh." I was surprised to hear he was back at work so soon, and it must have shown in my voice.

"He says he needs to keep busy," Kendra explained. "Hitting a ball, getting testosterone out. You know, that's how guys do grief."

I guessed I could understand. Hey, if retail therapy helped me through hard times, who was I to judge someone using baseball therapy?

"I'm actually headed to the ballpark today to speak with the management about the charity fund in Lacey's name. Would you like me to put your name on the security list?" Kendra asked.

"Please!" I agreed, quickly jumping on the invite.

Kendra gave me direction to the player's entrance and told me she'd leave my name with the guard.

I detoured only long enough to hit a drive-through Starbucks for a mid-morning pick-me-up before jumping on the 2 and heading toward the stadium.

The Stars stadium was located in Echo Park, at the apex of the 5, 101, and 110 freeways. It was the kind of neighborhood where you could pay a half-million for a two bedroom cottage down the street from a massage parlor that offered "happy endings" for twenty bucks. Transitional might have been the word to describe it, only this neighborhood had been transitioning for the last fifteen years. Its residents called it "eclectic," but Geico called it "high risk."

I pulled into the stadium parking lot, driving around to the east side where the players' entrance was located. Without a game today, the lot was a ghost town except for a small section near the players' entrance where rows of sports cars and luxury SUVs stood gleaming in the sun. I slipped my mini-van into a slot near the back, hoping it didn't stick out too badly, and made my way to a tall guy in a black security uniform standing by the entrance.

"Maddie Springer," I told him. "I'm a guest of Kendra Blanco."

"Just a moment," he told me, pulling up an electronic tablet and gliding his finger over the surface. A moment later he must have found my name on the list, as he nodded. "Mrs. Blanco is already here. She said you could go on in." He moved aside and held open the glass doors for me.

I thanked him and stepped into an air conditioned corridor.

Like much of Los Angeles, the stadium was built on a hill, the field and concessions above ground, while the business offices and private areas were carved into the hillside as an underground world. One large corridor ran the circumference of the stadium with several smaller walkways and doors leading off to the left and right. As I wound my way through the inner workings of the Stars' world I spied break rooms, training areas with weight machines, and a ton of offices housing the administrative arms of the franchise. I was starting to worry that I'd be lost forever in the maze of cool, white hallways when I finally spotted a ramp to the field about halfway through my stadium lap.

I took it and found myself once again in the bright, warm sunshine, squinting at a scattering of guys in various work-out gear tossing balls to each other on the field. Most were working in groups of twos and threes, coaches shouting directions as players worked out their kinks.

But I spotted Bucky thankfully alone.

Near the dugout, Bucky was swinging a bat at a pitching machine. It shot a white blur toward him, and the crack of his bat sent it back toward the far stadium seats, echoing in the empty arena. I watched him hit three or four in a row, then pause to sip from a Gatorade bottle as a young kid in a Stars jacket emerged from the dugout to refill the machine.

"Bucky Davis?" I asked, approaching him from behind.

"Yeah?" he answered, not turning around, his attention still completely focused on the fake pitcher in front of him as if staring the machine down.

"Uh, hi. I was wondering if I could ask you a couple of questions?"

"Shoot," he told me, swigging his drink again.

I cleared my throat, having a hard time broaching the subject of his dead girlfriend to the back of his head. "Uh, it's about Lacey."

I watched his back stiffen, then he spun around, his blue eyes narrowing at me. "You a reporter?"

"No," I shook my head quickly. "No, I'm…with the salon. Where she was…" I trailed off.

I watched Bucky's jaw clench. "What do you want?"

"I wanted to ask you a few questions about Lacey."

"Why?"

Great question. I doubted that saying because I thought he killed her was going to get me very far. Instead, I went with a small half-truth. "For our insurance purposes." I was pretty sure Faux Dad had some kind of insurance.

It seemed to work as some of the suspicion drained from his eyes. "Oh. Right. Sure, what do you want to know?"

"We noticed that Lacey was coming into the salon an awful lot," I started with.

He nodded. "Yeah. I guess. I mean, she liked to look pretty."

"She was spending a lot of money there."

He shrugged. "Hey, money spent on looking pretty is money well spent in my book, right?" He gave me his all-American smile, but it never quite made it to his eyes. Which, I noticed were rimmed in red like he'd spent more time crying than sleeping in that last couple of days. In fact, he looked exactly the way I'd expect a brokenhearted, grieving boyfriend to look. Which made me wonder if maybe he really *was* grieving. I'd seen him in the Stars commercials. And actor, he was not.

"Right. Well, we're a little concerned with how much she was spending," I said, trying to find a tactful way to put it.

His sandy brows drew together. "What do you mean?"

"I mean, she was spending upwards of three hundred dollars a week at our salon alone. Cash."

He blinked at me. "You gotta be joking?"

I shook my head. "No joke. And the clothes she was wearing?"

"What about them?"

"Designer. As in expensive."

"How expensive?" he asked, the confusion in his face making it clear that he was connecting the same dots about Lacey that I had. She'd had way more money to spend than she should have.

"Seven-hundred-dollar-heels expensive."

He did more blinking, the frown between his brows deepening.

"Do you know where she was getting that kind of money?"

He looked behind me, as if searching the ball field for the answers. "No. But, I mean, maybe she got a raise or something. She works at a boutique on Melrose. Tony DeCicco's wife owns it."

I bit my lip. "Actually, Liz told me Lacey didn't work there anymore."

He did more blinking, the surprise on his face plain. If he was faking, he was doing a bang-up job of it.

"She didn't?"

I nodded. "She didn't mention that to you?"

"Nuh-uh…" He trailed off, the realization that his dead girlfriend had been keeping secrets from him sinking in. I had to admit, I felt sorry for the guy. I was having a hard time keeping him in the suspect numero uno spot.

"Do you know if she had signed on to do the *Baseball Wives* show?" I asked. "Maybe received an advance from them?"

But he just shrugged. "I'm sorry. I don't know."

"I have to ask…someone said they heard you two fighting. Last week after a game."

His jaw clenched, and I could see his eyes growing wet. "Yeah. We did."

"Can you tell me what that was about?" I asked.

His eyes welled up, and he shook his head, suddenly sinking to sit on the wooden bench behind him. "It was so stupid. I mean now, with her gone, it seems like a totally petty thing."

"What was it?"

"I got home early from our series in Denver," he said, finally looking up. "I called her to go out, but she didn't pick up. All night. When I confronted her the next day after the game, she got all cagey."

"Cagey?" I repeated, feeling my suspicion radar perk up.

"Yeah, like she didn't want to tell me where she was. I got sorta upset and accused her of being out with someone else. Then she got *totally* upset and said I needed to trust her more. It got kinda loud, so I'm not surprised someone overheard."

"Did she ever say where she was?"

He shrugged. "She said it was a girl's night out at City Walk that went a little late. That's it. I mean, we made up the next day."

My heart sank. While I was 90% sure Lacey had been lying to her boyfriend, I also had a feeling Bucky was telling the truth to me now. And I didn't see him being the type to kill over a girl's night gone late.

* * *

Out of leads and out of ideas, I pointed my car toward home. Ramirez's SUV was parked in the drive, but the house was silent as I slipped my key in the lock.

"Hello?" I called, pushing the door open. "Anyone home?" I did a slow survey of the living room and felt my stomach clench. Again no toys littered the floor. No piles of diapers. No half-drank bottles or sippy cups on the coffee table. Ditto in kitchen. The sink was void of any dirty dishes, the counters were cleared, and the dishwasher hummed contentedly. If I didn't know better, I'd even say someone had washed the floors.

I hated to say it, but my husband was Super Mom.

I was just about to go check if he'd had time to do the laundry, too—then shoot myself for being such a slacker at this obviously easy mom thing—when the back door opened and Ramirez appeared pushing the twins' double stroller.

"Hey, look who's ba-ack," he sing-songed. "It's Mama."

This resulted in two rounds of giggles and raised arms from Max and Livvie.

I bent down, unbuckling Max from his seat, and gave Livvie kisses on the top of her head. "Everything go okay today?" I asked.

"Great," Ramirez said, pulling Livvie from her seat and setting her down on shaky toddler legs on the kitchen tile.

"They give you any trouble?" I asked, wondering what Livvie had been told to spit out earlier.

"Nope."

"You even had time to clean the house, huh?" I gestured to the spotless room.

"Yep," he answered, doing the one word thing again.

"Huh. I'm impressed," I admitted.

He grinned at me. "What? You think I can't be a domestic kind of guy?"

While it should have made me happy, I was slightly annoyed that he had done it. And better than I had.

"No, it's great. I'm glad it all went well."

"It did. And my buddy at the station got back to me with Lacey's financials."

Great. Super Mom, and he'd done more detective work than I had, too.

"You okay?" he asked, cocking his head at me.

"Peachy," I lied. "What did you learn about Lacey?" I asked, trying to hide my inexplicably foul mood.

"Okay, so here's what we know," Ramirez told me, crossing his arms and leaning his back against the kitchen counter, quickly shifting from domestic-kind-of-guy to Cop Mode. "Lacey was receiving regular deposits into her bank account. They started just over a month ago. Weekly deposits of large sums of cash."

"How large are we talking?"

"Ten thousand."

"Wow."

"Each."

I blinked at him, doing some mental math. "That's at least—"

"Fifty-thousand dollars over the last five weeks."

"I'm guessing the production company did not pay her fifty-thousand dollars in five cash increments?"

Ramirez shook his head. "Nope. Though, she *was* actually set to join the cast in the new season. But the producers confirmed that they paid per episode once production began. And not nearly that much for a first-timer on a reality show."

I bit my lip. Cash deposits, no paper trail, and no shortage of secrets. I could think of one way a gold digging celebrity girlfriend like that could come up with a money-making scheme.

Blackmail.

CHAPTER EIGHT

———

The next morning the first thing I smelled was freshly brewed coffee. The scent pulled me out of bed and toward its delicious caffeinated aroma, despite the fact the sun was barely peeking through the early morning smog layer.

"Coffee?" I croaked out.

Ramirez handed me a mug that read: Real Women Do it Backwards and In Heels. "Morning, sunshine."

"You're up early," I mumbled, gratefully taking a sip. Heaven.

Ramirez nodded. "Tox screen on Lacey is coming in this morning. I'm meeting my buddy for coffee to get a look at it." He paused. "That is, unless you've got some hot lead to follow this morning?"

I shook my head, ashamed to say I didn't.

"So you're good watching the munchkins today?" Ramirez asked.

I nodded, then, as if on cue, I heard tiny voices babbling through the baby monitor. I followed them to the nursery where both twins were wide awake and demanding their breakfast.

A whirlwind morning of diapers, bottles, mashed bananas, and flying Cheerios later, I decided I needed more info about the Baseball Wives. If Lacey had been blackmailing someone, the wives and Stars players were the most likely suspects. True, she hadn't been invited into their inner circle with open arms, but she could have been close enough to stumble on a scandalous secret that someone was willing to pay to keep quiet. And possibly even kill over.

I streamed every episode of *Baseball Wives* that Amazon had, trying to come up with any clue as to who Lacey could have targeted. But by the time I got to the last season, I'd had my celebrity gossip fix for the year but hadn't narrowed my suspect field any. Cheating husbands, backstabbing socialites, money, sex, rehab. It seemed that airing their dirty laundry was number one on the wives' list of to-dos. It all led to ratings. So what secret would they kill to keep?

I was just finishing up the last episode when my cell rang, displaying Marco's number.

"Hey," I said, picking up.

"You home, Maddie?"

"Yes," I hedged. "Why?"

"Good. We're on our way over."

"We?"

"Ling and I."

"To what do I owe this visit?" I asked, my suspicion radar humming.

"Clown auditions."

I prayed I'd heard him wrong. "What did you say?"

"Sorry, bad connection. Be there in ten!" he called, then hung up.

I sat staring at my cell, waffling between the options of grabbing the kids and hightailing it out of there before Marco showed up or locking the doors and pretending we weren't home after all. In the end neither seemed likely to work. Marco had a key, and there was zero chance of getting two toddlers out the door in under ten minutes.

Instead, I made another pot of coffee and was fortifying myself with a fresh cup when I heard a knock on the door.

"Yoo-hoo," Marco said, not bothering to wait for me to answer before stepping inside. Today he was a vision in Day-Glo orange pants in a paisley print, and a turquoise muscle T.

"Please tell me that connection was *really* bad and I didn't hear you mention clowns," I told him.

He shook his head. "No, I didn't say clowns."

I sighed with relief. "Oh good."

"I said *clown*. Singular."

I narrowed my eyes at him.

"I hope this is quick," Ling said, pushing into the room behind him. She was dressed in a tube top, tube skirt, and looked like she'd applied about a tube and a half of pale pink lipstick. "I gotta get in for the lunch crowd. Those truckers tip big when we have the lunch buffet."

I really hoped she was talking about chicken wings.

"Okay, don't hate me—" Marco said, settling himself on the sofa.

"Too late."

"But it turns out we can't get Johnny Weir. Something about the Ice Capades and a contract and, blah, blah, blah. Anyhoo, I've got the next best thing. A clown!"

I blinked. "How is a clown the next best thing to an Olympic figure skater?"

Marco waved me off. "The agency said they were sending their top performer over, so we're auditioning him today."

"You know, the twins really don't need a big performance," I told him, glancing at Max. He was lying on his back, currently enthralled with his big toe. "They're pretty easily entertained."

Marco gave me a horror stricken look. "How can we have a children's birthday party without a clown? Who will man the balloon animal station?"

"You're right. Let's just cancel the whole thing."

"Not funny, Mads," he said, wagging a finger at me.

I didn't have the heart to tell him I wasn't joking.

I was about to plead my case in earnest when the doorbell rang.

I shot Marco a look. "You sent the clown *here*? To my house?"

Marco was wise enough not to answer, instead scuttling to open the door.

On the other side stood a six foot tall, broad shouldered guy who looked like he belonged on the gridiron more than the circus train. He was dressed in a pair of yellow spandex pants, a polka dotted shirt, and had an afro of bright red hair that perfectly matched his round, red nose. His face was painted white, his wig was a little squished on one side, and I noticed a bicycle helmet dangling from his right hand and a messenger bag slung over his left shoulder.

"Hey. This the party place?" he asked, his voice a deep baritone.

"It is! Send in the clowns!" Marco said, then giggled at his own joke.

I didn't even try to hide my eye roll.

The linebacker clown came in and looked around. "Nice place. Cozy."

I narrowed my eyes. Was the clown commenting on the size of my house?

"I'm Marco, this is Ling, and these are the guests of honor," Marco said, gesturing to the twins.

The clown waved at them. Max and Livvie eyed him suspiciously. Smart kids.

"And this is, Maddie," Marco told him, gesturing my way.

"Hey. Big Red," he said. Then he stuck his hand out to shake mine and a spray of confetti flew out of his sleeve.

"Oh, geeze," he said, trying to stem the flow of colorful paper flying all over my living room carpet. "That's not supposed to come out until later. I think I got a hole in my sparkle bag or something on the way over. Sorry about that."

"No problem," I gritted out, mentally calculating if I had time to vacuum before the twins' nap.

"The agency said you were their best clown," Marco said, whipping out a notebook, all business.

Big Red nodded, his wig flopping up and down. "That's right. Of course, I was second best, but Sparky quit last week. Got a regular gig on Nickelodeon as a singing pirate. Lucky bastard."

"Right. So we're very eager to see what you can do," Marco said. He sat on the sofa and crossed one leg over the other in his casting-call mode.

"You want me to juggle or something? I'm real good at juggling. I've been practicing." He looked in his bag, a frown taking over his painted features. "Shoot. I musta lost one of my balls on the trip over. I gotta ride my bike on account the DUI I got," he explained. "Sometimes I lose stuff when I hit a bump."

I did some more eye rolling, more teeth gritting, more shooting daggers in the direction of one fab party planner.

"Hey, you got something else I could juggle?" Big Red asked.

"How about eggs?" Ling suggested. "I'm sure Maddie has some eggs."

"That sounds messy—" I started.

But Ling was already on it, scouring my refrigerator. "I got some! How many you want?"

"Three. Let's start with three," Big Red said. Ling shoved three brown eggs in his hands, and the clown stuck his tongue out in concentration. "Okay, here goes nothing." He tossed three eggs into the air.

And caught one.

The two others landed on the coffee table with a crack, splat, and gooey yellow yolks dripping down the legs.

Both twins giggled and laughed.

"Hey, what do you know, I'm a hit," Big Red said, smiling wide.

I shot him a glare.

"Okay, so honestly? I've only been juggling for a few days. I'm kinda new to this clown gig. I used to be a soap actor. You want me to do a monologue for you? I'm really good at that."

"No," I said.

"Yes!" Ling and Marco said, clapping their hands.

"*María, yo te quiero, pero tu marido me va a matar.*"

We all stared blankly at him.

"Well, it was a Spanish soap. But they tell me it's really good."

Mental forehead smack.

"Hey, you want me to try juggling something else? I could try melons?"

"No!" I shouted.

"Maybe you could do something other than juggle? We're having a very classy affair here, so we want a show that sizzles," Macro said, doing jazz hands in the air.

"Oh, I can sizzle," Big Red said, nodding again. "I got all kinds of sizzling tricks. Check this out—I'm about to disappear before your very eyes."

I should be so lucky.

Big Red pulled something round from his bag, did some gesture in the air with his hands, and threw the round thing on the ground. A huge puff of smoke engulfed him.

I coughed, the smoke overwhelming my *cozy* room. When it finally cleared, Big Red was gone. Or, almost gone. I could still see the top of his red wig peeking out from behind Ramirez's La-Z-Boy.

"Where's the big clown?" Ling asked the twins in a sing-song voice.

They blinked in response, and I had a feeling they were about as confused at why this might be entertaining as I was.

"Shoot," Big Red called from behind the chair. "There's usually more smoke. I usually have more time to hide. This thing must be broken." He grabbed the round ball from the floor and shook it. More smoke poured into the room. Only this time it was accompanied by a loud bang and sparks that jumped onto the La-Z-Boy.

"Fire!" Marco yelled.

Ling grabbed a sippy cup and dumped Livvie's morning apple juice on it. I grabbed a pillow and whacked at it. Big Red threw the remaining egg at it.

We looked down. There was now a soggy, smoking black hole in the center of Ramirez's favorite chair.

I looked up at the clown.

"Oh man. I hate it when that happens," he said.

"Out," I gritted through my teeth. "Get the clown out now."

"Uh, maybe you better go," Marco said, pushing Big Red toward the door.

"Maybe we need a new agency," Ling suggested.

"No. Clowns."

* * *

Once the clown, the stripper, and the queen (who promised me he'd somehow work a new easy chair into the party budget) were gone, I got the kids down for a nap and was just about to attempt cleaning up the living room when Ramirez walked in the door.

His eyes went from the gooey egg mess on the table to the confetti-strewn carpet to the hole in his chair. "And how was your morning?" he asked,

"Ha. Ha. Very funny. It's all Marco's fault."

"I'm not even going to ask," he said.

"That's a good plan," I agreed, grabbing a wet cloth from the kitchen and attacking the egg yolk first. "So what did Tox have to say?" I asked, turning the conversation from my inability to keep the house as spick and span as Mr. Mom.

"Well, it was very interesting. Lacey was, as we suspected, poisoned."

"No surprise there."

"What was surprising was the type of poison."

"What was it?"

"Methylated phenylethylamine."

I paused. "In English, please."

Ramirez grinned. "Amphetamines."

I frowned. "Like, meth?"

"Close," Ramirez told me. "Methamphetamine has almost the same chemical properties, but it also contains a whole bunch of other crap, too, which does nasty things like rot your teeth and make you see bugs crawling on your skin. What tox found in Lacey's system was more pure amphetamine."

"So how was it used to kill her?"

"The best the ME can tell, it was liquefied into a concentrate, then added in high doses to the spray. At the levels the ME found in Lacey's body, he figured she inhaled the spray, and the stimulant caused a massive heart attack almost instantly"

"Ouch." I pictured Lacey's contorted body lying on the tanning booth floor, immediately feeling sorry for her even if she was a gold digger and a blackmailer. "So how would our killer get his hands on some of this stuff?"

"Well, that's where it gets easy. Actually amphetamines are pretty widely used. They're in some prescription drugs, like the ones used as ADD medication, as well as sold on the street as recreational drugs. They give the user a jolt of energy, sort of like drinking four espressos all at once."

"Which would be super handy if you were, say, a baseball player in need of a pick-me-up," I mused out loud, my mental wheels turning.

Ramirez nodded. "Definitely. Amphetamines have been used for years by athletes. Ballplayers called them greenies, and guys have been using them since the earliest days of baseball. Heck, in the eighties, you'd be hard pressed to find a guy *not* using them. They're officially banned now, but that doesn't stop players from trying to fly under the radar. Rumor has it greenies are making a comeback in baseball lately."

"So it's likely one of our players could have easily had enough on hand to poison Lacey."

Ramirez nodded. "It's very likely."

"Okay, what about this: do any of the current Stars players have a history of using drugs?"

The corner of Ramirez's mouth quirked up a notch. "I can think of one. John Ratski. He was suspended a couple of years ago after testing positive for PEDs."

"PEDs?"

"Performance-enhancing drugs."

"Like the ones used to kill Lacey?"

Ramirez nodded again. "But before you get too excited, like I said before, it's likely a lot of players could be using the exact same thing. Just because Ratski has a history with drugs doesn't mean he killed Lacey with them."

"But it's a place to start," I protested. "Can't the police search his locker or something?"

"Not without a warrant. And to get warrants, Laurel and Hardy need probable cause. Some sort of evidence pointing to suspicion of our persons of interest before a judge will sign off."

I pursed my lips. If my one encounter with them was any indication, I had a bad feeling Laurel and Hardy were looking in a different direction for the killer—namely Faux Dad's salon. But, while the police might need a warrant to snoop through Ratski's life, I didn't.

I was gonna need backup for this one.

* * *

An hour later, Dana and I were at the players' entrance to the Stars Stadium where the same security guard stood sentinel with his clipboard.

If Ratski was using greenies as a way to enhance his on-field performance, chances were he had the stuff readily available before each game—like stashed in his locker.

I'd called Kendra earlier, asking if there was any way she could put our names on the security guard's list. Unfortunately, I'd heard the suspicion even louder and clearer than when we'd previously talked as she'd asked me just why I needed access to the stadium again. I'd lied and told her that I'd accidentally left my cashmere Magaschoni sweater behind the last time I'd been here and was hoping I could run in and grab it. Considering it was pushing eighty degrees outside, the lie was flimsy. But luckily it appealed to her sense of fashion—no designer label left behind!—and she'd agreed.

We quickly gave the guard our names and slipped into the cool subterranean part of the stadium.

"So where are the locker rooms?" Dana asked, our heels click-clacking on the polished floors.

"Your guess is as good as mine," I replied. "This place is a maze."

One that, as it turned out, branched off into locker rooms almost 180 degrees from our starting point. By the time we reached the pair of white doors labeled "Players' Lockers," my pale pink tank was sticking to my back despite the air conditioning, and my poor feet were regretting my decision to pair my white capris with two-inch leather pumps.

"Wait. Here," I panted. "I need. A lookout."

"Maddie, you need to come to the gym with me more often," Dana chided. I noticed that despite the fact she was dressed in leather pants and stilettos, she had barely broken a sweat during our indoor hike.

I shook my head. "Just let me know if anyone is coming," I told her. Then I quickly slipped into the locker room, leaning against the doors to catch my breath as I got my bearings.

The term "locker" was deceiving, as this place bore no resemblance whatsoever to those rooms full of metal lockers in high school. Instead, it was more like a room full of open closets lining the walls. Each closet was painted in the team's signature orange and blue colors and held a wooden rack, where pressed uniforms hung, shelves for shoes and cleats, and a cupboard for personal items.

I walked to the first locker. Above it a name plaque was affixed reading "Zander." The name was vaguely familiar to me. I gingerly tugged on the door to the cupboard, which swung open easily. While they were lockers it appeared they weren't actually *locked.* Inside was a variety of first aid tapes and creams and a sheaf of papers that looked like coach's notes. Nothing particularly interesting or incriminating.

Then again, Zander wasn't on my immediate suspect list.

I quickly moved down the row until I came to one labeled "Ratski."

I glanced over my shoulder at the doors. While I was alone for the moment, I had no idea how long that would last. Kendra had said the team was taking another practice day to prep for the doubleheader opening their series against the Tigers tomorrow. Which meant that at any minute some player might need to change his shoes or put on more deodorant or do whatever players did in locker rooms.

Which meant I had to hurry.

I tugged on Ratski's cupboard door and immediately regretted it. Something reeked to high heaven. If I had to guess, week-old socks. Eww. I gingerly poked around, not really wanting to encounter anything too personal of Ratski's. If I touched a jock strap, I was so leaving this evidence thing to Laurel and Hardy.

Unfortunately, I found much the same as I had in the other locker—a variety of muscle creams, first-aid braces, and some papers. Nothing that screamed "illegal drugs." No suspicious prescription bottles, no contraband baggies. No smoking gun.

Bummer. Call me crazy, but I'd really wanted Ratski to be the bad guy.

I looked down at the collection of papers grabbing one at random and quickly scanning it. Lots of notes in shorthand, some diagrams. If I had to guess, notes for the field. I put it back, shuffling through the stack.

And an envelope fell out.

I bent down to pick it up, glancing at the door as I did. Still closed. For now.

The envelope was unsealed, and I quickly slipped my hand inside, pulling out a single sheet of lined binder paper.

Being away from you while you're on the road is pure torture. I can't wait for you to get home so I can be with you again.

I felt my eyebrows rise. While I'd been hoping for a letter of blackmail from Lacey, this looked more like a love letter. I couldn't help myself. I had to read a little bit more. Ratski had struck me as the last type of guy to inspire love letters from his wife. Maybe I'd misjudged him.

Nobody here understands me like you do, schmoopy. I can't wait to see you again. All my love.

Schmoopy? I stifled a giggle.

Just as I heard a sound from the doorway.

"What are you doing here?" came a low, gravelly voice I knew all too well.

Ratski.

CHAPTER NINE

———

I quickly ducked behind a row of chairs in the center of the room.

"Oh, uh, well, I was just…waiting for a friend…" I heard Dana stalling at the door.

I quickly looked around for any place to hide. Unfortunately, the room was a wide open rectangle, offering precious few pieces of furniture to hide behind.

"Who are you?" I heard Ratski bark at Dana.

"Me? Oh, just a baseball fan. A big, big fan."

"Really?" I heard Ratski's voice soften. "Well, you're in luck, because *I'm* a fan of pretty baseball fans like you."

Gag.

While Dana was doing a bang-up job of giggling like Ratski's line had scored points with her, I knew she couldn't hold him forever. I scanned the room for another way out and spotted a door at the far wall.

"Hey, I recognize you," Ratski said.

I froze.

"You're that actress, right? The one who does the lawyer show?"

I let out a breath. Right. Of course he recognized her. As the star of *Lady Justice*, Dana's face was plastered all over the billboards gracing the 5 during sweeps week.

"You got me," Dana said. "But I am really such a fan of *yours*."

She was laying it on thick. Luckily, Ratski was eating it up.

"Hey, you think maybe I can get an autograph?" I heard Dana ask.

"I think maybe that can be arranged," he answered.

Dana did another flirtatious giggle.

"I've got a pen inside," I heard Ratski say.

Uh-oh.

I jumped up from behind the chairs and made a dash for the far door. I heard Dana mumbling something else, trying to keep Ratski at bay, but I knew she couldn't hold him forever. Luckily, the gods of breaking and entering were with me because as my hand grabbed the doorknob, it turned easily. I quickly pushed it open, slipping into a room that looked like a smaller version of the one I'd just been in.

"In the locker room?" I heard Dana say, unfortunately much closer. "Wait, is it okay for a woman to be in here?"

"Honey, I've had lots of women in here," Ratski crooned back, his footsteps echoing just on the other side of the door.

I quickly scanned the room. In the corner I spotted what looked like part of a Charlie Chaplin hat. I must be in the mascots' changing room. I opened one of the lockers, and sure enough there was the Marilyn Monroe outfit.

"Look, dollface, I gotta get changed. But, you can stick around for the show if you like," I heard Ratski say.

Eww. Unless I wanted to subject Dana to Ratski au-natural, we had to get out fast. I grabbed Marilyn's cheap polyester replica of her famous seven-year itch dress and threw it on over my tank-top and capris. Then I plunked the heavy foam head on top of my own, blinking to adjust my eyes so I could see out of the mesh hole that was Marilyn's mouth.

"Uh, wow, look at the time. I gotta go," I heard Dana say on the other side of the door.

"What's your rush, doll?"

It was now or never. I opened the door and quickly wobbled my way into the players' locker room, bouncing off the doorframe a little as I did. Marilyn's head must've weighed fifty pounds, easy.

"Hey, watch it," Ratski shouted as I tipped toward him. I noticed his right eye still bore a purple-ish ring around, courtesy of my husband.

"Sorry," I mumbled. Then I grabbed Dana by the arm. "Come on, you're late for practice," I told her, hoping she played along.

"Practice?" Dana asked

"You know, for the celebrity halftime show."

Dana blinked at me. "Uh...seventh inning stretch?"

"Yeah that's what I meant," I said, feeling Ratski's eyes on my back. "Come on, let's go." I shoved her ahead of me, almost knocking her over with my giant head as I waddled toward the door.

We made it into the hallway without incident, and several wrong turns and collisions with the corridor walls later, we finally made our way to a door marked "West Parking Lot Exit." I ditched the costume in an empty office, and we made a break for it back into the warm sunshine.

Unfortunately as I blinked against the natural light, I realized we'd lost our way in the underground maze.

"Crap," I said scanning the vast empty parking lot on the west side of the stadium.

"I don't see our car," Dana stated.

"Yeah, that would be in the east lot."

* * *

After a half-mile hike back to the car, both Dana and I were sweating and panting. We both agreed that our first order of business was cold drinks. We drove to the nearest Jamba Juice— me ordering a Peach Pleasure with frozen yogurt on the side, and Dana ordering a fresh squeezed orange juice with a wheatgrass shot on the side.

"You were so right about Ratski, Mads," Dana told me sipping her OJ across from me in the blessed air conditioning of the Jamba bar. "He is a total pig. Please tell me you got something on him?"

I shook my head. "Sorry. Nothing in his locker screamed drug use. The only thing I found was a love letter from his wife which was interesting but hardly a smoking gun.

Dana scrunched up her nose. "Poor Beth. Here she's writing him love letters, and he's asking me out."

I raised an eyebrow. "He asked you out?"

"Oh yeah." She nodded. "He slipped me his card and said his wife has a book club meeting tonight, so if I met him for dinner he'd make me his 'MVP' all night long." Dana made a gagging motion with her index finger then shook off invisible Ratski cooties.

I bit my lip, that teeny tiny little light bulb going off in the back of my head again. "What would I have to do to persuade you to keep that date?"

Dana shot me a horrified look. "Maddie, what would I tell Ricky?"

Ricky Montgomery was Dana's fiancé, who, like her, was an actor. Only Ricky had already achieved movie star status and was currently shooting an action movie starring as a Marvel comic book character. And the only thing hotter than Ricky's shirtless pecs on a thirty-foot tall movie screen was his jealous temper where Dana was concerned.

I shook my head. "I'm not saying you should *date* date him. But it could be a great way to pump him for information about whether or not he's using."

Dana sighed. "I guess. But are we sure that Ratski is even the one who killed Lacey? I mean, if these performance enhancers are so easy to get, it could be any one of the players?"

I slurped at my Jamba, sucking extra hard to get a large piece of peach up the straw. "Okay, let's play devil's advocate for a moment and say that Lacey was killed by someone else."

"Someone she was blackmailing over something," Dana added before pounding back her wheatgrass shot. Amazingly she didn't even shudder.

"How about this," I started. "What if Lacey found out one of the other players was using PEDs and threatened to go public with that info."

Dana nodded. "That would be some dirty laundry you wouldn't want to air on network television."

"It's also great blackmail fodder."

"Okay, so how would Lacey find out?" Dana asked.

I pursed my lips together. "Through Bucky?"

"I don't know," Dana said. "It seems like those guys are all pretty tight. I can't imagine him sharing that kind of pillow talk."

"Well maybe it wasn't *pillow* talk that got her the information. More like *girl* talk."

Dana raised an eyebrow. "You think one of the wives told Lacey her husband was doping?"

"Not necessarily. But Lacey worked for Liz, and she was at a lot of the same events as the wives. It's possible she overheard them talking about it."

Dana nodded. She looked down at her watch. "I've got an hour before I have to be on set. Plenty of time to catch up on some girl talk of our own."

* * *

While *Baseball Wives* was a "reality" TV show, Dana found out through a few well-placed calls that they were actually shooting on the Sunset Studios lot today. According to her agent's assistant's assistant who was dating a PA on the show, several of the Baseball Wives favorite haunts were actually located inside studio walls for convenience purposes. Kendra's elegantly furnished parlor where she hosted intimate get-togethers, which often turned into knock-down, drag-out cat fights, was actually a re-purposed sitcom set. The gourmet kitchen where Beth was known to mix up the girls' night cocktails, famous for loosening the ladies' lips, did double duty as a celebrity cooking show set. And today the wives were on the set of Liz's Bellissima boutique…only this version was not on Melrose. Apparently filming in the actual location required such a number of permits, not to mention extra security and local police efforts to control curious tourists, that it had been more cost effective for the producers to build an exact replica of the boutique within the studio walls.

After Dana showed her credentials at the guardhouse, we swapped out my minivan for a golf cart—the studio lot's preferred means of conveyance. We quickly made our way to Studio 4B, home of Bellissima 2, and slipped in the warehouse doors, unnoticed among the myriad of sound guys, PAs, wardrobe consultants, and makeup artists rushing around like an underpaid yet fabulously dressed army. In the center of the commotion was Liz DeCicco, being simultaneously powdered by a makeup artist, sprayed by a hairstylist, and miked by a sound guy.

Beside her stood two unfortunately familiar figures in cheap, public-servant salary suits that stuck out like polyester thumbs.

"Oh, great," I groaned.

"What?" Dana asked.

I gestured to Laurel and Hardy. "The gruesome twosome beat us here." I quickly explained who they were as a PA settled the pair of detectives onto two giant X's made with electrical tape on the floor.

"Can we get makeup over here?" one asked, eyeing Laurel's shiny forehead. The woman powdering Liz immediately abandoned her subject and descended on Laurel.

"Am I okay here?" Hardy asked a guy sitting behind a bank of monitors. "You can see me okay, right? I mean, maybe I need to cheat toward the light more?"

"Is this guy for real?" Dana mumbled to me.

"Unfortunately."

"And we're rolling in ten," the guy behind the monitors said.

Hair and makeup abandoned the people on set, and a pair of cameraman replaced them, one moving in close on Liz, the other taking an opposite stance in front of the pair of LAPD homicide detectives turned reality TV subjects.

"Marker. Speed. And…action," someone shouted.

The director pointed at Hardy.

Hardy blinked at the camera. "Oh, me? Are we…are we ready? I wasn't sure when I should start."

I thought I saw the guy behind the monitors roll his eyes

Hardy cleared his throat and danced a bit from foot to foot, trying to "get in character."

"So, Elizabeth DeCicco, is it?" Hardy asked, intonating like he was in a school play.

"Yes, Detective," Liz said without missing a beat.

"We need to ask you some questions about your whereabouts on the day Lacey Desta was killed." Hardy pulled out a small, spiral notebook. I'd bet my favorite Via Spigas it was a blank prop.

He elbowed Laurel. "Your line," he whispered.

"Right!" Laurel cleared her throat loudly, her forehead starting to shine again despite the copious powdering. "Uh, where. Were you. On the day. Of the murder." Her words came out in a painful staccato like a stage-frightened kid at her first grade spelling bee.

But again, Liz answered like a pro, almost sounding like she was genuinely surprised at the questions. "Well, I started the morning here at my boutique." She waved her arms around her.

"And what time would that be?" Hardy jumped in.

"It was early. I was preparing for the semiannual clearance sale we have scheduled for Labor Day. All of our jewelry and apparel is buy-one, get-one-half-off. We expect a very large crowd, so if you're in the market for a new look, Detective McMartin, I would suggest you come in early." Liz sent a wink in Laurel's direction.

The mousey detective's cheeks pinked.

"The time we're most interested in is between ten AM and eleven-thirty, Mrs. DeCicco," Hardy said, still booming in a theater voice.

"I was filming. We all were. My fellow Baseball Wives and I were doing a promotional piece for the Network. I only have the entire cast and crew of the show to alibi me out." She did another knowing wink at Laurel. "If you were implying I needed one, Detective."

"Just routine questions, Ma'am," Hardy assured her, sounding laughingly like a Dragnet character.

I looked around the set. People were milling in every dark nook and cranny of the sound stage. PA's, makeup artists, hairstylists, directors, catering, and, of course, the wives themselves. How anyone could tell where everyone was at any particular moment was beyond me. Fernando's salon was only fifteen minutes from the studios, give or take for traffic. I wondered how hard it would be for someone to slip away unnoticed for a half hour?

But Hardy seemed perfectly satisfied with Liz's response. "I'm sure your alibi—needless as it may be—is sound," he assured her.

"Can you think. Of anyone who would. Want Lacey dead?" Laurel asked in her unnatural staccato again

Liz's eyes went big and round. "Why I can't imagine. Lacey was such a sweet—"

"Cut," yelled the director behind the monitors. "You're blocking Liz's light!" He pointed at Hardy

Hardy glanced around at the lighting techs. "Oh, sorry. I just thought you'd want to have my good side to the camera. Should I be standing more over here?" He shuffled a couple of steps to his left. "Maybe I need one of those spotlight things of my own."

"Take it again from Laurel's last line," the director said, ignoring the prima donna detective.

Laurel licked her lips and nodded, looking like a deer in the spotlights.

"And…action!" the director said, pointing at Laurel.

She blinked and took a deep breath. "Can you think of anyone who would want Lacey dead?" she asked again

Again Liz did the big, innocent eyes. "Why I can't imagine. Lacey was such a sweet girl. I can't imagine anyone wanting to harm her."

"Thank you very much for your time," Hardy said shutting his notebook.

"And…cut," yelled the director.

If I rolled my eyes any farther I'd be staring at my roots. This was Laurel and Hardy's idea of questioning a suspect? Ramirez was right. There was zero chance of these two figuring out what really happened to Lacey.

Dana and I hung back while the cameraman and lighting crew dispersed. Liz called again for hair and makeup, and I spied Kendra and Beth come onto set, presumably to take their turn under the rain of Laurel and Hardy's hard-hitting questions.

I nudged Dana. "Let's talk to Kendra before the dorknamic duo gets to her."

Dana nodded, leading the way to where the craft services table was set up. Kendra grabbed a bottle of water, and Beth looked longingly at the plate of glazed donuts.

"Dana?" Kendra said, a note of surprise in her voice as she looked up and saw us approaching. "And Maddie. You found your sweater, I trust?"

"Uh, yeah. Thanks, Kendra," I said, ducking my head to avoid the words "liar, liar, pants on fire" being written across my guilty features.

"I'm shooting *Lady Justice* in a bit, so we thought we'd stop by and see how you're holding up," Dana answered coolly, clearly much better at improv than I was. "I see the police are here." She gestured to where Laurel was being re-powdered.

Kendra snorted. "Trust me, they are no match for our producers." She grinned, a wicked thing that confirmed my suspicions—no one was asking the wives any questions they didn't want to answer.

"Have the detectives questioned you yet?" I asked the two. And, yes, I died a little inside using the term "detectives" when it applied to Laurel and Hardy.

"No, they're shooting my interrogation tomorrow afternoon," Beth told me.

"I'm up next," Kendra said, adjusting the top of her blue silk blouse that perfectly matched the color of her eyes. She'd matched it with a simple gray pencil skirt and a pair of white pumps that looked like they'd never seen the grime of a real L.A. sidewalk.

"The police seem to be asking some deep questions," I lied. "They just asked Liz if she knew who would want Lacey dead."

Kendra snorted. "I can't imagine it's a short list."

"Did she talk about her life outside of baseball? Mention anyone who stands out to you?" What I really wanted to ask was did the *wives* talk about *their* lives, but that felt like a subject I had to tiptoe into lightly.

Kendra just shrugged. "It's not like she was my bestie, you know."

"Sure, but you must have spent a fair amount of time together at baseball events," Dana pressed.

Kendra nodded. "I suppose."

Then Beth cut in, "God, she was always around. It was almost like she was stalking us. Doing everything she could to become one of us, you know?"

Kendra shot her a look. "We all attended functions together," she enunciated quite clearly.

Beth looked down, a guilty look spreading across her face.

I jumped on it. "That must have been so annoying," I sympathized. "I mean, having an outsider always tagging along with you, trying to join you, listening in on your private conversations…"

"Just what are you implying?" Kendra asked, her eyes narrowing.

"Nothing. Just that everyone has things they don't want a stranger to overhear. Things they don't want the press to get hold of, right?"

"Well, that's why we have the producers. To screen what the press hears," Beth said.

If Kendra could have smacked her across the face with a look she would have. "*My* life is an open book," she said pointedly. "That's why I agreed to do this reality show."

"Oh, so is mine," Beth amended quickly. "I mean it's not like I have secrets or anything."

Riiiight. I was beginning to like the theory that Lacey had gained some blackmail fodder from the wives more and more. Clearly these two were hiding something.

"Well, I guess now that Lacey's out of the picture, you won't have to worry about your tagalong anymore," Dana said, a wide, innocent smile on her face that said it was all fine and dandy to talk ill of the dead among *girlfriends*.

But as good of an actress as Dana was, Kendra wasn't buying it. Her eyes narrowed again, turning into fine, mascara rimed slits. "Look, I don't know who killed Lacey or why, but I assure you it had nothing to do with us."

"Kendra!" a guy with a headset hailed her from the center of the action in the fake boutique. "They're ready for you on the set."

Laurel was freshly powdered, and Hardy was standing on his X adjusting his microphone.

"I'll be right there," Kendra said. Then she turned to Dana and me. "I don't know what your fascination with Lacey is. She was a nobody in life, and she's a nobody in death. Give it five minutes, and this whole thing will blow over. So I suggest dropping it, okay?"

Why did I have a feeling I was not going to get on her guest list to the stadium again?

I watched as she stomped to the set on her spiky heels. Lacey might've been a nobody in Kendra's book, but she certainly wasn't going to hurt the *Baseball Wives* ratings any. I suddenly felt very sorry for Lacey. I'm sure she hadn't envisioned getting her part on the show this way. All she'd wanted to do was be in the wives club.

Then again, I was pretty sure she'd been blackmailing her way in.

"You'll have to excuse Kendra," Beth said coming up behind us. "This has all been very difficult on her."

I raised an eyebrow. "Difficult on *her*?"

"Oh, yes," Beth said nodding. "I probably shouldn't say anything, but…"

I leaned in. Those words always preceded something juicy.

"…but I guess Lacey's death has actually been something of a relief to Kendra."

"Really?" I asked. While there was clearly no love lost between the two, "relief" implied something a little more sinister.

"Well, you know Bucky is her husband's catcher, so you can imagine…" she trailed off.

Unfortunately, knowing about as much about baseball as Ramirez knew about the spring Prada collection, I couldn't imagine.

"Sorry, I'm not super baseball savvy," Dana piped up beside me. "How does her husband being a pitcher make this difficult?"

"Oh, sorry," Beth stammered. "I forget not everybody's life revolves around the diamond." She sent us a shy smile through her curls. "What I meant to say was when Bucky's game is off, so is Blanco's. Bucky's his catcher, so it's up to him to call the right pitches at the right time to Blanco."

"I see," I said, nodding alongside Dana.

"Kendra's just been beside herself all season. Ever since Lacey came into the picture, Bucky's been, well, distracted while he's behind the plate. It's like his mind just isn't on his work, you know?"

"And this has been affecting Blanco's game?" I asked.

Beth nodded vigorously, her curls bouncing up and down on her head. "Unfortunately, yes it has. His season started out with a bang, but then his game started being hit-and-miss. I honestly think Kendra's dreaming if she thinks he's still in the running for MVP. And now that Bucky's mourning Lacey...well the whole situation has everyone turning into a bundle of nerves, wondering how the distraction is going to affect the team. Especially Kendra. Her husband is up for a new contract this year, you know?"

I quirked an eyebrow her away. "No I didn't know that." I wondered just how badly Kendra had wanted Bucky's distraction out of the picture. I glanced back at Kendra in the middle of her interview with Laurel and Hardy, suddenly seeing a motive standing in those gleaming white pumps.

"When is their next game?" Dana asked.

"Tomorrow," Beth said. "The team management is hoping they clear everyone by then." She cocked her head at Laurel and Hardy. "It's not good for anyone to play under a cloud of suspicion, you know?"

All the more reason for Laurel and Hardy to wrap it up quickly. A situation that did not bode well for justice for Lacey...but greatly favored her killer.

CHAPTER TEN

―――――

"So it looks like Kendra had a big fat motive for wanting Lacey dead," Dana said, as we made our way back to our golf cart.

I nodded. "Agreed. What I want to know is if she has a big fat alibi."

"You think she did it?" Dana asked.

I pursed my lips together. "I'm not sure. There's still the issue of the blackmail. Did Lacey have anything on Kendra?"

Dana shrugged. "Maybe. But just because Lacey was blackmailing someone doesn't necessarily mean that person was the one who killed her."

"Good point." No matter where I turned it seemed Lacey had made more fast enemies than good friends. Which meant that there were just as many motives floating around as there were shaky alibis.

"Well promise to keep me posted," Dana said as we pulled up to Studio 6D, where she was filming that afternoon. "*Justice* calls!" She hopped out of the cart with a little wave.

"Will do!" I promised. Then I navigated the golf cart back to the front of the studio parking lot where my minivan awaited me.

I checked my cell. No calls or text from Ramirez. I resisted the urge to call home to see how things were going. Partly because I didn't want to hear that he had just put the children down for a nap, cleaned the entire house, pressed and folded the laundry, and baked a loaf of bread from scratch. Not that a worry Ramirez made a better mom than I did was niggling at the back of my head or anything.

Instead, I decided to indulge the niggling in my stomach, reminding me that I'd skipped lunch. I navigated my way through the noon traffic-clogged streets around the studios, avoiding the trendy delis and hotspots. Instead I pulled up to one of my favorite out-of-the-way burger joints, Chubby Burger, ordering a double bacon cheeseburger with curly fries, onion rings, and a thick chocolate milkshake. Hey, being an investigator burned a lot of calories, right?

I was halfway through my meal when my cell trilled to life in my purse. Wiping my fingers on a napkin to blot out *most* of the grease, I picked it up and saw Marco's name flash across the screen.

"Hello?" I said, swiping it on.

"Madds, darling, where are you?" Marco's voice came over the speakerphone

"At lunch."

"Fabulous. Where?"

"Uh…" I looked around myself. "New place. Trendy. I'm sure you've never heard of it. Anyway, what's up?" I asked, glancing guiltily at my pile of calorie laden onion rings.

"We're taking you shopping," Marco said in a voice that broached no argument.

Not that I wasn't going to try broaching a little.

"I'm not sure I have time to go shopping right now, Marco." Not to mention the fact that his supersized party meant my bank account was sporting a mini-sized balance.

"Nonsense," Marco answered. "Dahling, *everyone* has time for *shopping*."

I couldn't help a small grin. "Okay, okay, you're right. What is it I'm shopping for?"

"Birthday outfits of coooourse," Marco, responded, drawing out the vowels with gusto that would make an opera singer jealous. "Your little darlings will be the stars of the show on their big day, and they need to look it!"

While I could've argued with him, I had to say that I wasn't entirely opposed. Part of the fun of having babies was dressing them up in little too-cute outfits. And a birthday was a great excuse to do just that. I nodded agreement. "All right, fine. Meet me at the Beverly Center?"

"Perfect! Be there in ten!"

I snuck a furtive glance at my half-eaten cheeseburger still sitting on my plate. At least a bouncy jaunt around the mall would burn down some of those calories. Besides, some retail therapy was exactly what I needed to get my investigative muse kick-started. So far I was having a hard time connecting any dots between Lacey's death and the baseball crew. At least any that contained enough evidence for that warrant.

The truth was, any one of the players or wives could have snuck away to add poison to the tanning solution. Fernando had said Lacey had a regular tanning date. It wouldn't have been a hard thing for someone to have found out when. Which left means and opportunity wide open.

And then there was motive. Clearly if Lacey had been blackmailing someone, that was great motive to want her gone. However, if Kendra was afraid her husband's game was suffering because Lacey was around, that was a great reason, too. For that matter, any of the Baseball Wives might have wanted Lacey gone if she was signing on to the show and they thought she might upstage them as the top players' girl.

Which led me back to Bucky himself. While I was having a harder and harder time putting the grief-stricken boyfriend in the role of killer, it wasn't outside the realm of possibility he was faking. Let's face it, he wouldn't be the first killer to fake grief. And Marco and Ling were right—most of the time it was the boyfriend whodunit.

All of which left me with motive as wide open as means and opportunity.

I tossed the rest of my burger and made sure I didn't have any little bits of onion rings stuck in my teeth. Then I pointed my car in the direction of the Beverly Center.

* * *

After circling the garage a mere fifteen minutes I found a spot near Macy's and, via text messages, quickly located and caught up to Marco at the Little Lovin' baby boutique on the sixth floor, sandwiched between Godiva and The Body Shop. Firmly telling myself that a chocolate dipped strawberry was *not* the perfect dessert to cap off my burger, I made my way into

Little Lovin', where I spied Marco pawing through a rack of christening dresses.

Standing beside him was Ling, wearing a sequined tube top, hotpants, and platform heels. She was holding up a purple onesie with a fuzzy monster on it. I would've laughed at the juxtaposition if I didn't have a sinking feeling that purple fuzzy thing was going on one of my children.

Marco looked up and spied me first. "Maddie, my love, you will not believe the fabulous things we've already picked out for your children."

I glanced at the purple thing. "No."

Marco waved my dissention off. "But you have to see it *on*, darling."

"See it on?" I asked, hoping Marco hadn't kidnapped my children for this excursion.

"The models." Marco gestured to a row of dolls on a shelf by the dressing room doors.

"You're kidding?"

Marco shook his head. "Isn't it clever? Look, they have all different hair colors, eye colors, skin tones. Now you can shop for baby without bringing baby!"

"It look okay on Caucasian Baby, but I think it look way better on Hispanic Baby," Ling said, holding her purple onesie up against a doll with dark hair and cafe-latte skin. "You think maybe you wanna to spray tan your guys before the party?"

Marco got a look of glee in his eyes. "Ohmigod, that would be so fabu—"

"No!" I said, empathically. "I am not spray tanning *babies*!"

Marco's shoulders sagged. "Killjoy."

Ling sighed, putting the purple thing back on a rack. "I guess dying the hair is out then, too."

"They hardly have any hair!"

"Okay, what do you think of this?" Marco asked, holding up a teeny tiny white suit with Zebra striped lapels and a pair of matching zebra booties.

"I think it probably belongs to a teeny tiny pimp," I told him honestly.

Marco swatted my arm. "Maddie, animal print is *so* in this season!"

"I like this one better," Ling interjected, holding up a red, velvet suit that looked like it belonged on a dwarf Santa Claus at his junior high school prom.

Before I could protest, Marco shook his head. "Oh, honey, that will never work."

I did an internal sigh of relief.

"It totally clashes with the fuchsia taffeta in Livvie's bloomers."

So much for relief.

"Okay, okay," I said, halting the madness. "Marco, I will concede that you are the party planning expert here."

"Thank you," he said, beaming from ear to ear.

"However, who among us is the fashion designer?"

Marco's smile faltered. "You."

"Correct. Which means I'm taking over choosing the twins' outfits."

Marco opened his mouth to protest, but must have seen the serious-as-a-heart-attack look on my face, as he quickly shut it. "Fine," he conceded, sending a wistful look toward the teeny tiny pimp outfit. "But just promise me one thing."

"What?" I hedged.

"Make sure they coordinate with the peacock's feathers. We can't have our guests of honor clashing with our exotic petting zoo!"

Heaven forbid.

* * *

Once we'd shopped till we'd almost dropped, I had the most adorable pink and blue matching outfit for the twins that were still in the realm of tasteful, yet flashy enough that they didn't "clash" with any of Auntie Marco's plans. We celebrated our fashion victory with iced mochas at the Coffee Bean, where I caught Marco and Ling up to speed on the investigation, telling them about the laughable "interrogation" Laurel and Hardy had done in the fake Bellissima boutique.

"The real one's on Melrose, right?" Ling asked. "I've been there a couple of times."

"What did you think?" I asked, only having experienced the "reality" version of it myself.

"Pricey."

"That sounds like Melrose."

"Yeah, but her stuff is way overpriced. Hey, I don't mind paying for quality, but her stuff is junk."

I felt a frown pull between my brows. The replica version of the store hadn't looked like it was populated with junk. "What do you mean?"

"I mean, my friend, Laquisha, bought a handbag there, and the lining ripped out in a week."

"What kind of bag was it?"

"Louis Vuitton."

Marco choked on his latte. "Dahling, Vuittons are not *junk*."

"Yeah, well my grandmother in China sews higher quality 'Vuittons,'" Ling said, doing air quotes with her acrylic fingernails.

"Are you sure it wasn't a high end replica of some sort?" I asked. "I can think of a handful of designs that are very similar to a Vuitton."

Ling shrugged. "Laquisha said it was the real deal designer."

"Well, did she take the bag back?" I asked.

"You bet your skinny butt she did! Laquisha's no fool. She asked for a full refund. I told her to go for pain and suffering compensation, too. She almost lost an earring down that ripped lining."

"What did Liz do?" I asked.

Ling shrugged. "She gave her the refund," she admitted. "She said it must have been a manufacturer defect. But I tell you, Laquisha wasn't buying it. She said those ladies at that boutique were profiling."

"Profiling? Like, racial profiling?"

Ling blinked at me. "What are you talking about? Laquisha is white."

"Oh, I, uh, didn't mean…" I stammered.

But Ling waved me off. "No, profession profiling. Like, give the stripper the defective bag 'cause she won't know the difference."

"Wait—how would they know she's a stripper?" Marco interjected.

Ling gave him a get real look. "What do I look like I do for a living?"

Marco and I looked down at her hotpants, hair extensions, and platform shoes.

"Point taken," he mumbled.

"Anyway, that's one place I refuse to shop on principle," Ling said, sipping at her coffee.

I sipped too, making a mental note to visit the real Bellissima soon myself.

* * *

By 6 o'clock I was shopped out. I turned my car in the direction of home, tuning in to KIIS FM as I inched my way through the traffic on the 405. Until Ryan Seacrest started talking about the "Tanning Salon Murders." Ugh. I switched it off and cued up an audio book instead.

I finally pulled up to our little bungalow in West Hollywood almost an hour later. I pulled into the driveway, turned off the engine, and sat there staring at the front door of my house. How wrong was it that I almost wished to hear sounds of screaming children or see sticky handprints all over the windows? Why I dreaded coming home to a clean, tidy house and happy children was a heavy enough question to make me consider therapy. I shook it off and got out of the car, forcing my pumps up the front walkway.

"I'm home," I called turning my key in the lock and walking across the threshold. As expected the living room was clean, the play yards organized, and nary a stray crumb or toy was in sight. I was beginning to worry Ramirez was keeping the twins caged up all day.

"That you, babe?" I heard Ramirez's voice from the kitchen. Which, as I stepped toward it, smelled suspiciously like tamales.

"Yep. Where the kids?" I asked.

"Playing in their room."

I paused, listening for sounds of shrieks, squeals, or screams. Nada. "Did you drug them?"

"What?" Ramirez gave me a funny look.

"Nothing," I mumbled. I peeked in the oven and found two trays of delicious smelling Mexican food. "You cooked, too?"

Ramirez grinned at me. "Oh, I'm not brave enough to take on tamales," he said. "Mama stopped by with a couple of trays earlier."

Ramirez's mother was known as "Mama" to everyone, young and old alike. She was round in the middle, wrinkled in the face, and had the skills to cook a feast for a crowd of a hundred on twenty minutes notice. If this woman ever went on a cooking show, she'd mop the floor with the competition.

"Smells like heaven," I told him honestly.

"Heaven will be ready in ten minutes." Ramirez crossed the kitchen and gave me a quick peck on the cheek. "How was your day?"

"Well, let's just say I feel like I'm spinning my wheels and not much closer to knowing much of anything." I told Ramirez about our busted visit to the stadium, and our conversation with Beth, pointing out an excellent reason Kendra might have wanted Lacey dead. Unfortunately I didn't have any excellent evidence to procure any kind of excellent warrants. "And," I added "I have a sinking feeling Laurel and Hardy aren't finding any either."

"Why's that?" Ramirez asked.

I recounted the almost comical scene Dana and I had witnessed on the set of the *Baseball Wives*. Only when I finished Ramirez certainly wasn't laughing. In fact he turned to the fridge, pulled out a beer, popped the top, and downed half of it in gulp. "And I'm the one on suspension," he mumbled. I could see that tell-tale vein in his neck threatening to bulge, so I quickly changed the subject.

"On the upside, I did get some super cute outfits for the twins' for the birthday party," I told him.

He shot me a look. "Yeah, speaking of the birthday party…"

Uh-oh. What had Marco done now?

"…take a look in the backyard," Ramirez directed me.

I walked to the back door and peered out the sliding glass. While our bungalow was what could be described as cozy-sized, the upside of being in an older home was that we were one of the lucky few in Los Angeles to still have a yard. Ours was a decent size, bordered by a high fence, with a couple of mature trees and some low maintenance hedges flanking the perimeter. In the center was a lawn that Ramirez had hinted on more than one occasion would be ideal for a swing set in a year or two.

At the moment, however, it was occupied by a giant inflatable waterslide, a five-foot ball pit, and a grass covered tiki bar.

I turned to Ramirez. "What is this?"

He shrugged. "They told me Marco ordered them."

Mental forehead smack. "No wonder he was keeping me busy at the mall today," I mumbled.

"Crafty fellow," Ramirez said, though I noticed the vein was going down and the twinkle was returning to his eye.

"Well at least there will be alcohol," I said pointing to the tiki bar

Ramirez's face broke into a grin. "Let's hope there's lots of it."

CHAPTER ELEVEN

———

After I'd practically consumed my weight in tamales (which, by the way, was rapidly climbing after the cheeseburger luncheon and a decadent dinner) all I wanted to do was snuggle on the couch with my husband and watch DVRed episodes of *American Idol*. Unfortunately, Dana and I had a date with Ratski.

"You sure this is a good idea?" Ramirez asked, his eyebrows furrowing together when I told him about it.

I shrugged. "No, but it's the only idea I got."

The brows furrowed further, my candor clearly not upping his confidence in his "eyes and ears."

"Look, we'll be perfectly safe," I assured him. "Dana is meeting him in a public place, and she's only there to get him to spill the kind of info one might let slip to a hot movie star and not the LAPD."

Eyebrows were joined by a downturn of his mouth. Clearly my reference to Ratski not talking to the LAPD was also not doing much to lighten his mood.

I cleared my throat, trying again. "It'll just be a couple of drinks, maybe an appetizer. Dana will pump him for information, then we'll head home."

"And what if Ratski recognizes you?" Ramirez asked.

I perked up. "Trust me, I've got that covered." While out shopping with Marco and Ling earlier I'd had the forethought to pick up a very sneaky disguise. I'd be going to La Pastaria Italian restaurant in a sliming, navy blue Donna Karan dress, a brand-new pair of grey Grecian style platform heels, and a cute little brunette bobbed wig. After I added some smoky eye makeup and a few fake lashes, there'd be no way Ratski would recognize me.

While I could tell my husband wasn't 100% convinced of our plan's success, it was, as I'd mentioned, the only plan we had. So twenty minutes later I was parked in front of La Pastaria, adjusting my adorable (even if I did say so) bob and watching in my rearview mirror as Dana emerged from her sleek little black sports car and handed her keys to the valet. I wasted no time, locking my own car and following her through the front doors.

La Pastaria was one of those trendy little restaurants that seem to pop into the L.A. nightlife scene and pop out just as quickly. It had a tiny little storefront featuring lots of sleek chrome glass and natural woods, a menu with very few choices, servers who were incredibly slow, and prices that were incredibly high. It was no wonder it was currently one of the hottest spots in L.A. Though, in six months, the space would probably be a Chipotle Grill.

I spotted Dana giving her name at the hostess stand and watched as she was quickly led to a table near the back where Ratski was already waiting. If the empty glass in front of him was any indication, he'd gotten there early. Good. Liquor loosens lips, and loose lips were all we were banking on.

Ratski stood and kissed Dana on the cheek as she approached. I credited her great acting skills to the fact she hardly even cringed.

As soon as the hostess returned to the stand, I slipped her a twenty and asked her to please seat me near the baseball player.

She shot me a look. "You're not a reporter or something, are you?"

"Do I look like I'm with a tabloid?" I asked.

She narrowed her eyes at me, doing an up and down.

"It's Donna Karan," I told her.

More eye narrowing.

"Look, I'm just a really big baseball fan."

"We value our customers' privacy," she said.

"I'm not going to disturb him. I just want to sit near him."

The hostess looked down at the twenty in her hand. "I don't know if we have any empty tables near him..." She trailed off, staring pointedly at the lonely bill.

I rolled my eyes and slipped her another one.

"Right this way, ma'am," she said.

I followed her to a *clearly* empty table two over from Ratski and Dana. While it might have cost me, it was perfect. I was close enough to hear them but far enough away that I was pretty sure Ratski wasn't going to notice me.

Though in all honesty, I had a feeling he wouldn't be taking his eyes off of Dana at all. She'd arrived in a silver sequined mini dress with a racer back tank that showed off her broad gym-built shoulders. At a good six inches taller than I was, she'd accentuated her long legs with four-inch heels that had her almost eye-to-eye with Ratski when she stood. She was playing pure movie star tonight, and if the look on his face was any indication, Ratski was loving it.

"Well don't you look nice tonight?" Dana said, arranging a napkin on her lap.

He leaned back in his chair, a slightly buzzed grin snaking across his face. "I could say the same for you, doll."

Dana shot him a wide smile. "It was so fortunate running into you earlier. All I was hoping to get was an autograph, and now here I am with the opportunity to learn *all* about you."

"I guess it's your lucky day that my wife had a book club meeting, isn't it," Ratski said, his grin widening.

I cringed, picturing poor Beth. Even though she was still on my list of snarky Baseball Wife suspects, nobody deserved to be saddled with a guy like this.

Luckily the server arrived at that moment with a bottle of wine, so Dana didn't have to come up with a witty reply to a married man bringing up his wife on a clandestine date. Instead, she snuck me an eye roll as Ratski inspected the bottle.

I turned my head away, stifling a laugh.

"I've been reading about the team's troubles online," Dana said, clearly eager to cut to this evening's chase.

"Troubles?" Ratski's eyes glazed as he swirled wine in his glass. Then he took a big sip followed by a hiccup.

Geez, we needed to make this quick before he got too drunk to give us any information.

"Yes," Dana said, clearing her throat again. "You know, the death of that poor girl Lacey."

I watched Ratski's face. At least he had the decency to wipe the grin off of it as he responded. "Yeah, it sucks. Totally distracting to the team. We got killed yesterday. Total shutout."

His concern was touching.

"How terribly upsetting for you." Dana reached across the table and laid a hand on Ratski's.

"Yeah, upsetting." Ratski furled his eyebrows as if trying to create the appropriately "upset" expression.

"Is your game suffering too badly?" Dana asked.

Ratski shrugged. "We'll recover. We got a lot of season left to play."

Dana shot him a fake smile. "Sure, but doesn't the *distraction* kill your momentum? Make it harder to perform on the field?"

"Nah." Ratski drained his glass and refilled it from the bottle on the table. "Not much fazes me."

Dana bit her lip. I could tell she was running out of polite ways to hint at Ratski's need for performance enhancers. "I heard you guys are playing a doubleheader tomorrow. That must get tiring. That's, what, six hours of play? How do you guys have enough energy to do that?"

"Oh, I got stamina, baby," Ratski leered.

Ick.

"Don't you ever need a little energy boost or something?" Dana pressed.

"Yeahlikewhat?" Ratski said, his words slurring together as he downed another gulp.

Dana shrugged. "I don't know. I mean, you naughty baseball boys must have *some* clever way to pep up before a big game." She gave him a knowing wink.

"Riiiight," he agreed, drawing out the word as the grin returned to his face. "You have a thing for the naughty boys?"

"Maybe I do," Dana persisted, leaning forward so that just a bit more of that cleavage showed beneath her sparkly dress.

Ratski leaned in on his elbows (or elbow, singular…The other slipped out from under him, almost crashing into his plate with intoxicated grace.). "Well, let me tell you a little secret then, Miss Dana…"

"Good evening, ma'am, my name is David."

"Shhh!" I shushed the server beside me on instinct.

The poor guy jumped.

"Uh, what I mean is, I'm not quite ready to order," I quickly amended, sending him a smile.

He gave me a funny look but thankfully walked away. I tuned in again to the conversation two tables over.

"…I had no idea," I heard Dana say.

Damn. I'd missed something juicy. I closed my eyes trying to hone in on only their voices over the myriad of conversation happening around me. The other tables nearby had quickly filled, and the conversation was starting to roar as the trendy nine o'clock hour approached.

"Yeah, well, what can you do, right?" Ratski shrugged, sitting back in his seat and downing the rest of his drink.

"So what did Bucky do then?" Dana asked.

Double damn. Whatever Ratski had told her must have involved Bucky. Was he the one popping PEDs?

"Nothing. The coach might have been all over him, but management knows he's the golden boy. They'd only be screwing themselves if they took him out of the game."

"Hmm," Dana said. "You know, it was Bucky's girlfriend who was killed, wasn't it?"

Ratski nodded, drinking again.

"I wonder…" she trailed off thoughtfully. "Oh, but of course I remember reading that Bucky has an alibi, right?"

Ratski grinned. "Don't we all."

Dana shifted showing a bit more cleavage. "Whatever do you mean by that, naughty boy?"

"Well, Bucky and I—"

"Are you ready yet, ma'am?"

I closed my eyes and thought a really dirty word directed at one overly-vigilant server standing by my table yet again.

"Martini," I shot out, hoping the drink order would keep him busy for a few minutes.

"Very good ma'am. And would you like that shaken or stirred?"

"Shaken," I spat back, leaning in to try to catch the end of the conversation two tables over.

"Perfect. And would you like olive or onion?"

I ground my teeth together. "Neither."

"Wonderful. Now, would you like to hear about the specials—"

"No!" I said. Clearly a little too loudly as heads at the neighboring tables turned my way. Including, unfortunately, Dana and Ratski's. I quickly ducked my head toward the server hoping to avoid recognition. "What I mean is, I've already decided I'll have the…" I glanced at the menu finding the first thing my eyes landed on. "…roasted chicken in mushroom sauce."

"Very good, ma'am." The server scribbled my order and thankfully walked away from the table.

I heaved a small sigh of relief, then furtively glanced through my brunette locks toward Dana's table again. They were giving their order to another server. Crap. I'd missed the juicy stuff again. I sincerely hoped Dana was taking great notes.

I waited while Dana ordered an arugula and watercress salad and Ratski ordered fried calamari and another bottle of wine.

As soon as the server walked away Dana leaned forward again. "So you and Bucky are close, then?"

"Sure. We all are. We're one big happy team," Ratski drawled, his eyelids looking decidedly heavy.

"*Everyone* is tight *all* the time?" Dana probed.

Ratski shrugged. "You know, we have our moments."

"Like what?"

He paused, looking over his glass at her. "Why?"

"Oh, you know, we girls just love a little gossip." Dana sent him another flirtatious wink.

Ratski chuckled, taking another sip. "Alright, you like juicy stuff? I've got gossip for ya."

I was leaning so far toward their table my right butt cheek was halfway off the chair, and I was precariously close to toppling to the floor.

"Oh, do tell," Dana crooned.

Ratski opened his mouth to speak.

Unfortunately, he never got the chance as I heard a faint clicking sound from the table just behind Ratski and Dana. They must've heard it too as the pair immediately turned their eyes on the culprit. A young guy in slacks and Converse held a cell phone up toward the couple, rapidly firing off shots like a great amateur paparazzi.

"Uh, I'm wondering if this was such a great idea," Dana stammered, her eyes glued to the phone. She'd been in show business long enough to know that those pics could either be someone's bragging material at their next dinner party or the headliner for TMZ tomorrow.

"It's just a couple of photos," Ratski drawled, shrugging his shoulders. "No biggie."

Dana didn't look convinced. "But what if your wife sees them?"

"Huh?"

"Your. Wife." Dana clearly enunciated, trying to break through his intoxicated fog.

"Oh. Her. Yeah, well, you know I wouldn't worry about her too much…" Ratski trailed off.

At the table just to my right another person whipped out a cell, and I heard a whisper of "Dana Dashel" followed by more soft clicks.

Uh-oh.

Dana shot a panicked look my way. I did a curt half nod toward the front door.

Unfortunately we hadn't gotten much from Ratski. But if we didn't get out now, there was a bad chance we'd be hearing from his wife tomorrow.

"You know, I'm not really comfortable," Dana said, rising from the table. "I've got to go."

"I tell you what, honey," Ratski said, wrapping a hand around Dana's arm. "How about we go somewhere a little more private?"

"Private?" Dana asked

"How about my place?"

Double uh-oh.

Unfortunately, that was all I heard of their conversation as my server arrived with not only my martini, but a plate of chicken, mushrooms, rice, and a side of vegetables. I couldn't help the groan that escaped my lips as I took in the humongous meal. After the tamales I'd already eaten there was no way I could even make a dent in this.

Out of the corner of my eye I saw Ratski throw a few bills down on their table then steer Dana toward the door. And not a moment too soon as three more cell phones flew out of back pockets, snapping shots of the two escaping from the restaurant.

"Is anything wrong, ma'am?" the server asked.

"Uh, yeah," I rushed. "Can you wrap this up to go?"

By the time I finally got the slowest server in the entire L.A. basin to wrap up my gargantuan meal, paid my bill, and rushed outside, both Dana and Ratski were nowhere in sight. I cursed my timing. Had I just sent Dana out alone with a murderer?

I was just about to start freaking out when my cell buzzed in my pocket. I looked down and heaved a sigh of relief when I saw Dana's name flash across my screen with the text:

Ratski drunk. driving him home.

An address was listed below it. I quickly typed out a response as I walked to my car.

Two minutes behind you

I jumped behind the wheel of my minivan and pulled into traffic with such force that my tires squealed. While it was nice of Dana to drive Ratski home, I was pretty sure Ratski had an agenda other than avoiding a DUI.

Luckily, traffic was light at this time of night and only fifteen billboards and two freeways later I was pulling into a trendy neighborhood in Brentwood filled with multimillion dollar homes, gated manicured lawns, and so many celebrities people practically used their Golden Globes as lawn gnomes.

I spotted Dana's sports car crawling up the circular drive of a colonial flanked by tall cypress trees halfway down the street. I cut my lights and waited at the curb until I saw her shiny silver dress exit the car, walk around to the passenger side, and pull an unsteady Ratski out beside her. It took him three tries to shove his key into the front door.

I tapped my fingers on the steering wheel, waiting in the dark, wondering what I should do next. If Dana was in trouble, I wanted to be close. But it would totally blow our cover if I went busting through the front door. After five agonizing minutes of silence, I finally texted Dana.

You okay?

Almost immediately a reply came back.

Fine. Ratski passed out.

I raised an eyebrow. Iiiiiinteresting. Ratski was out, and we had free access to his house? Me thinks me felt some snooping coming on.

front door, I texted back, exiting my car and jogging toward the house.

A beat later Dana opened the door and quickly ushered me in with a finger to her lips. I tiptoed inside and softly closed the door behind me. Though as I peeked into the parlor off the foyer, I could tell there was very little that was going to wake Ratski. He was flat on his back on a petite floral sofa, snoring like a bear with a sinus infection.

"You get anything good from him before he passed out?" I asked.

"Maybe," Dana said, leading me away from Sleeping Ugly. "I didn't get Ratski to say one way or another if he was using, but he did tell me something interesting about Bucky."

"I'm dying here. What?" I prodded.

"Well, Ratski said that just last month Bucky was caught with something he shouldn't have had."

"No! PEDs?"

"Sort of. ADD meds."

I nodded. "Right, Ramirez said that some ADD meds contain amphetamines."

"Apparently Bucky's cousin has ADD, and Bucky popped a couple of pills before a game to give him a pick-me-up."

"But he wasn't suspended? It wasn't in the news."

Dana shook her head. "No. Ratski said the coaching staff swept it under the rug. They didn't want to risk taking Bucky out and potentially losing games. So everyone involved was told to forget it ever happened."

"Did Lacey know about this?" I asked, suddenly wondering if maybe the person she'd been blackmailing had been none other than her boyfriend.

Dana shrugged. "I didn't get a chance to ask Ratski before he went comatose."

"What did he tell you about Bucky's alibi?"

Dana grinned. "Only that it's shaky. Look, all three guys *did* go to the gym together that day. But they didn't work out together. He told me Bucky wanted to get in a basketball game, Blanco was in the weight room, and Ratski spent most of the time at the pool and sauna. But when Lacey died and the police started asking questions, they all agreed to alibi each other out."

"Just like Ramirez thought." My husband really was a good detective. I cursed Ratski again for getting him suspended. "So Bucky has no real alibi *and* had access to the murder weapon. The only thing he's missing is a motive." I paused. "Let's face it, even if he and Lacey were on the outs, the simplest thing to do would have been to dump her, not kill her."

Dana nodded. "Unless she was blackmailing him over his PED use."

I pursed my lips together. "Possibly. But Bucky doesn't have the kind of money Lacey was depositing. However…" I glanced around myself at the decorator-designed opulence in Ratski's foyer.

"…Ratski does," she finished for me.

I nodded. "He's also got the same shaky alibi."

"But we still don't know if he was even using PEDs or not."

I grinned. "Well, there's no time like the present to find out." I glanced around the marble tiled entry. Rooms led off in all directions in a semicircular pattern, with a sweeping staircase going up the center. A landing stood at the top, off of which I could see more doorways. To say this place was massive was about the same understatement as calling my place cozy. "Which room do you think holds his medicine cabinet?"

"Upstairs?" Dana suggested.

We tiptoed up the stairs as quietly as we could in our heels, trying not to clack them against the polished hardwood floors. Once we got to the top of the landing we both paused trying to instinctively feel our way toward the master bathroom. We poked our heads into the first room. It looked like a home office, a desk sitting in the center and sports memorabilia framed on the walls. The next one was a guestroom, if I had to guess from the lack of personal touches and pristine floral quilt on the queen-size bed.

One hall bath, two more unused guest rooms, and one work-out room later, we finally hit upon the master. A set of double doors led into a large room decorated in tasteful pale grays and lemon yellows. Two nightstands flanked the bed—a four poster, mahogany item in California King size. The walls were covered in wainscoting, the bed in a contemporary designed duvet, and the floors in plush wool rugs that spanned from the bed to a large reading nook on the other side of the room. Beyond that stood an arched doorway leading into the master bath.

"I'll take the bathroom," I told Dana. "Want to see if you can dig up anything in here?"

Dana shot a reluctant look to the nightstands. "Okay, but if I find anything kinky, I'm outta here."

I quickly crossed to the master bath. An oversized jetted tub sat on the far end of the room under a massive bay window. A glass-enclosed shower was to the right and two large vanity sinks to the left. Above the second was a built-in medicine cabinet. I made a beeline for it, quickly opening the craftsman inspired cabinetry (Did these guys know how to mix their architectural styles or what?) and peered inside.

If I'd hoped to find some sort of prescription bottle, I'd hit the mother load.

Three small shelves filled the cabinet, all of them lined with little orange bottles with prescriptions written on them. I blinked, momentarily overwhelmed before quickly scanning the labels. All of them were prescribed to Ratski. Unfortunately, most of them seemed benign enough: Propecia, Viagra, Zoloft, a couple of different painkillers. I pulled my phone out and took photos of a couple of labels I didn't immediately recognize, but I didn't see anything that mentioned ADD, "speed," or "greenies."

I moved on to the vanity drawers. Like the medicine cabinet, they were a treasure trove of bottles. Hair products abounded, and it took me a moment to realize these were *men's* products. Geeze, Ratski was high maintenance. Hair straighteners, hair curlers, nail growers, nail trimmers, exfoliators, moisturizers, acne creams, and wrinkle creams. I shuddered to think what Ratski might look like *without* this stuff.

I was just about to give up on the idea that Ratski had kept his murder weapon in his house when I spied a walk-in closet to my right. With a quick over-the-shoulder, I tiptoed in, switching on a light.

The thing was the size of my frickin' living room. Drawers, cupboards, and racks of clothes filled every wall, all of it lined in cedar that smelled like pure fashion heaven. Rows of slacks and dress shirts lined one wall, blouses and skirts the other. And the back wall held shoes…dozens of pairs of beautiful shoes in tidy little rows of cubby holes. I couldn't help myself. I ran my fingers over a pair that I knew were in the four-digit price range. I suddenly had a good idea why "poor Beth" stuck it out with a guy like Ratski. Heck, these might make *me* consider a guy like Ratski.

I think I let out a little gasp when I saw a pair of vintage Martin Margiela pumps on the bottom row, and crouched down to get a better look.

That's when I saw the duffle bag.

Shoved behind the legs of some hanging trousers on the clearly "man" side of the closet, a bit of blue nylon peeked out. I gingerly reached under and tugged at it, extricating a gym bag that smelled suspiciously like Ratski's locker at the Stars stadium. Saying a silent prayer to the gods of not-touching-icky-things, I stuck my hand in and rummaged around. Unfortunately, there wasn't much in the bag other than the usual water bottle, running shoes, and ear buds.

I was about to concede this whole trip had been a bust when I heard Dana cry out from the bedroom.

"Eep!"

In three quick strides, I was by her side. "What? Are you okay?"

Dana blinked at me, holding up a pair of hot pink silk bikini briefs in a leopard pattern.

I felt my heart rate immediately slow down. "Geeze you scared me."

"And these don't?" Dana argued.

"Well, they're a little wild for Beth—"

"They were in Ratski's drawer."

"Eep."

"Thank you!" Dana said, tossing the panties back into the open drawer in front of her.

"Find anything else interesting?" I asked, peeking into it.

"Not really. There were some letters in the nightstand. They started getting dirty, though, so I put them back. Who'd want to 'shtup schmoopy'?"

"Ick," I agreed.

"You find anything?"

I was about to answer in the negative when a noise from the first level made me freeze in my tracks.

I immediately cut my eyes to Dana's. "Ratski?" I mouthed to her

Dana shrugged. She opened her mouth, about to respond when the answer came floating up the stairs to us loud and clear.

"John? Johnny I'm home," came Beth's voice.

Oh snap. The wife.

CHAPTER TWELVE

―――――

Instinctively, I ducked, even though I was pretty sure that she couldn't see us all the way up here. Something that wouldn't hold true for very long.

"Johnny?" I heard her walking farther into the house. "Whose car is that outside?"

Dana's eyes went big and round. "What are we going to do?" she whispered to me, the panic I felt rising in my stomach clear on her face.

I quickly whipped my head around the room, looking for an escape route. Unfortunately the only way out was the way we'd come up. I grabbed Dana by the hand, speed tiptoeing out of the master bedroom as quickly as possible. When we reached the landing I peeked out.

"Great. Passed out again," I heard Beth say out loud. She stood in the doorway to the parlor, narrowing her eyes at the sleeping Ratski.

I flattened myself against the wall as she turned around. She paused at a credenza in the foyer, shuffled through some mail, then grabbed her handbag and started up the stairs.

Oh, crap.

Dana squeezed my hand tighter as we crabbed walked as silently as we could down the hall toward one of the guestrooms, slipping into the dark doorway just as Beth hit the top landing. I held my breath, crouching behind the guestroom door. I heard feet padding along the carpeting toward the master and held my breath, praying she didn't notice anything out of place. I couldn't be 100% sure I'd put everything back in exactly the spot I'd found it.

A couple of tense moments passed before we heard bathwater running from the master. I took it as a sign to bolt.

We both took our shoes off before padding barefoot down the wooden staircase and across the marble foyer. I closed my eyes and thought very, very quiet thoughts as I slowly turned the front door knob and slipped outside.

Dana and I both jumped into her roadster, and I crossed my fingers that the master bath was far enough toward the back of the house Beth either wouldn't notice the sound of the engine turning over or would attribute it to a neighbor as we peeled out of the driveway and onto the street. Dana parked just in front of my minivan, and we sat in the silence for a few moments taking deep breaths.

"That was close," I said. What can I say? When I'm nervous I state the obvious.

"No kidding. Bad enough I was out on a date with her husband. I can't imagine what I would've said to Beth if she'd caught me in her house."

"Poor Beth," I said, not for the first time thinking about what life must be like married to Ratski. Despite her to-die-for shoe collection, I suddenly felt incredibly fortunate for my own loyal lug at home.

"You know, when this is all over I have half a mind to tell her what a cheating scum her husband is," Dana said.

I nodded. "Agreed." And if we were lucky, he might just be a murderer, too.

* * *

The house was dark by the time I got home, save for the flicker of the television coming from the living room. And I was happy to say that instead of a completely pristine room, there was one empty water glass sitting on the coffee table. I guess Mr. Mom wasn't *completely* perfect after all.

Ramirez was lying on the couch, snoring lightly, his eyelashes casting long shadows on his cheeks. His jaw was slack, dusted with a day's worth of stubble, creating an oddly vulnerable pose for my usually intimidating husband.

I grabbed an afghan his mother had knitted for us from the back of the sofa and covered his legs with it. Then I picked up the remote and switched off the volume on the TV. He stirred, and I felt an arm snake around my middle pulling me back onto the sofa beside him.

"How'd the date go?" he asked, his voice husky with sleep.

I couldn't help a small smile as I snuggled next to him. "Ratski passed out drunk. His wife came home and almost found us snooping through his underwear drawer."

I felt Ramirez's chest rise with a deep chuckle. "You girls know how to have a good time."

"We try."

"Learn anything useful?"

I quickly told him about Bucky's lack of an alibi and availability of amphetamines in the form of ADD meds.

"I'll call it in tomorrow," he told me. "It's possible it will be enough for a warrant to go through Bucky's things."

I felt pride bubble up in my chest.

"Though, all this will prove is that he has access to the drugs, not that he killed Lacey."

Bubble burst.

"Well, it's a start," I mumbled.

"That it is," Ramirez agreed, hugging me closer.

"When did the twins go down?" I asked.

"Couple of hours ago."

"They wore you out, huh?" I asked, tilting my head to see his face.

A slow smile snaked across his cheeks. "I might have a little energy left in me…" he trailed off, his lips finding the back of my neck.

I felt myself go warm in all the right places as I shut off the TV.

* * *

I woke up to the sound of insistent pounding on my front door. I groaned, peaking one eye open. I had no idea what time it was, but the sun was barely dusting the sky with the palest pink color. I closed my eyes, hoping the noise would go away.

No such luck. More pounding.

I rolled over to check my bedside clock. 7 AM. On the upside, it was the latest the twins had slept in the last six months. On the downside, somebody at the front door was demanding that I *not* sleep in. I was about to roll over and put a pillow over my head when I heard the worst sound the parent of sleeping children can ever hear.

The doorbell.

I jumped out of bed, grabbed a robe from the back of the chair, and sprinted toward the front door. I had just reached it when the soon-to-be dead man on the other side went to hit the doorbell button again.

"Do not touch that button!" I yelled at him.

The portly guy in a gray uniform with a bunch of balloons on the lapel blinked at me, his finger hovering over the button.

"Well, what do you want?" I asked. So clearly I'm not a morning person.

"I got a delivery here for Springer?" he said, a question in his voice.

"I didn't order anything."

The guy consulted the clipboard held in his other hand. "Three helium tanks and a cotton candy machine for a kids' birthday party?" he asked, looking me up and down from my bed head to my hastily thrown on robe to the scowl that I'm sure was marking my features.

I took a deep breath. I counted to ten. Okay, I only got as far as five before I started counting ways to kill Marco.

"Fine. In here," I said pointing to the living room.

He looked behind me. "I'm not sure it's all gonna fit. I mean, your house is kinda—"

"Small. I know. Just cram it in, okay?"

He took a step back. "Okay, okay, lady. I'll do my best."

I closed my eyes and told myself it wasn't this guy's fault that my party planner was out of control. I left the door open to let the party guy cram items into our living room, and I shuffled into the kitchen and put on a pot of coffee. I was just taking the first divine sip when the party guy yelled an, "All done!" and scuttled back to his truck as fast his feet would go.

Cup in hand, I walked back into the living room.

And stopped short.

My sofa had been moved out of the way to accommodate a machine almost as tall as I was with colorful painted balloons on all sides, three nozzles sticking out of the front. Beside it sat an equally tall cotton candy machine, dripping what looked like pink syrup into the burnout hole in Ramirez's chair.

I grabbed my cell from my purse by the door and immediately stabbed through my contacts, hitting Marco and listening to it ring on the other end. Five rings in, I got a voicemail.

I stabbed the phone off. Clearly *Marco* was sleeping in this morning. I took a deep breath, then another, and another. Then I decide this was an excellent way to hyperventilate, and took a sip of coffee instead.

It was just one day. One little party. By Monday, this would all be over.

I held onto that one comforting thought as I showered, dressed, and threw on a pair of black skinny jeans, a red silk tank, and cute grey high-heeled ankle booties. Then I fired up my computer just as I heard Livvie and Max rousing their dad from dreamland. The first thing I did was scroll through my photos on my phone and google the drug names I'd found on Ratski's prescription bottles, in hopes that one of them contained the lethal drug. After reading through pages of medical jargon, I found that Ratski had prescriptions to combat acne, hair loss, erectile dysfunction, and high blood pressure. But nothing that contained the lethal amphetamines. If Ratski was using PEDs, he wasn't getting them legally.

I chewed on my lower lip as I stared at my computer screen. If Lacey had been blackmailing someone over drug use—or anything else—how had she found out? As much as I'd liked the idea of her overhearing a tidbit from the wives, I was getting the impression that they were pretty tight lipped around outsiders. So where had she stumbled on some crumb of information scandalous enough to kill over?

On a whim, I googled the Bellissima boutique.

Lacey had worked for Liz there before becoming a tag-along member of the Baseball Wives crew, and it had been where she'd met Bucky. Maybe she'd found her blackmail worthy item while in Liz's employ?

I scanned through the first page of hits getting mostly references to the *Baseball Wives* TV show. Two pages in, I saw a couple of articles about the grand opening of the boutique, just over a year ago. I clicked, the screen in front of me filling with pictures of Liz and her husband posing as the happy couple. I scrolled through but didn't see anything out of the ordinary—nothing to indicate a blackmail-worthy secret. I squinted at the photos for a glimpse of the handbags on the shelves behind her. Unfortunately I couldn't see much more than colorful blobs on the shelves which could've easily been the Michael Kors' spring collection or the Jaclyn Smith Kmart collection.

Which meant just one thing. A shopping trip to Melrose was in order today. Oh, the sacrifices I made.

* * *

Bellissima was nestled along a trendy shopping corridor where small boutiques rubbed elbows with big-name designer stores and dozens of coffee houses. Tourists carrying cameras mingled with housewives from Beverly Hills toting their Birkins, with a few young Hollywood "It" kids sprinkled in between, loitering in the cafes in their short-shorts, Ugg boots, and gargantuan sunglasses. Parking was scarce, but I must have been on the traffic gods' good side as I found a spot on the street just two blocks from Bellissima.

Large glass windows faced the street on either side of the door, flanked by displays of mannequins with skin in neon hues, dressed in tasteful black-and-white, each sporting a pair of pewter kitten heels that had me drooling. I pushed through the doors and was greeted with the familiar scent of retail—new clothes, fresh leather bags, and a slight hint of expensive perfume. I inhaled deeply as I took in my surroundings.

The boutique was an eerie duplicate of the Sunset Studios set. The walls were stark white with shelves in the same neon hues as the mannequins lining them, artfully displaying handbags, shoes, and belts, while the main floor of the boutique was occupied by racks of blouses, skirts, and dresses. Along the back wall sat a large sofa, two chairs, and some curtained-off sections which I guessed to be dressing rooms.

I went to the first rack pretending to browse as I scanned the place for Liz. (Okay, I might have *actually* browsed a little too. Liz had good taste!) I spied a young woman with Bambi eyes, Lindsay Lohan lips, and long, pale blonde extensions behind the cash register, ringing up a purchase. Another blonde with almost identical make-up and hair stood near the dressing rooms, and a third clone was straightening shoes on a wall rack. I silently wondered if Liz had a hard time telling them apart.

Blonde Number Three spotted me and approached. "Welcome to Bellissima. May I help you with something today?"

"I was wondering if the owner was in?"

She nodded. "She's in the back. May I get your name?"

"Yes, Maddie Springer," I said, hoping Liz remembered me.

The blonde nodded, then scooted away toward a door behind the cash register.

I browsed for a few moments, wandering to the wall of handbags. Designer labels in leather and nylon stared back at me, assuring me that Bellissima was as high end as its address promised.

"Maddie?" I heard behind me. I turned to find Liz, her brown eyes blinking at me. "How wonderful to see you again."

"Lovely to see you too. I love the boutique," I told her honestly meaning it.

She brightened up right away, a genuine smile of pride on her face. "Thank you. It's sort of my baby."

"How long have you been here?" I asked, even though I knew full well from my handy dandy googling earlier.

"Just over a year now," she said.

"And business is going well?" I fished.

Liz paused, the smile faltering for a fraction of a second. "Of course! I mean, look around. We're always busy."

She was right. The place had a healthy number of well-dressed women browsing the racks, the dressing rooms looked full, and all three blond clones were busy.

"Well it's amazing that you got this piece of real estate," I told her. "This is a prime location. I hope you're not paying a mint for it."

Liz laughed, but it lacked the genuineness of her earlier beam of pride. "Well, you get what you pay for," she said noncommittally.

"You must have a lot of overhead here." I gestured to the triplet girls handling the floor.

A frown formed between Liz's perfectly threaded brows. "You're awfully interested in our business operations, Maddie," she said with a laugh, though I could see suspicion creeping into her gaze.

Fortunately I had a plan.

"Well, I'll confess something to you Liz. I'm not here purely for personal reasons. I'm looking at expanding the distribution of my footwear line. And your boutique," I said, spreading my arms out around me, "seems a perfect venue for my heels."

Once again Liz's face brightened up. "Well, as you can see we have several top-of-the-line shoe designers here. You know we'd love to add your collection. Here, let me show you." She led the way over to the wall of shoes I'd spied earlier and began telling me about each designer. I'll admit, had I not pegged Liz as a potential suspect in a murder, I might have actually been tempted to enter into a business partnership with her. I hadn't been lying when I'd said the boutique was in a prime location, and it did seem to be doing a brisk business.

"Liz?" Blonde Number One said, tapping her employer lightly on the shoulder. "You have a call in the back. Mr. Frinkelstein?"

"I'm so sorry, Maddie, I have to take this. You don't mind, do you?" Liz asked backing towards the rear room on her stilettos.

"Of course not," I assured her, even though I was a little bummed at not having extracted anything juicy from her yet.

I wandered over to a rack of clothing near the dressing rooms, browsing through pastel, chiffon tops. I picked up one in a pale peach color that was cut on the bias, holding it up in front of me.

"That cut is very on-trend for spring," Blonde Number Three piped up from behind me.

I turned to face her eager customer-service smile. "It's lovely," I said.

The Blonde nodded. "You're the shoe designer, right? Maddie Springer?"

I nodded, sending her a questioning look.

"I overheard you and Liz talking," she admitted.

I raised an eyebrow. An eavesdropper might be useful.

I nodded. "Yes, I'm thinking of selling my line here. I see you do a good business?"

"Oh, sure, we're always packed," she said.

"Have you worked here long?" I asked.

Blonde Number Three shrugged. "A few months."

"So, then you worked here when Lacey was here?" I asked, lowering my voice the appropriate amount when speaking of the dead.

But if the Blonde was spooked by mention of a dead coworker, she didn't show it. She just nodded her head, her extensions bobbing down her back. "Sure. But she wasn't here very long."

"Oh, really?" I asked. "What happened?"

Blond Number Three smirked. "She was fired."

I raised an eyebrow. This was a tidbit no one had mentioned. Liz had made it seem like Lacey had quit when she'd started dating Bucky. "Do you know why?"

She frowned at me. "Well, I don't know *for sure* why, but I can tell you that Kylie," she said, pointing to Blonde Number One at the register, "heard something about some unaccounted for money."

"No!" I said, doing a little gasp which wasn't all acting on my part. Had Lacey been stealing and that's why she was fired? Or…was it the other way around? Maybe Liz had been skimming money from her own business. If Lacey had found out, and Liz fired her for it, I could see Lacey not losing sleep over blackmailing her former boss.

"Did Lacey tell Kylie this?" I asked.

Blonde Number Three shook her head. "No, she overheard an argument between Lacey and Liz in the back room. But I do know that Lacey was for sure fired."

"You do?"

She did the extension-bobbing nod again. "Yep. I ran into her at dinner at City Walk, like, a week ago."

My ears perked up at the mention of the trendy City Walk. Was this the "girl's night" that Bucky said he and Lacey had fought about?

"What did she say?"

"She told me Liz totally gave her the boot. We didn't really get into it too much, though, 'cause she was out with that ball player whose name I can never remember."

"The ballplayer—you mean with Bucky Davis?" I asked, confused.

Blonde Number Three laugh-snorted, the sound coming out a cross between a horse whinnying and a two-year-old blowing raspberries. "No. God, everybody knows Bucky Davis. No, it was some other guy. Tall but has kind of a gut."

I felt my heart rate speed up. "Ratski?"

She stabbed a finger at me. "That's the one! I totally didn't get why Lacey was out with him. He's, like, way old and kinda smarmy. I mean, if I had Bucky at home, trust me, I'd be at home!"

My mind reeled over the possible reasons Lacey would be having dinner with Ratski…and lie to her boyfriend about it. Had Lacey been meeting Ratski to extract blackmail from him? Or had she been seeing him behind his wife's back? While it was certainly possible Liz's "unaccounted for" money had something to do with Lacey, it was now starting to look like there could have been one other baseball wife who might have wanted Lacey out of the way badly enough to kill her.

Beth Ratski.

Blonde Number Three brought my attention back to present, asking, "Did you want to try that on?" She gestured to the blouse in my hands.

I looked down, almost having forgotten my browsing cover. I shoved the blouse back on the rack. "No thanks. But…"

I couldn't help myself. "...do you have those kitten heels in a seven?"

CHAPTER THIRTEEN

———

The first thing I did when I got back to my car was dial Dana's number. She picked up on the third ring with a, "Hello?" followed by loud noises in the background.

"Hey, it's me. Is this a bad time?"

"Nope. Just getting a makeup touch-up between scenes at the moment. Today's my big trial where I get a hooker off."

I stifled a giggle at her pun.

Lady Justice was based on the concept of a lawyer who inadvertently becomes an advocate for female porn stars, fighting for their rights in a male-dominated industry. At least, that was how *Variety* put it. Dana and her cast & crew usually just referred to it as the "porn lawyer show." Clearly, sex sold, because *Lady Justice* had been one of the top rated shows on the network for the new season. My fingers were crossed they picked it up for another thirteen episodes. As much as Dana loved being "movie star Ricky Montgomery's girlfriend," she was ready to step out of his shadow.

"I was hoping you were on the Sunset Studios lot today. I need to get in to see Beth Ratski. She should be filming her interrogation scene this afternoon."

"Ooo," Dana cooed. "New development?"

I quickly filled her in on what Blonde Number Three had told me about seeing Lacey out with Ratski.

"What a jerk. He really can't keep it in his pants, can he?" Dana said.

I nodded as I turned on my car and let the welcomed air conditioning wash over me.

"Do you think you could put me on the list at the gate?" I asked.

"Sure. I've got to shoot another scene right now, but then we'll be breaking for lunch around noon. Ricky's supposed to meet me here, too, so we can all go eat together."

"Perfect," I agreed. I heard more noise in the background and someone shouting.

"Hey, I gotta go. They're calling me on the set. See you later," Dana said, as she hung up.

I looked down at my cell. It was just past eleven, which gave me almost an hour to brave the traffic toward the studios. I decided to take the long way there, doing a little drive-by experiment.

Ratski all but told Dana that the gym alibi was a joke last night. Which left Bucky, Ratski, and Blanco alone at the time someone was tampering with Lacey's tanning booth. It begged the question: just how far from Fernando's salon was this gym?

I pulled up a web browser on my phone. After a little surfing of the tabloid sites I found out that Bucky was frequently seen leaving the L.A. Fit Gym, which I had never heard of. While my best friend Dana was an exercise devotee all the way, I had a definite love-hate relationship with gyms. I love to avoid them and hated to go. Google told me it was located on Blake Street, and according to my GPS, it was only a mile from Fernando's. Of course, in L.A. a mile could mean a two minute drive or twenty, depending on the time of day and what part of town it was in. I pulled my car into traffic and pointed it toward Fernando's.

Twenty minutes later, I was slowly driving past Faux Dad's salon, which, sadly, looked as deserted as ever. I spied Marco through the front windows, idly picking at his cuticles. As tempting as it was to park, storm in, and yell at him for dropping a cotton candy machine in my living room at 7 AM, I instead noted the time on my cell and continued on toward Blake Street.

Six minutes later I was idling in the parking lot of L.A. Fit. Any of the three players could have made their way to Fernando's, slipped in the back door to add the poison to the tanning solution, then made their way back here in under half an hour. All the killer would have had to do was find out when Lacey was going tanning, then casually suggest a trip to the gym to the other two to create an alibi.

Which left me back at square one. Again. Plenty of suspects, plenty of motives, no alibis. I really hoped that Ramirez was making more headway on getting that warrant than I was today.

With that depressing thought, I jumped back on the 2 toward Hollywood, and, after braving both the tourist traffic and the Wilshire corridor lunch rush, I finally made my way up to the gate of the Sunset Studios. True to her word, Dana had put my name on the visitor list, and the guard waved me through, gesturing to the massive parking lot to the right where I swapped out my real car for a golf cart. I hopped in, slowly motoring my way toward Studio 4B.

Quite frankly, I wasn't sure what I was going to ask Beth when I got there. It seemed a little forward to come right out and say, "Did you kill Lacey Desta because she was sleeping with your husband?" Even hinting that Lacey might've had a relationship with Ratski was treading on thin ice. I knew the Baseball Wives might not be the sharpest crayons in the box, but Dana and I were likely to lose our "girl talk" status if we didn't tread lightly.

Unfortunately, any ideas I had of hinting at her husband's infidelity disappeared as soon as I parked my golf cart and entered the studio. Standing next to the crafts services table, with an arm around his wife, was Ratski himself.

I paused suddenly wondering what to do now. Ratski was sure to recognize me the second he saw me. I ducked into a narrow hallway to the left and took refuge behind a rack of sparkly cocktail dresses. I watched Ratski shove a donut into his mouth, licking the icing off his fingers one by one, as I wondered how to get Beth alone. I spied Laurel and Hardy standing on their X's, already being miked. It wouldn't be long before Beth was called to set.

"I told you to keep quiet about it."

I froze. I slowly peeked out from behind the wardrobe rack and spied Kendra Blanco on her cell, stomping down the empty hallway. Her lips were tight, her forehead pulled taught in a way that suggested if she could frown through her Botox, she would.

"That's not good enough!" she hissed into her phone.

I ducked down lower, hoping I'd hit the eavesdropping jackpot. Kendra was clearly upset about something.

"Look, we had a deal. I've kept up my end, now you keep up yours." She paused. "Well, you better do something! The cops are nosing around enough. I don't need them looking at me."

I felt an eyebrow rise. And just why would the cops look to Kendra?

"Oh, you better care," she spat into the phone. "You and I both know that if I go down, I'm taking you with me."

With that she stabbed her phone off and stalked back onto the set.

I moved out from my wardrobe hiding place. Very interesting. Just what was Kendra afraid of "going down" for? Did it have something to do with Lacey's murder? The fact that she didn't want the cops looking into it was a good sign it wasn't 100% on the up and up. Whatever "it" was. I bit my lip, wondering just who had been on the other end of that call.

I didn't have long to contemplate that as my cell vibrated with the text from Dana.

Ricky and I on our way to meet you

I quickly texted back that I'd meet her out front.

I slipped out from my hiding place, keeping one eye on Ratski as I made my way back out into the assaulting sunshine. Two minutes later I spied Dana and Ricky approaching. Something seemed to be in the air today because the two of them were arguing as well. An odd occurrence for them. Ricky had proposed to Dana just a few months ago, and ever since then you would swear that the two had already started their honeymoon phase. Only today it looked like the honeymoon was on hiatus, Ricky's features pulled into a frown, Dana waving her hands rapidly in the air.

I took a step forward, hesitant to interrupt.

But as it turned out, that wasn't an issue. Ricky stopped dead in his tracks, staring at the open doors to Studio 4B.

"You!" Ricky pointed an arm toward the doorway.

I whipped my head around just in time to see Ratski and Beth emerging.

Ratski's eyes bounced from Dana to Ricky. "I…I…" Ratski started.

"You were putting the moves on my fiancée last night!"

Uh-oh.

"Uh…" Ratski's eyes shifted to his wife with a deer-facing-the-business-end-of-an-SUV look in them.

So much for me delicately broaching the subject of her husband's infidelity. I watched her reaction carefully. If I had to guess, confusion was the overriding emotion playing across her face. "John?" she asked.

"I…I don't know what he's talking about," Ratski protested,

"Like hell you don't!" Ricky yelled back. And like a shot, Ricky closed the few feet between them, cocked his right fist back, and hit Ratski square in the nose with a blow that sent him reeling backwards.

CHAPTER FOURTEEN

———

Ratski fell backwards, knocking into a wardrobe rack by the door and taking down a dozen dresses with him as he hit the ground. Dana shrieked, diving for Ricky. Beth shrieked, diving for Ratski. And two guys in security shirts appeared from inside the studio, rushing out at the sound of the screams.

"Ohmigod! Oh, my poor pooh bear," Beth cried, trying to disentangle Ratski from the mess of cocktail dresses and pant suits.

"Poor pooh bear, my ass," Ricky shouted. Though all of Dana's hours at the gym were paying off. She had him around the waist, just barely able to hold him back from hitting Ratski again. "You stay the hell away from my fiancée, you got that, pal?"

"I don't know what you're talking about," Ratski sputtered again, scrambling to his feet.

"It's all over the *L.A. Informer's* website. I saw the pictures of you two at dinner last night."

Mental forehead thunk,

"Ricky, I told you it's not what you think," Dana started.

But neither of the guys was paying attention to her. They were completely focused on the pissing contest going on in the middle of the studio lot.

"What's a friendly little dinner?" Ratski said, grinning.

Ricky growled and lunged for him. Ratski jumped out of the way just as the security guards made it to the center of our group, the larger of the two restraining Ricky.

"What's going on here?" one of them barked.

"He's a two-timing jerk!" Ricky yelled stabbing a finger Ratski's way.

Ratski was still wearing a superior smirk on his face. He held his hands up in a surrender motion. "Me? I'm a married man. What would I want with that floozy?"

"Hey!" Dana cried.

I stepped in just in time to save Ratski from being punched twice in one day. While he was still smirking I could see blood trickling from his nose, his whole face starting to swell. He might be enjoying riling Ricky up, but I'd wager he'd be feeling that tomorrow.

Beth must've noticed too, as she started bawling. "Oh, my poor pooh bear! How could you do this to him? How dare you accuse him of something like that! He would never!"

I barely restrained myself from rolling my eyes. How one woman could be so clueless about her husband, I had no idea.

Beth put an arm around Ratski, dabbing at the blood on his upper lip with her thumb like the mother wiping gook off her kindergartner.

"You stay away from her, you understand. Or next time no one will be able to hold me back," Ricky growled, still under the vice-like grip of the security guard.

"Are you threatening me, pretty boy?" Ratski asked. Then he turned to the second guard. "You heard that, right? That was a threat. I want to file charges. I want a restraining order. Knowing these Hollywood types, he's probably hopped up on something."

Ricky growled again, lunging forward, and the security guard lost his grip.

Ratski jumped back behind his wife with a terrified yip. Good grief.

"All right, all right, enough!" the second security guard said, inserting himself between the two. "Ratski, if you want to press charges I'll call an officer down here and have this guy arrested. Is that what you want?

Ratski looked from the security guard, to Ricky, to Dana shooting daggers at him, and then to his wife, still sobbing beside him. He must have realized that if he brought the police in, what he'd planned that night with Dana might be called under closer scrutiny. I didn't have great respect for Ratski's intelligence, but at least he had the brains to know the whole thing was better swept under the rug.

"No," he said. "You just keep this guy on a leash," he told Dana.

The security guard turned to Ricky. "If I find you anywhere near this set again, I will call the police."

Ricky shook the guard off and straightened his shoulders. "Trust me, I don't want to be anywhere near this place. Come on, Dana, let's go." He grabbed her arm and turned away.

Dana made a motion with her hand at her ear like she'd call me later. I nodded my agreement. I had a feeling the two of them needed some alone time.

I wasn't much in the mood for lunch, anyway. Truth was, I'd had enough of the Stars gang for one day. I drove my golf cart back to the lot entrance and was just swapping it out for my minivan when a text came in on my phone. I looked down to see Ramirez's name on the screen.

A pony just arrived. A live pony.

I pursed my lips, wondering if Ricky's fists of fury were available for hire. There was one party planner I wouldn't mind seeing decked at the moment.

Before I could even respond Ramirez shot off another text, saying he was taking the kids and going to Mama's.

I was tempted to join him, but I was worried about what might arrive next at my humble abode.

I hopped into my minivan and quickly pointed it towards home, only stopping once at a drive-through for a Double-Double and some Animal Fries. If I was going to face the worst, better not to do it on an empty stomach.

One precarious drive down the 101 later, I was happy to report I did not drop any pink sauce on my pants. However, as I pulled up to the front of my house I felt my good luck disintegrating.

A catering truck blocked my driveway, and a Jeep with a cheetah-print custom paint job sat at the curb. A magnetic sign on the driver's side door read "Aaron's Exotic Animals," and I could've sworn I recognized the bike parked by the front door as that of one former Spanish-soap-star-turned-clown.

I parked my car. I closed my eyes and counted to ten. I tried to get the tick twitching over my left eye under control before grabbing my purse and making my way into the house.

I had to look at the number on my mailbox twice just to make sure it really *was* my house as I walked through the door.

My furniture had been moved out to God knows where, replaced with a pinball machine, a vintage Pac-Man arcade game, and a foosball table. Huge decals sporting balloons and rainbows had been stuck on one wall, elephants and hippos with party blowers in their mouths on the other side. People in various company uniforms filtered in and out through the sliding glass doors, carrying folding chairs, flowers, dishes, and plastic novelty blowups of various circus animals.

And in the center of it all stood Marco, waving his arms in the chaos like some sort of mad conductor while chatting into his Bluetooth.

"…well, of course we can't have a pony without a Wild West gunslinger. What did you say you charge by the hour?" Pause. "*That* much? Wow. Well, what if the pony's handler just puts on a cowboy hat?"

"Ahem." I cleared my throat loudly.

Marco turned around, a bright smile lighting up his features. "Dahling, I'll have to call you back," he said into his Bluetooth before enveloping me with air kisses.

Which I did not return.

"What's going on here, Marco?"

"Don't you just love it?" he asked, spreading his arms wide. "I'll admit the decals might've been a bit much. But we have to have *some* décor in here. I mean, not to say there's anything *wrong* with your décor, darling, but it is a bit…well…" He scrunched up his nose, "…on the pedestrian side. Drab. Ish. For a *children's* party, mind you."

"Did you just call my décor too pedestrian for children?"

"Well, once the belly dancers arrive, they're going to totally stick out like sore thumbs without a pop of color somewhere in the room."

I blinked at him. "The what?"

Marco took a deep breath to launch himself into another monologue but was interrupted as a guy in a chef's hat crashed through my kitchen door.

"I simply cannot work in zat kitchen. It eez much too small."

"And you are?" I asked.

"Oh, Maddie, meet François LeRue. He's classically trained. In Paaaaaaris," Marco said, drawing out the words.

I stared at Marco. "You realize my children's palates run from mashed bananas to mashed sweet potatoes?"

Marco waved me off, addressing the chef. "François I'm sure you can find some way to work around the size."

"Impossible! There eez no counter space. I cannot even find room to lay out zee crepe station."

I rolled my eyes. "It's not *that* small."

"Dahling, I'm sure we can work something out," Marco addressed the chef. "I know! You can use the banquet table on the patio."

"We have a banquet table?" I asked, craning to see around him out the sliding glass doors to our yard.

"Of course you have a banquet table, silly," Marco said, giving me a sly grin. "Where else was I going to put the ice sculpture?"

That tick was coming back with full force, "Marco I think we need to talk," I started.

However, that's as far as I got before a guy in a Crocodile Dundee outfit burst through the back door. "I've lost Matilda!"

I shot Marco a look. "Do I want to know who or what Matilda is?"

Marco shrugged. We both turned questioning eyes on Dundee.

"My Amethyst."

"Amethyst…" I had a bad feeling about this.

"Python. Snake," he said, looking in the bushes near the door. "My poor baby snake."

I froze, the creepy crawlies slithering up my spine. "Uh, just how big is this 'baby?'"

"She's just a young thing," Dundee assured me.

I sighed in relief.

"Only about ten feet."

"There's a ten foot snake loose in my yard?!"

"Not for long," Dundee said, shaking his head. "Matilda prefers warm, cozy places. Small, dark." He paused. "A bit like your house."

I threw my hands up. "I get it! My house is small!" I took a couple of deep breaths, that tick starting to vibrate my entire brain, causing a headache that it would take copious amounts of alcohol to fix.

"Maddie, now, don't you stress," Marco said, putting an arm around my shoulder. "Auntie Marco will take care of everything. That's why I'm here. You just go relax. Take a bubble bath or something."

I shot him a death look. "I'd love to. But there might be a *python* in my *bathtub*."

Marco shook his head. "Nonsense. Big Red is practicing his juggling in there. I'm sure he'd see a ten foot snake if it was in the bathtub."

I ground my teeth together. "The clown is back?"

Marco blinked innocently at me. "You weren't serious about firing him, were you?"

I heard a low, menacing growl. I'm pretty sure it came from me.

I whipped out my cell, pushing past the guy in the safari outfit crawling on all fours, crooning, "Here, Matilda, baby." I pulled up Ramirez's number and quickly shot off a text.

To avoid another murder, I'm joining you at Mama's.

* * *

Ramirez's mother lived in Hacienda Heights, which was a quick half-hour drive down the 60 into the San Gabriel Valley, a sleepy little suburb of Los Angeles. The yards were generous, the houses 50's style ranches, the neighborhoods unpretentious, and the occupants lifers of the burbs. There was something I always found comforting about driving into these family neighborhoods which had sat largely unchanged for the last fifty years. Go karts might've been swapped out for Razor scooters and checker boards for iPads, but the rhythm of life was still the same: work hard, come home, eat pot roast, and mow the lawn on Sunday.

Mama's house was nestled between two others of the identical style, with minor additions of converted garages and picket fences over the years. There was a tricycle outside on her lawn, a couple of soccer balls wedged into the bushes, and a driveway filled with late-model sedans in various states of wear. Even as I parked at the curb, I could smell the heavenly scents of cinnamon, cumin, and chocolate wafting from Mama's kitchen. Instantly my blood pressure went down ten points.

I knocked twice on the door before pushing inside. "Hello?" I called.

I was greeted by the hum of a television in the corner, tuned to an old Western movie, mingled with the sounds of low snoring emanating from the older man snoozing in an easy chair under a brightly colored Afghan. The screeches and squeals of children carried in from the back yard, accompanied by someone singing a soft melody with an acoustic guitar. And above all of that was the high pitched sound of five different women speaking in rapid Spanish in the kitchen.

"Hello?" I asked, poking my head into the room.

Five heads turned my way.

"Ay, *linda*, so good to see you!" Mama said, enveloping me in a warm hug. Mama was a few inches shorter than I was, a few pounds heavier, and a whole lot more domestic.

"Good to see you too, Mama," I told her, meaning it.

"You came at just the right time," Mama told me.

"Oh?" I asked, looking over her head to the rest of the women assembled in the small kitchen. Three smiling, well-lined faces rimmed with salt and pepper hair—and one scowling face punctuated with heavy Goth make-up—stared back at me. Ramirez's aunts, Swoozie, Cookie, and Kiki, collectively just known as The Aunts, were the owners of the smiling faces. The scowling face belonged to Ramirez's sister, BillieJo. Then again, if I'd been saddled with a name like BillieJo, I might spend life scowling as well. As Ramirez had told it, when his parents had immigrated from Mexico, his mother had learned English watching reruns of TV Westerns and named each of her children after one of her favorite characters. He'd just been glad he hadn't been stuck with Maverick.

"Yes," Mama told me. "We need you to settle a dispute."

Uh-oh. A "dispute" was never good, and the one who settled it was never popular with everyone. "Uh, what kind of dispute?"

"Well," Cookie said, gesturing toward a tray with circles of fried dough, sitting on the counter. "Clearly we should sprinkle these *buñuelos* with cinnamon and sugar now."

"And I say," Mama piped up loudly, "you drizzle with honey."

"Nonsense," Kiki argued. "Cinnamon and sugar is the traditional way to do it."

"*Abuelita* always used honey and cinnamon," Swoozie countered.

"*Abuelita* was ninety years old and half blind," Cookie said. "She mixed Bengay in her *pozole*."

Mama sucked in a quick breath. "Don't you disparage *Abuelita*'s cooking. *Abuelita* made the best *pozole* in all of Mexico."

Kiki leaned in close, whispering to me. "Well, it loosened up the joints at least." She gave me a wink.

"I say we stick with tradition," BillieJo piped up. "Our Hispanic heritage is very important for us to pass down to the younger generation. Don't you think, Maddie?" She gave me a pointed look.

"Uh…yes?"

BillieJo narrowed her eyes at me.

"You *loco*," Mama said, rolling her eyes. "What is tradition if it tastes bland?"

"Maddie, you are the deciding vote," Kiki told me. "How do you make your *buñuelos*?"

"Uh…*my buñuelos*?" The truth was, I made all of my Mexican cookies by going to the bakery three blocks down from our house. "Well, you know, I really think there's no wrong way to top a cookie."

Five voices gasped in unison. Mama put a hand to her heart. BillieJo's eyes narrowed into fine slits. Kiki grasped onto the counter to keep herself upright.

"Maddie," Mama whispered reverently, "*buñuelos* are fritters. Not cookies."

Oh boy.

"Is that Margaritas?" I asked pointing to a pitcher of lime colored deliciousness sitting on the well-worn kitchen table. Before anyone could answer, I quickly poured myself a glass and made for the back door.

Luckily, I spied my husband across the yard, sitting at a long wooden picnic table under a tree strung with twinkling white lights. The twins were sitting happily on a blanket on the grass nearby, surrounded by an army of cousins who tickled their cheeks and spoke in rapid Spanish. The babies giggled back.

I sank down beside my husband and took a long sip of my drink, ending in a contented sigh. Tequila had never tasted so good.

"This was a good idea," I told him.

He nodded and held up his own Margarita glass in a cheers motion. "How's the house look?" he asked.

I shook my head. "You don't want to know."

"He's not going to do this every year, is he?"

"I can't make a promise like that," I told him.

He grinned and sighed, tossing an arm around my shoulders. "I'm sure it'll be a wonderful party."

I raised an eyebrow at him. "Okay why are you in such a good mood?"

Ramirez gave me a lopsided grin, holding up his glass again. "You got a little catching up to do, kid. This isn't my first round."

I laughed, taking a sip from my own glass.

"So how was your day?" Ramirez asked.

I quickly filled him in on what I'd learned at the boutique about Lacey being fired, the "unaccounted for" money, and her dinner out with Ratski. I was just about to tell him about Kendra's interesting phone call when my cell buzzed with the text. I looked down to see Dana's face on my screen and swiped it, bringing up her message.

Check LA informer website.

Uh-oh.

I quickly pulled up the site on my phone, fearing I'd find more photos of Dana and Ratski pasted all over the internet. I had to stifle a giggle when I saw what actually came up. Apparently one of the extras on the Sunset Studios lot must've had a phone handy when Ricky went after Ratski, because there, in bold living color, was a picture of one of the Stars players being laid out by a "pretty boy" movie star. He'd gotten Ratski just as he'd gone to the ground, blood trickling from his nose, a look of complete surprise on his face. Ricky towered over him, looking every bit the action star.

I quickly shot a text back to Dana.

Ricky okay?

Couple seconds later, her response buzzed in.

He's great. He's totally trending. His agent says he should punch more celebrities.

I stifled another giggle. (Wow, the margarita was working its magic!)

"What's so funny?" Ramirez asked, leaning over my shoulder to take a look at the phone. I showed him the picture as I relayed the entire scene between the two men. When I finished, Ramirez chuckled softly, the rumbling sound warm and vibrating through his chest. "I knew there was something I liked about that Ricky. I'm assuming Ratski didn't press charges?"

I shook my head. "No. He thought better of it." I paused. Something about the scene was niggling at the back of my head. Something that just wasn't right. I took another sip of my margarita. "His wife, Beth, was beside herself. I feel sorry for her," I said, meaning it not for the first time.

Ramirez nodded. "I feel sorry for anyone forced to spend time with that *pendejo*."

I wasn't quite sure what that meant, but I had a feeling it wasn't a warm-fuzzy.

"Hey, any luck getting that warrant on Bucky's place?" I asked, sipping my drink again.

He nodded. "Yep. Turns out Bucky had a whole bottle of his cousin's ADD meds."

I perked up.

"Unfortunately, the crime lab confirmed that these meds were not the same chemical composition as the stuff that killed Lacey. Close, but not exact."

"Damn. Did they find anything else?"

Ramirez shook his head. "They did a pretty thorough search of his place, but didn't find anything to indicate Bucky pulled the trigger, so to speak."

"Great, so we're back to square one with the murder weapon."

"Sorry, babe," Ramirez said, nuzzling his lips into my hair.

And as my husband used his term of endearment to comfort me, it suddenly dawned on me what had been wrong with the scene I'd witnessed today.

"She called him pooh bear!" I said, sitting up straight in my seat.

Ramirez looked over at me. "What?"

"Ratski's love letters. They weren't addressed 'pooh bear.' They all called him 'shmoopy.'"

"So his wife used a different term of endearment in her letters?"

I shook my head. "I don't think so. I think those letters were from someone else."

"Lacey?"

"Possibly." I bit my lip. "But, you know, everything I've learned about Lacey doesn't suggest that she was the sentimental type. I have a hard time picturing her writing schmaltzy letters. Going out to dinner with him, shaking him down for money, maybe even sleeping with him and threatening to tell his wife. But those letters were more like love letters than sexting, you know?"

"Okay, how about scenario number two," Ramirez offered. "Ratski was seeing someone else and Lacey found out about it. Then she blackmailed him, threatening to tell his wife."

I chewed my lip some more. "I like that theory."

Ramirez took another sip from his glass. "All right. So who do we think Ratski was seeing? One of the other wives?"

I shrugged. Honestly, I really wish I knew. I didn't see either Kendra or Liz being the type to go for Ratski. Then again, who was the type to go for Ratski, I had no clue.

Fortunately I knew one person who apparently had the 411 on all the celebrity gossip. I looked down at the website displayed on my phone's screen. While Felix Dunn and I hadn't always seen eye-to-eye, my friendship with the *L.A. Informer*'s editor had, at times, proven useful. I hoped this was going to be another one of those times.

CHAPTER FIFTEEN

———

I woke up with a hell of a hangover, surrounded by pink sheets covered in Hello Kitty designs. I blinked, sitting up, and almost knocked over my husband who was crammed into the twin bed beside me.

"Unh," he grunted, grabbing me around the middle to keep from hitting the orange shag carpeting beneath him.

That's when I remembered. After telling Mama about the disaster at my house, she'd insisted that we spend the night in BillieJo's old room. BillieJo had given me more of the eye, which, considering her current Goth craze was almost disconcerting enough to have me scheduling a hex cleansing with Mrs. Rosenblatt. But when I weighed her evil eye versus my snake and clown infested house the evil eye had won, hands down.

"Don't get up. Babies still sleeping," Ramirez grunted out, caveman style. His hand strayed from my middle to cup my panty-clad booty.

I swatted it away. "Not here," I hissed. Besides the dozen or so eyes of BillieJo's discarded Cabbage Patch dolls staring at me from the pink dresser by the door, the babies were slumbering softly in a pack-n-play in the corner.

Ramirez paused, opening one sleepy eye. "You got somewhere else in mind?"

I swatted him again. "You have a one track mind," I whispered.

"Yeah, but you love it." He nuzzled his lips into the crook of my neck.

He had me there. I did love it.

And on any other day, I might have suggested an early-morning jaunt to the shower. But as it was, the long day ahead was looming over me. On my to-do list: 1) get a tabloid editor's help to catch a killer, 2) attend my kids' 1st birthday party, 3) not kill my party planner. All three seemed equally daunting at the moment.

I slipped from beneath the sheets, awkwardly trying to climb over my husband.

"Where you going?" he asked, sleepily cocking one eye at me.

"I have a couple of things I need to follow up on," I said, hoping he wouldn't question me more. While I viewed Felix Dunn as an old friend, Ramirez might have had a slightly different opinion of the tabloid editor.

My history with Felix had more ups-and-downs than a Six Flags rollercoaster. I'd first met him after he'd reported on one of my run-ins with a dead body. Since then, Felix's and my paths had crossed several times—some of them good, some bad, but all unforgettable. Felix had been the thorn in my side, my partner in crime, and I'd even viewed him once or twice as my road not taken.

There'd been a point before our marriage when Ramirez and I had almost ended things over my complicated relationship with Felix. While I had no regrets about the direction of my life, I knew my husband and Felix were not destined to be the best of buddies. Which is why, while I wasn't exactly lying to my husband, I was going to spare him the details of my morning's plans.

"I promise I'll be back in time for the party," I reassured him as I scooted to the end of the bed.

Ramirez groaned. "Do we really have to go to that?"

"Probably." Even though I'd been wondering the same thing myself.

He grunted and rolled over again, causing the sheets to fall down his torso. Even after years of marriage, I couldn't help a warm little flutter in my stomach at the sight of his bared pecs and six-pack that would make Budweiser jealous. I briefly contemplated that shower again…

* * *

I'm woman enough to admit it had been a while since I'd braved the morning L.A. traffic. I twiddled my thumbs along the 60. I did a little drumming on my steering wheel to the radio as we crossed to the 101. And I did a little cursing at the other drivers as I crawled along the 170 into Hollywood behind an SUV with a stick figure family in the window.

I stopped off at home just long enough to grab a fresh change of clothes—a pale peach wrap dress that was soft, summery, and appropriate for both morning snooping and an afternoon party for tiny tots—and an hour and fifteen minutes later I was finally pulling into the lot behind the big gray building that housed the *L.A. Informer* offices. I rode the elevator up to the second floor, and as the doors slid open I was immediately assaulted by the sound of computer keyboards clacking and conversations via speaker phone about everything from Miley Cyrus's tongue acrobatics to Madonna's latest grill.

I gave myself a moment to overcome the sensory overload before crossing the crowded newsroom floor to Felix's glass-walled office in the center. The doors were closed, but I could see him inside, shouting and waving his arms wildly as he talked into his earpiece. I did a short rap on the door, causing him to spin around midsentence. He raised one eyebrow in question but motioned me in with a wave.

"No, that is absolutely not what I said we were printing," came Felix's voice, his British accent more pronounced than usual as he shouted at the person on the other end of the line. "I said we would be going with the swimsuit pictures, not the yacht photos." He paused, listening to someone on the other end of his tirade. "I don't care what her manager said. If she's going to go traipsing around Belize in a thong, her cellulite is fair game for our photographers."

Felix motioned me to a chair in front of his desk as he paused for the unfortunate soul's response again. I sat self-consciously, crossing one leg over the other as I smoothed down the skirt of my dress.

"Damn right we are. And you can tell her manager that, too!" he yelled, hitting a button on his earpiece to end the call.

Then he turned to me. "And to what do I owe this unexpected pleasure, Maddie?" His voice was suddenly all charm, no sign of the previous tirade in it.

Felix was old enough that fine laugh lines creased his eyes but young enough that he could still pull off a look of boyish charm when his mouth curved into a lopsided grin. His sandy hair was slightly tussled, his blue eyes always sharp and assessing, and since getting the upgrade in occupation from tabloid reporter to editor-in-chief, Felix's wardrobe had undergone a slight upgrade as well, morphing from khakis and sketchers to wool slacks and Oxfords. Though he still sported his white button-down shirt, open at the collar, sleeves rolled to the elbows, and in need of a good ironing. His look was casual and somehow polished all at the same time. It fit considering the *L.A. Informer* was slowly becoming one of Hollywood's premier entertainment news sources...yet they still ran the occasional story on Bigfoot's alleged love child with one of the Honey Boo-boo girls.

"I need your help, Felix," I said, coming straight to the point.

He raised one of his sandy brows at me. "I see," he said slowly. He shoved his hands into the pockets of his slacks, coming around his desk to lean casually against the front corner. "Always happy to do a favor for a friend, Maddie. You know that. What can I help you with?"

"I need some information on John Ratski."

"Ah. Our fist-fighting ballplayer," Felix said with a smile as he moved around the desk to sit behind his computer monitor. "I can't say we have tons of coverage on him. I'll be honest with you, Bucky's usually our target. Ratski has been mostly off our radar, until yesterday."

"Where you hit the jackpot," I mumbled.

Felix's eyes shot up to meet mine, and if I didn't know him better, I'd say there was the tiniest hint of guilt in them. "You know I don't write the news, love. I just report it."

"Nice try. You had to know you were inciting a celebrity feud with those photos of Dana and Ratski at dinner."

"Ricky was pretty angry, huh?"

I nodded. "Angry enough to hit Ratski, obviously."

"What did he say?"

I grinned. "No way are you getting a quote out of me, mister."

He shrugged. "Can't blame a bloke for trying."

That was debatable.

"Well, Ricky can't be too angry with us," Felix continued, switching computer screens. "He's exploding all over the Twitterverse this morning. Right-Hook-Ricky is the top trending hashtag at the moment."

I couldn't help a snicker.

"Followed closely by," he continued, reading off his monitor, "Ratski-struck-again and Battle-Royal. If there was any better press Ricky could get for his action star career, I don't know what it is."

"Well, in that case, I guess I always have a second career as a celebrity publicist," I joked.

"Sorry, love," Felix said, "but everyone knows any real self-respecting celebrity has a gay publicist."

I opened my mouth to argue when I realized he was right. I didn't know anyone who had a straight publicist. "Listen, I need to know who else Ratski has been seen with lately," I told him. "Specifically, if he's been seen with any of the other *Baseball Wives*. Liz DeCicco or Kendra Blanco maybe?" I paused. "Or possibly Lacey Desta."

Felix's eyebrow rose. "The dead girl?"

I nodded slowly.

"You think Ratski had something to do with that?"

I bit my lip, hesitant to respond in the affirmative. As I well knew, anything said in the presence of the tabloid reporter was sure to end up public knowledge.

"I'm looking into several Stars players."

Felix's eyes cut to mine, that questioning eyebrow lifting again.

"Just to be thorough," I quickly added.

"Uh-huh." He still eyed me. "Well, we can run a search through our archives." He slid his keyboard drawer out and typed in Ratski's name. "I take it this is one of Ramirez's cases?"

"Uh, sorta," I said, sidestepping the issue of Ramirez's suspension.

"And how is the husband?" Felix asked.

The question was benign enough, but I heard the sudden tightness in Felix's voice.

While Felix was my road-not-taken, I sometimes wondered if I was his one-that-got-away. Shortly after I married Ramirez, Felix started dating one of his junior reporters, Allie Quick, who some had described as a younger, perkier version of me. I'd encountered Allie a handful of times, and while part of me wanted to hate her, another part of me sort of wanted to take her under my wing. However, both parts often wondered if Felix was dating *her* or me-light.

"He's fine. And Allie?"

"She's fine."

"Good. I'm glad."

Felix cleared his throat, breaking the awkward exchange. "All right, I got a blank for Ratski and Lacey, but I found four articles in the last two months which mention Ratski and either Liz or Kendra by name."

"That's promising," I said, getting up from my chair and coming around the desk to peer at the monitor over his shoulder. "What do they say?"

"Well, the first mentions the Stars shooting a KPIX commercial in Burbank. There's not much to it, but if you'd like to take a look…" Felix trailed off, pushing his chair back to give me more room.

I quickly scanned the article but didn't see anything to suggest the outing had been anything other than straightforward Stars promo.

"And the next article?" I asked hopefully.

Felix moved his mouse. "Ratski at a restaurant opening."

I looked at the screen, seeing a photo of the woman on his arm. Beth. Again a strikeout.

Felix must've seen the crestfallen look on my face as he asked. "You know, it might help if I knew exactly what we're looking for?"

As much as I wanted to play my cards close to my chest, Felix was right. I was looking for a needle in a haystack, and without his help that haystack was scattered over millions of paparazzi hours. "I'm looking for anything that might indicate Ratski was dating someone."

"Besides Dana?" Felix asked, a teasing note in his voice.

"Ha. Ha. Very funny. Yes, besides Dana. Clearly Ratski can't do much in Hollywood without one of your reporters knowing about it, so I figured if anybody knew who he'd been seeing, it would be you."

Felix nodded. "Well, I can't promise anything. Clearly, if there was any hint of him having an affair with someone else, we would have reported on it."

I was afraid of that.

"However," Felix went on. "I can have Cam pull photos of Ratski from the last month or two and see if anyone shows up with him more often than she should."

I figured that was about as good as I could get. I stood. "Thank you," I said, sincerely meaning it.

Felix shook my hand, holding onto it just a second too long before turning to the speakerphone on his desk again. "I'll have Cam email you pictures as soon as she can compile them. Might be a day or two though. She's following Bieber around, and you know how unpredictable *that* can be."

I nodded. "Thanks again," I said before turning on my heels and walking back to the *Informer*'s elevators.

* * *

I still had a couple of hours before the party, so I pointed my car toward Melrose. It was unlikely Liz would come right out and admit if she or Kendra had been having an affair with Ratski, but I figured it wouldn't hurt to do a little well-placed hinting and see how the reality actress reacted. Besides, I was sort of regretting leaving that biased-cut blouse there the other day.

Street parking was non-existent, so I opted for the garage on the corner, driving to the absolute top before finding a spot. I figured that jogging down the stairs in my two-inch heels would be my workout for the day.

As I pushed through the glass doors of Bellissima, I immediately spotted Blonde Number One and Blonde Number

Two helping other customers. Liz was behind the cash register today, ringing up a purchase for a purple leather handbag that I silently thought would go marvelously with my new kitten heels.

"Maddie, what brings you here?" Liz asked when she finished.

"I, uh, just wanted to see if my manufacturer had spoken to your buyer yet?" I lied.

Liz's eyebrows drew together. "No, I don't think we've heard from him."

Probably because I hadn't called him, but I glossed over that.

"Oh, darn," I said, faking a frown of my own. "I guess I'll have to put in another call." I paused. "Say, how's Beth doing?"

"Beth?" Liz frowned.

I did my most sympathetic face—eyebrows drawn, lips pursed, head tilted to the right. "I saw the pictures in the *Informer* last night. It must be so hard to be faced with proof of your husband cheating on you."

Liz snorted. "Yeah, like that's the only time he did it."

Bingo.

"What do you mean?"

"I mean that guy is always chasing some tail. He even tried to hit on *me*. Can you believe that? His teammate's wife?"

"No!" I said. Though I had to admit to feeling a little deflated. If she was admitting he hit on her so quickly, it was looking less and less like she and Ratski had anything serious going on.

"Oh, yeah. That guy would have done anything that moved. I'm pretty sure he hit on Kendra when he got drunk at the Christmas party, and he was all over Lacey the first couple of weeks she and Bucky were dating."

"Really?"

"Yeah, but I'm sure he struck out there," Liz said, echoing my earlier thoughts on the idea of the two of them having any sort of romantic relationship. "Lacey said he was a total loser. I guess that's one thing the two of us agreed on."

"But there isn't anyone special that you know of? Anyone he was actually seeing?

Liz screwed up her face. "Not that I know of. And, I mean, Ratski didn't exactly try to hide his exploits."

Unfortunately, she was right. In fact, now that I thought about it, Ratski hadn't seemed particularly worried about being photographed out with Dana the other night. Which made me even more curious about this affair that he was trying so hard to keep under wraps.

"Poor Beth," Liz sighed. "The woman is in complete denial."

"You mentioned that he hit on Kendra," I said, backtracking. "Did she tell you this?"

Liz paused, uncertainty flickering in her eyes as if not sure how much to say about the leader of the Wives pack without her prior approval. "She might have mentioned it."

I took a leap of faith and leaned in. "You know, between you and me, Kendra seems awfully controlling. I think *Ratski* might have dodged a bullet there."

"Ha!" Liz let out a short bark of laughter, quickly covering it with her hand. "You don't know the half of it," she confided.

I grinned. "Oh, really?" I prodded.

Liz looked over both shoulders, as if Kendra might magically appear, before leaning in close. "Look, you didn't hear this from me…"

I shook my head, putting a finger to my lips. "Of course not."

"…but Kendra told the producers what to say to the police. She said if they didn't, she'd walk. I mean, talk about controlling, right?"

Sadly I had a feeling Laurel and Hardy were only too happy to take the producers' word for anything. "What did she tell them to say?"

"Well," Liz said, getting a wicked twinkle in her eye, "On the morning that Lacey died, we were shooting a promo spot for the show. But Kendra was late."

"How late?" I asked.

"*Late* late. She always has an earlier call time for make-up than everyone else, because, well, Kendra takes the longest." She paused, leaning in to faux whisper. "She's over *forty*."

I feigned a gasp while mentally calculating just how many years I had left before hitting the age-of-no-return in Hollywood.

"Anyway, make-up was totally freaking when I got there because Kendra was nowhere to be found, and they knew it was going to take forever to get her presentable."

"What time was this?" I asked.

Liz shrugged. "Our call time was at nine, and the first anyone saw of Kendra was eleven."

"Did she say where she was?"

Liz waved her hands in the air. "She said something about car trouble or some such excuse."

"Excuse?" I asked, jumping on the word. "Where do you think she *really* was?"

Liz gave me the same big wide-eyed stare that she'd given to Laurel and Hardy, blinking her false lashes up-and-down. "Well, I really couldn't say, now, could I? But I know that she made sure the producers left her call time out of the segment she shot with the detectives."

As interesting as the information about Kendra's lack of alibi for the time of the murder was, I found it equally interesting that Liz was giving this information out so freely. Why was she throwing her friend under the bus? Was she trying to get Kendra in trouble? Or was she just trying to divert suspicion from herself?

I was still trying to decide the diva's motives when the bell over the front door jingled, and we both turned to see Beth walk in.

"Speak of the clueless," Liz mumbled to me, giving me a wink as if she and I were besties who'd just shared juicy gossip. Then she quickly crossed the boutique, switching gears to all-smiles as she gave air-kisses to Beth.

"Hello, darling! You ready for lunch?"

Beth nodded and gave Liz a big smile. One that faded significantly when she saw me.

I gave a little wave. "Hi."

Beth narrowed her eyes. "What are you doing here? Is Dana here too?"

I shook my head. "No. Just me."

The frown between her brows eased some, but she still gave me the wary eye.

"I am so sorry about what happened. It was all a big misunderstanding." A total lie. The only one misunderstanding anything here was Beth. But as long as she remained on my suspect list, I figured it was better to smooth things over. "The press has blown everything out of proportion, haven't they?"

Beth bit her lip and nodded in agreement. "Yes, they have."

"How is your husband? Is his nose okay?"

My words had the desired effect as the tension in Beth's shoulders released a little.

"He'll be fine. It's not broken, just a little bruised," she conceded.

Liz cleared her throat. "Well, let me just grab my purse and lock up, I'll be right with you, okay, Beth?" She didn't wait for a response before flouncing into the back room.

Beth glanced after her friend nervously, as if hesitant to be alone in the same room with me. Geez. It wasn't as if *I* had hit Ratski

"Liz has some lovely designs here," I said, trying to ease the tension in the air.

Beth nodded. "Yes." She paused. "She mentioned that you were thinking about stocking your shoes here?"

"I think they'd be a great fit."

"Hmm." Beth pursed her lips together.

"What?" I asked.

Her eyes cut to the doorway Liz had just disappeared through. "You didn't hear this from me..."

These women were too good to be true. Must be my lucky day as I "wasn't" hearing a lot.

"Yes?" I prompted encouragingly.

"I don't know if I would invest too heavily in this particular boutique."

"Why not?" I asked.

"Well let's just say I'm not sure it's the most financially stable business decision."

"Oh?" I asked.

"Let's just say I'd steer clear of it if I were you."

She was "just saying" a lot of very vague things, and I had a feeling Liz wouldn't be much longer. Time to cut to the chase.

"Are you saying that Liz's boutique is in financial trouble?" I asked, remembering what the blonde clone had told me about some "unaccounted for" money.

Beth pursed her lips together again but nodded.

"But it always looks so busy here," I countered. Which was true.

Beth shrugged. "I guess Liz just doesn't have a head for business."

"Did she tell you she was in trouble?"

"Well, not in so many words. But I overheard her asking Kendra for a loan."

"When was this?"

"About six weeks ago."

I perked up. That was right before someone started paying Lacey blackmail.

"How much did she ask for?"

Beth looked nervously toward the back room. "Thirty-thousand."

Which theoretically would have covered the first three payments to Lacey. Which would have meant that two payments later, Liz could have been desperate.

"But please don't tell anyone you heard this from me," Beth pleaded. "Especially not Liz."

I did a zipping-the-mouth-shut-and-throwing-away-the-key motion and nodded reassuringly at her.

"I'm ready," Liz said, flouncing back into the boutique, a beautiful navy blue cashmere wrap thrown over her shoulders. "And, boy, after the day I've had with my suppliers, those pomtinis are calling my name."

Beth cleared her throat and shifted from foot to foot as if she'd just been caught, well, ratting out her best friend. "Yeah, me too."

"Maddie, would you care to join us?" Liz asked.

I shook my head. "Sorry, I've got somewhere to be." Even though pomtinis sounded a whole lot better than what I had planned.

"Okay, well, I'll be awaiting that call from your manufacturer," Liz said, leading the way out of the store.

I watched them go, my mind turning over the possibilities. Were Liz's "financial difficulties" due to paying off a blackmailer? Or, had the financial difficulties been the subject of blackmail? Was that the "unaccounted for" money they'd argued about before Liz had fired Lacey? Had Lacey threatened to expose it? If so, just how far would Liz have gone to protect her baby?

CHAPTER SIXTEEN

————

I thought about stopping at the Starbucks drive-through. I thought about going to the shoe sale at DSW. I thought about buying a plane ticket to Brazil. But, as much as I was dreading this big first birthday party, I realized there was no avoiding it. Sort of like the pimples that come with puberty or the high price tag that comes with California real estate. In the end, it was worth it.

At least that's what I told myself as I pointed my car toward home and ignored the anxiety building in my gut.

As I pulled up to my house, I realized that not only had Marco made good on his word to make this party memorable—huge, wacky waving inflatable arm flailing tube men (yes, plural) sat in my front yard—he had also made good on his promise to invite everyone he knew. Because my entire block was bumper-to-bumper parked cars.

I slowed in front of my house (honestly more gaping at the waving inflatable tube men than looking for parking), and a guy in a bright red uniform with the sort of box-shape hat that belonged on a grinder monkey came running out of my front door.

"Valet! Would you care to valet your car, ma'am?" the monkey boy asked.

I cautiously rolled down my passenger side window. "We have valet parking?"

"But of course! What kind of party would this be without valet parking?"

I closed my eyes and did a ten count to get my temper under control, quietly wondered how much I was paying this valet. "Where are you parking these cars?"

He blinked at me as if not understanding the question.

"Valet parking indicates a parking *lot*," I enunciated clearly.

"Oh, sure. Yeah, Marco said we should use the Ralph's lot down the street as overflow."

I could've argued, but I didn't feel like walking all the way to my house from the Ralph's two blocks away. I hopped out of the car and handed the monkey boy my keys, figuring, quite honestly, he was going to be the least offensive thing I would encounter today.

With my trepidation at an eleven, I opened the front door to my house.

As I had guessed from yesterday, my entire front room had been turned into an arcade of sorts. I spied my cousin Molly's two oldest children and her husband, Stan, bopping between the pinball machine, the vintage Pac-Man machine, and the cotton candy machine, clearly working his sugar high to become the top scorer on both of the games.

Strong scents carried from the kitchen, telling me that my Parisian chef was at work. Though I had to admit they weren't altogether unpleasant. Maybe there would be a high point to this day after all.

I crossed the living room to the back sliding doors and into the yard where I could see the bulk of the festivities taking place. I had to admit Marco knew how to throw a party. The tiki bar was in full swing, surrounded by several of Ramirez's brothers and sisters-in-law, and children were running and shrieking all over the yard, going up and down the giant inflatable waterslide and jumping into the ball pit. I spied Dana and Ricky feeding each other deviled eggs on the shaded patio, clearly having made up and gotten back to their usually honeymoon-ish selves. On the other side of the yard, a pony was trotting around in a circle led by a cowboy, for whom I sincerely hoped Marco hadn't paid full price. And in the other corner sat Mr. Crocodile Dundee himself with his exotic animal pen. I spied a peacock, a small animal that looked like it was a goat on steroids, and a ten foot long snake wrapped around Dundee's neck.

In the center of it all stood Ramirez, a baby on each hip. God bless him, I didn't know how Mr. Mom did it, but they both looked immaculate. They were dressed in the outfits I had picked out for them—Livvie in a pink, ruffled dress that flared like a bell around her diaper-padded hips, and Max in a pair of pint-sized denim jeans and a baby blue button-up shirt—both complete with teeny tiny little baby shoes in coordinating ivory. Both kids were giggling and laughing at their surroundings. Even Ramirez was wearing a smile. Maybe this party wasn't such a bad idea after all. I mean, everyone seemed to be enjoying themselves, and I didn't see a single clown in sight.

I quickly crossed the yard and gave Ramirez a quick kiss on the cheek. "Hey, you," I said taking Livvie from him and giving her a little nuzzle in her soft neck.

"Hey, yourself, Springer."

"Sorry I'm late."

Ramirez shook his head. "No problem. Mama came early to help get the babies ready. You learn anything interesting? "

"Possibly," I said, filling him in on Kendra's lack of alibi and the state of Liz's boutique. I was just finishing when I heard a high-pitched voice behind me.

"My babies!" I turned to find my mom and Faux Dad coming straight at the children—arms outstretched, lips in the puckering position, ready to drop kisses all over their chubby little cheeks. Though which one of their high-pitched voices had screamed, "My babies," I wasn't sure.

After an appropriate amount of kissing, pinching, and squishing, Faux Dad and Ramirez drifted off to the tiki bar.

I turned to Mom. "How's he doing?" I asked, gesturing toward Faux Dad. I could see that even though he was trying to put on a happy face for the children's party, the bags under his eyes were growing exponentially.

Mom shrugged and averted her eyes.

"That well?" I asked, a pang of guilt hitting my stomach. I'd hoped to have better news for him by now, but it seemed all I was doing was running around in circles lately.

"He's doing the best he can, Maddie. You know the salon is his life. Without the salon, your stepfather is…well…just Ralph."

"But we love Ralph," I said, trying to be more upbeat than my voice came out sounding.

"Of course we do, Maddie," my mom said, sending me a sad smile. "You love Ralph, and I love Ralph. But the women of Beverly Hills love *Fernando*. As do their bank accounts, their credit cards, and their checkbooks. Without those, I'm afraid the salon won't be open much longer."

Geeze, talk about a guilt bomb. I was just about to go drown my sorrows in one of the fruity looking drinks I'd seen coming away from the tiki bar, when I spied my party-planner du jour.

"…and over here we have the exotic animal pen," Marco said, waving a hand to his right with flourish. He was wearing a lemon yellow suit and bright turquoise tie, speaking to a small group of people I didn't recognize. They all looked in their twenties, most wearing what I would describe as geek-chic attire—colorful leggings, beanies, and T-shirts with sci-fi sayings on them under open flannel shirts.

"…and this lovely little lad and lady are the guests of honor!" Marco said, doing jazz hands as he bowed and pointed to Livvie and Max on the hips of my mother and myself, respectively.

His geek-chic crowd clapped.

"Now, enjoy the party, mingle, and don't forget to check out our exotic animal zoo!" Marco told them as they dispersed.

"Marco," I said. "Lovely party." I leaned in for air-kisses, though as I got to his left cheek, I whispered in his ear, "And who are those people?"

"The press, of course!"

Mental forehead thunk. I'd had more than enough of the press for one week.

"You invited the press to my *children's* birthday party at my *home*?!" I hissed to him.

To his credit, his wide smile only faltered for a second. "This is your children's big debut party, darling. Their society moment. What's a coming-out party without a little publicity, right?"

"They're one. They're not coming out of anything except their diapers."

But Marco completely ignored me. "That woman over there?" He pointed to a redhead in neon pink and purple flannel. "That's Mary Mags who does a fantastic fashion blog, focusing on tiny tot couture. And the guy next to her does the Big Baby twitter feed. You know Big Baby, don't you?"

I gave him a blank stare.

"Oh, darling, you must get out more."

"Tweeting is not getting out."

"Big Baby," he continued, ignoring me (for a change), "is only the most subscribed-to celebrity baby news feed." Marco leaned in and faux whispered, "He's the one who broke the news about Suri Cruise's Easter dress fiasco." He made a tsking sound through his teeth. "So sad."

"Marco, I—"

"And that fine duo over there," he plowed ahead, "Are FuzzyBunny and BinkyBear."

I looked to where he was pointing, half expecting a couple in animal costumes. Instead I spotted two more chic geeks, the female of the two wearing Google Glass and filming everything in sight.

"Fuzzy who?" I hesitated to ask.

"The famous YouTubers? They get simply millions of hits for their funny baby videos. The Happy Baby Meets Cranky Cat series? That is all them." Marco nodded reverently.

I took a deep breath. I counted to ten. Then I realized I'd been practicing my counting more often than my children's favorite red monster on *Sesame Street*.

Where was that tiki bar?

I pushed past Marco, handing Livvie off to one of Ramirez's aunts, and made a bee-line for the tropical bar wearing what looked like a grass skirt in the center of my lawn. Luckily, Ramirez must have seen me coming as, good man that he is, he quickly slid me a pink cup that read "Livvie and Max's First Birthday Extravaganza" in scrolling letters.

I downed it in one gulp, then asked for another. By the third, I almost didn't care that my children's party would be all over the internet in various forms of baby fashion policing and cranky-cat memes.

And then I heard it.

To anyone else it might have seemed unassuming enough. But I knew that Australian accented voice, and I knew the name it was calling.

"Matilda, love, where are you?"

My squick radar shot to a hundred just like that. I spun around, half expecting to see a ten-foot python crawling up my leg. Fortunately, she was nowhere to be seen. Unfortunately, the top to her cage was off and *she was nowhere to be seen.*

I clutched Ramirez's arm in a claw-like grip. "Matilda's loose," I whispered.

Ramirez turned to me. "And she is…?"

"Oh, God, please don't let Matilda be—"

Only I didn't get to finish that thought as I heard the whinnying of a horse from the other side of the yard. No, not quite a horse. Smaller, fainter, higher pitched…like a spooked pony.

It all happened in slow motion.

My cousin Molly's son, Connor, sat atop the pony, which reared up on two legs. Presumably to avoid the ten foot snake slithering in its path. Connor screamed as he was thrown backwards through the air…and luckily hit the side of the inflatable waterslide, bouncing off to land face first in the ball pit.

The pony charged forward, trotting at full speed toward the banquet table where the ice sculpture of two babies posing as cherubs sat, taunting him. The pony crashed through them, a cacophony of wings and frozen halos crashing to the patio, accompanied by a dozen trays of raining hors d'oeuvres.

"Matilda!" cried Crocodile Dundee

"Nelly!" cried the pony-wrangler in the cowboy outfit.

"My canapés!" cried François, running from the kitchen.

"Awesome!" yelled the chic-geek with Google Glass, catching every gory moment of it in digital glory.

"Marco," I threatened under my breath.

Unfortunately it seemed neither Matilda nor Nelly were very well-trained, as they completely ignored their owners. Matilda was slithering through the party-goers—now screaming and lifting their legs to high step out of her way. Ramirez's brothers chased the pony, who was charging, whinnying, and leaving nervous little pony droppings all over my yard.

They almost had him corralled into one corner when my cousin Molly's husband, Stan, walked through the sliding glass door.

"I beat the high Pac-Man score!" he announced to the yard at large.

Two seconds before a rampant pony with the runs charged into him, knocking him to the ground, and running straight into my living room.

"No!" I cried, making an attempt to move toward the door.

Only it was too late. Nervous Nelly had already let loose on my living room carpet.

* * *

It took us the better part of the evening to clear all the guests from the party, the animals from my house, and the pony poop from the yard…not to mention my rug. Which, as I'd pointed out to Marco in a tirade of words I never wanted my children to learn, was now ruined. He'd tried to cheer me up by joking that it matched my La-Z-Boy. I told him that it was a good thing my husband worked out, because he was the only thing holding me back from strangling the fab party planner. Marco had wisely made his exit at that point. By the time the party rental place had hauled away the last helium machine, I was exhausted. Ramirez and I both fell into bed, and I'm pretty sure I began snoring even before my head hit the pillow.

The next morning I woke to sunlight streaming through my bedroom window and the faint smell of rotting deviled eggs on my back lawn. I groaned and rolled over.

As much as the party had ended (and started…and continued) in disaster, in the light of day, I felt the teeny tiniest bit of guilt creeping into my peripheral about yelling at Marco. Okay, he had turned my backyard into a pony potty, he owed me a complete new living room, and if I never saw another reptile again it would be too soon. But I knew Auntie Marco's heart had been in the right place. Even if his head and my pocketbook were not. He put his all into the party, and I knew he'd be sulking today. So my first stop after I dropped a kiss on my husband's cheek and wished him luck cleaning up the rest of the canapés from the yard was Starbucks for a Venti mocha frappuccino with extra whip, extra espresso, and lots of chocolate shavings on top. As far as peace offerings went, I hoped this did the trick.

Unfortunately, business didn't seem to be any more brisk at Fernando's than the last time I'd been there. Empty cut and color stations lined the walls, and there was just one lone woman getting a pedicure. Probably the only woman in the L.A. area who hadn't heard about the Tanning Salon Murder.

Marco looked up as I pushed through the glass doors, his expectant-receptionist smile quickly morphing into a look of pure fear.

I bit my lip. I walked up to the desk and shoved the Starbucks out in front of me. Marco looked down at the cup, back up to me, down at the cup. He didn't say anything, though his expression softened a little

"And this is?" he asked.

"Peace offering."

Marco eyed me suspiciously out of the corner of his heavily lined lids, as if it might contain poison.

"Look, the party did not end well yesterday, but I shouldn't have yelled. And threatened to kill you. And said you couldn't plan your way out of a paper bag."

Marco crossed his arms over his chest.

Boy, I sucked at apologizing. I cleared my throat and made another go of it. "I know you were doing your best to make a memorable party for the twins."

Marco raised one eyebrow. "Well, if we were going for memorable, I think I succeeded." A hint of a smile peeked out from behind his words. "You know how many hits we've had on YouTube this morning alone?"

I clenched my teeth together, remembering I was here to restore our friendship. "Goody for us."

Marco reached for the coffee. "But you were right, Maddie. I'm starting to think maybe I did go just a bit overboard."

I couldn't help myself. "Ya think?"

"I know, I know," Marco said, taking a sip of his peace offering and waving his hands. His black and gold crackle manicure sparkled in the air as he emoted. "But I just wanted everything to be perfect. I've had other clients before, even some big celebrity clients," Marco added. "But, I've never done a big party for a friend-ebrity before."

I couldn't help but get a little emotional, my hand going to my chest. "I'm a friend-ebrity? I'm not a celebrity. I just design shoes. Dana's the celebrity."

But Marco shook his head from side to side so violently that even his gelled spikes seemed to wobble in the air. "Honey, you are both dazzling stars in my book. And little ol' me is just manning the phones here while you two superstars are into the stratosphere with your careers." Marco paused, a frown taking over his features. "I was just trying to keep up with you ladies. I'm sorry for going a little overboard."

I moved around the reception desk and grabbed him in a big hug. "Honey, you *are* one of us ladies. You're a party planner to the stars. And I'm sure after everyone hears what a...memorable party you threw for my twins, they'll be clamoring to book you for theirs."

"Really?" Marco said, the same sort of disbelief on his face that I'm sure I'd displayed when I saw the pony in my backyard.

"Really," I promised. Just as my cell buzzed to life in my pocket. I pulled it out to see Ramirez's name with an incoming text.

Laurel and Hardy calling press conference. 11:15 Stars Stadium.

Oh boy. Whatever they had to say couldn't be good.

CHAPTER SEVENTEEN

———

After a quick text exchange with Ramirez, we both decided that I was much more likely to get into the press conference than Ramirez was. Not to mention I was a lot less likely to piss off his captain, who was most certainly planning to be in attendance. Especially if Laurel and Hardy had good news he could take credit for.

So, forty-five minutes later I was pulling into the Stars Stadium parking lot. Once again it was still freakishly empty compared to game day. However, at the far end of the lot near the players' entrance there sat a smattering of cars, mostly of the beat-up or news van variety, signaling that members of the press had gathered. I parked my car next to a Channel 4 van with a huge satellite dish stuck on its roof and made my way inside. Unfortunately I only got as far as the front entrance as the bodybuilder/gatekeeper was in attendance today as well. He took one look at me and shook his head.

"Press pass?"

"I'm a friend of Kendra Blanco," I said, hoping he remembered me from previous visits.

No such luck. He just gave me a steely stare and repeated the words. "Press pass?"

I shrugged. Unfortunately, there would be no sneaking around him today.

I was about to give up and go queue up the Twitter app on my phone to get the breaking news secondhand when I heard a familiar voice behind me.

"Well, if he doesn't want his picture on the front page he shouldn't go around inciting celebrities."

I spun around to see Felix, Bluetooth firmly in one ear, waving his hands and yelling as he stalked across the parking lot toward the stadium entrance.

"Oh, please. Slander? This picture has Ratski trending higher than any mere homerun ever will." Felix paused, shook his head, and threw his hands up in the air. "Listen, I've got a press conference. I've got to go. You want to talk slander, you can call the paper's legal department." He hung up, then lifted his eyes and spotted me.

I gave him a little one finger wave as he approached.

"I take it Ratski's lawyer isn't a fan of your recent headlines?" I asked, referencing the conversation I'd just overheard. In my defense, it was hardly eavesdropping if the person you overheard was yelling at the top of their lungs in a crowded parking lot.

Felix shrugged. "Par for the course. He has to say something or he's not earning his retainer now is he?" He paused, looking over my shoulder. "I don't suppose that your husband has any inside information on what's about to break in there?"

I shook my head. "Sorry, this time he and I are as out of the loop as anyone."

Felix raised one eyebrow.

Oops. I'd forgotten that I hadn't told him about Ramirez's suspension. "Anyway," I glossed over it, "it seems I need a press pass to get past the gatekeeper." I blinked my lashes and did my best innocent little smile at Felix.

Felix raised the other eyebrow. "Are you asking for *another* favor, Maddie?"

"Yes, I'm asking you for another favor. A small one," I clarified.

Felix grinned again. "And in return I get…?"

"The warm fuzzy feeling of helping out a friend?"

"Hmm." He pursed his lips together and shook his head in the negative.

"The satisfaction of helping to bring a killer to justice?"

More head shaking.

I sighed. "An exclusive interview with an eyewitness to the Ricky versus Ratski's altercation?"

Felix's face broke into a wide grin. "Now we're talking." He reached into his jacket pocket and pulled out a rectangular laminated pass on a lanyard emblazoned with the *L.A. Informer*'s logo, identical to the one I noticed he was wearing around his own neck.

I quickly snatched it from his hand before he had second thoughts and slipped it over my head, making tracks toward the gatekeeper. I triumphantly held it up and couldn't help feeling just a little gratification as he stepped aside and let us past him.

Felix and I followed a thin but steady stream of reporters, anchor persons, various freelancers, and bloggers down a short corridor to the Stars press room. As soon as I stepped inside, I recognized the podium and back drop as having graced my living room TV screen on many an occasion as Ramirez either celebrated or grumbled about the night's game. The back wall was papered with the team's logo—a bright red star with the letters L and A in scrolling calligraphy—and in front of the wall sat a simple, long wooden table, outfitted today with several microphones and scattered pitchers of water.

Right away I noticed Laurel and Hardy, sitting behind the table. Hardy was checking his teeth in the reflection of his microphone stand while Laurel guzzled water like it was going out of style, her deer-in-the-headlights eyes bouncing around the quickly filling room.

Behind them, I could see several guys in suits, whispering to each other and shuffling papers back and forth. Whether they were publicists for the LAPD or the Stars, I wasn't sure. What I was sure of was that they were about to deliver some news that would cast both in a favorable light...though I had a sinking feeling that light would not extend to Fernando's.

"Any chance they arrested a suspect?" Felix whispered to me, as we found two seats near the back of the room.

"Unlikely," I mumbled back, ignoring the nervous flutter in my stomach.

"Unlikely because?" Felix pressed.

"Those two investigate a murder about as well as I catch a foul ball."

Felix had barely covered his snicker when the owner of the Stars stood up behind the microphone, raising his hands to the room to signal quiet.

"I want to thank the members of our esteemed local journalistic outlets for attending our conference today," he started.

I barely concealed *my* snicker as I glanced around. Esteemed was probably the last word I would use to describe the assembled group. "Tabloids," "yellow journalists," "hacks," maybe.

"I'll make this quick," the owner said. "And I'd like to turn the microphone over to detectives Laurel McMartin and Jonathan Hardy with the LAPD to give you a brief update on their investigation into the tragic death of a member of the Stars family, Lacey Desta."

At the mention of Lacey's name there was a pall of simultaneous silence and eager anticipation that hit the crowd. I found myself jiggling my knee up and down and biting my lip as Hardy stood up, clearing his throat and squaring his shoulders as he preened for the cameras.

"Thank you, Mr. Shwartzheimer," Hardy began. "And thank you to the esteemed members of the press."

Oh, brother. My eyes rolled so far up in my skull I could almost see my brain.

"After an exhaustive investigation where my partner, Laurel McMartin," he said pointing to his apoplectic deer, "and I have explored many avenues of inquiry, gathered ample evidence, and done exhaustive analysis, we are happy to come to the conclusion that none of the players of the L.A. Stars baseball team have any connection whatsoever to the death of Lacey Desta."

The room immediately erupted into quiet murmurs, tapping keyboards, and rustling coats as members of the press tweeted, typed, and emailed this development to their respective editors.

I narrowed my eyes at the detective, wondering exactly what sort of *exhaustive analysis* he'd done. So far all I'd seen him analyzing was his B-roll from *Baseball Wives*.

"We have officially cleared all members of the team and their spouses," Hardy emphasized, nodding toward Mr. Schwartzheimer, "of any suspicion whatsoever in this tragic death. It is our conclusion that persons unknown and unaffiliated with this baseball family perpetrated a random crime upon the unfortunate Miss Desta."

It was all I could do to keep myself from jumping up and shouting, "Not true!" Random crime at Fernando's salon was exactly the sort of thing that would shut him down for good. Who knew when the next *random* tanning salon killer would show up, right?

"I assure you that myself, detective McMartin, and the entire LAPD will continue to tirelessly look for this unknown individual. However, I would just like to repeat they have nothing whatsoever to do with the Stars family."

I crossed my arms over my chest, glaring at the detective and wondering just what sort of season tickets the owner had promised him in exchange for this declaration of "not under cloud of suspicion."

"Quite interesting," Felix said beside me.

"Interesting is one word to use for it."

"I take it your husband doesn't agree with this assessment?"

It was on the tip of my tongue to say that my husband thought that Laurel and Hardy were the two biggest losers on the LAPD. However since I was talking to a tabloid reporter, I chose my words carefully.

"My husband would prefer to focus on the persons unknown rather than the Stars publicity."

Felix gave me half a grin. "You realize that gives me nothing printable."

"Thank God for small favors."

* * *

Felix left me in the parking lot with a promise to check in with Cam about those photos of Ratski as soon as he got back to the *Informer*'s offices. Once I got back to my car I looked down at my cell and saw it was just past noon. I had a brief thought of going home for lunch, but it faded as soon as I spotted the enticing beacon of the Del Taco sign down the street from the stadium. A Macho Burrito was just what I needed to plan my next move. I hit the drive-through and parked under a tree in the lot as I dug into my cheesy, spicy, heaven on a tortilla, letting the flavors dance on my tongue as my mind wandered over the case.

While Laurel and Hardy had cleared the Stars and their wives, I had exactly the opposite feeling. It was clearer than ever to me that Lacey had been blackmailing someone in the team "family," and that someone had wanted her dead. My favorite suspect was still Ratski. He was dating somebody; that much was clear. "Who" was another question, but if Lacey had somehow found out and was blackmailing him over the sort of affair that his wife couldn't ignore, it gave Ratski good motive to want to shut her up.

Then there was Beth herself. Lacey *had* been seen having dinner with Ratski. Maybe Lacey had been the one having the affair after all, and Beth wanted her out of the picture.

Of course it could have just as easily been one of the other players who wanted Lacey out of the picture. If someone was using performance enhancers, say someone like Gabriel Blanco, that would've been excellent fodder for blackmail as well.

I paused to take a near orgasmic bite of my burrito, chewing thoughtfully as my mind worked over the rest of my list. In addition to the players there were the other two wives. Liz had been Lacey's former employer, and they'd been seen fighting over money. If Liz's boutique really was in such financial dire straits, Liz wouldn't have been able to keep up with the designer-label-wearing blackmailer's demands for much longer. Getting rid of Lacey would've been a faster solution to her problem. And then there was Kendra. She wanted Lacey gone for reasons that had nothing to do with blackmail, but if she really was worried about her husband's contract not being re-upped due to seemingly poor performance on the field, she had an excellent reason for wanting to keep Bucky's head in the game. Hadn't it been Kendra who had told me Bucky was eager to get back to work? Maybe keeping his mind in the game, and off his girlfriend—dead or alive—had been Kendra's main goal all along.

I mentally went through my list of suspects as I wiped a dab of guacamole from my chin. The problem was any one of them could've wanted Lacey gone. They all had excellent reasons, and they all had shaky alibis. I could see why detectives with an aversion to work might rule this case the way Laurel and Hardy just had.

I was just finishing up the last of my churro (Hey, I needed something sweet to chase the burrito with!) and wiping cinnamon sugar crumbs off my black capris when my phone pinged with an incoming email. I scrolled down to find that, true to his word, Felix had sent me a file full of photos.

This is everything Cam could pull from the past two months, Felix texted.

thanks, I wrote back before quickly opening the file. I turned my car on, letting the AC run as I scrolled through. Some of the photos seemed vaguely familiar, like I'd probably seen them on the *Informer* website when they'd gone live. Others were untouched, and I could tell they were raw footage Cam had taken that never made it to publication. Many of them were of Ratski at various Stars functions, press conferences, and charity events. A couple were candid shots of him coming out of the club or going into a trendy restaurant. I squinted down at the screen, wishing I had a larger device as I zoomed in and out with my fingertips, trying to catch the faces of Ratski's companions, scanning for anybody who seemed to appear more often than they should. I found a couple of photos where Beth was present. A few featured his teammates, a guy with a headset and a tablet wearing horn rimmed glasses that I pegged as a publicist, and a dark-haired woman with an L.A. Stars jacket. The woman in the jacket was interesting. Could it be Ratski was sleeping with someone on the Stars admin team? I quickly whipped through the photos for any other sign of the brunette. But as far as I could tell she only appeared in the press event pictures. The only recurring character in the candid about-the-town photos was the publicist with the horn rimmed glasses.

Wait.

I paused, flipping back to the first photo, then looked at the pictures one by one. In almost every photo the publicist was there—even in places where I wouldn't assume Ratski would need his publicist's attention, like shopping at the 3rd Street Promenade and grabbing a bite to eat on Sunset. What was it Felix had said about publicists? Anyone who was anyone in Hollywood had a gay publicist.

I did a happy dance in my seat, the burrito jiggling around in my belly. Was it possible that I'd found the salacious affair just too scandalous to let public? The fans would forgive Ratski for being a womanizer. Heck, they might even eat it up, boosting both the *Baseball Wives* ratings and his ticket sales. But it was another thing to ask the fans of America's favorite sport to embrace a gay baseball player.

CHAPTER EIGHTEEN

———

The first thing I did was google "John Ratski publicist." I quickly came up with the name of Theodore Schwimmer of Image Public Relations, who had offices on Highland. If Lacey had somehow found out about Ratski and Theodore, it would have been perfect blackmail fodder. The last thing Ratski would want is for his wife to find out. However, if Lacey really was about to be on the *Baseball Wives* show with Beth, it was about to become much harder for Ratski to keep his secret life from his wife. Unless, of course, Lacey was out of the picture.

It was a great theory, but what I really needed was proof—proof that Lacey had somehow found out Ratski's secret and was using that information to her advantage. And if there was one person Ratski would have confided in about the blackmail, I had a feeling his offices were on Highland.

Unfortunately there was a wreck on the 405, meaning it took me over an hour before I reached the offices of Image Public Relations. I parked on the street a block down and fed the meter before hoofing it in my new pewter kitten heels back toward the office. I pulled open the glass doors to a blast of welcome air conditioning and rode the elevator to the third floor offices of Image.

"May I help you?" a blonde woman behind the desk asked in a pleasantly efficient voice.

"Yes, I was wondering if Theodore Schwimmer was available?" I replied.

"Do you have an appointment with Mr. Schwimmer?" The woman consulted a screen behind her desk.

I shook my head. "No. But it's relating to one of his clients. John Ratski of the L.A. Stars."

"And you are?"

"Maddie Springer," I replied. "I'm with the *L.A. Informer.*" I reached into my purse and pulled up the press pass I'd borrowed from Felix.

The receptionist nodded, and, to my surprise, instead of calling back to Schwimmer's office, she got up and made the trek down a short hallway to a closed-door near the back herself.

I only had to wait a few minutes before she returned and informed me, "Mr. Schwimmer will see you now."

I nodded my thanks to her and made my way down the hall.

While Schwimmer's office wasn't overly large, it was clean and furnished in a contemporary style that exuded impeccable taste. A small black sofa graced one wall, flanked by wooden bookcases, and a dark wood desk sat in the center of the room. Behind the desk sat the man from the pictures with the horn rimmed glasses. In person he was shorter than I had anticipated, though slightly chunkier. He had dark hair and a pale complexion that said he didn't spend much time in the California sunshine drifting in through his window. He was dressed in pressed slacks, a starched shirt, and a tie that lay across his chest straighter than an arrow. His appearance gave off an air of tidy organization. If I had to pick someone to be the opposite of Ratski, I couldn't have gotten closer than this.

His blue eyes blinked at me with anticipation behind his lenses. "My client has no comment on the celebrity battle being played out in your tabloid, Ms. Springer," Schwimmer started.

I nodded. "Actually, I was wondering if I could ask you a few questions of a different nature about John Ratski."

He raised an eyebrow at me, but indicated that I sit in the leather chair opposite his desk. "Don't you think that you people have done enough to him this week?"

I bit my lip, thinking fast back to the partial conversation I'd overheard earlier in Stars parking lot. "That's why I'm here, Mr. Schwimmer. *The Informer* doesn't want any legal trouble. We realize every story has two sides, and there's a possibility that photo of Ratski and Ricky was taken out of context. I'd like to do a piece on Ratski to set the record straight and get the real story"

Schwimmer raised his dark eyebrows at me again. Clearly he wasn't used to members of the tabloid press asking for a *real* story. "All right," he said slowly, as if choosing his words like a witness on the stand. "What can I tell you about John?"

The way he said Ratski's first name only heightened my suspicions.

"We ran a picture of Ratski with Dana Dashel the other day, implying that they were on a romantic date." I watched Schwimmer's reaction carefully.

But like the pro he was, he kept his poker-face in place. "Yes, I'm aware of this inference."

"But Ratski didn't have any romantic intentions toward Dana, did he?" I pressed.

"No," Schwimmer answered slowly.

"In fact, Ratski doesn't have any romantic intentions toward any of the women he's been rumored to be interested in, does he?" I said pointedly.

Schwimmer paused before answering. "Ratski is happily married," he replied.

"He's married, all right. But I'm not sure it's exactly what you call a happy marriage."

"I'm sorry, Ms. Springer, I'm not really clear about what you're implying. But if you are looking to help clear Ratski's name in your tabloid..." he trailed off, standing.

I knew when someone was about to give me the boot out of his office, and this guy was close. Time to pull out the big guns.

"Ratski's gay, isn't he?"

Schwimmer paused about halfway up from his seat. He gave me a long look, and I could tell it was on the tip of his tongue to deny it. But instead he sat back down and steepled his fingers, giving me an assessing stare.

"What makes you think that?" he asked.

"Sorry, I can't reveal my sources," I hedged, not quite ready to confess that I'd been going through Ratski's things and found his love letters. But I charged on, hitting Schwimmer with all I had before he had a chance to come up with a good denial.

"Lacey Desta knew it. She had proof that Ratski was batting for the other team, so to speak. She blackmailed Ratski, and when he got tired of paying, he killed her."

Schwimmer jumped up from his seat. "That's completely false! John would never do such a thing. He doesn't have a violent bone in his body."

"But Lacey *was* blackmailing him?" I pressed.

Schwimmer looked from me to the door of his office. He quickly crossed and shut it before turning back to me.

"This is all off the record, and I swear to you if I see this in print in your newspaper, I'll not only deny it, but I *will* sue you for slander."

Since I clearly had no intention to print any of this, I nodded my agreement.

Schwimmer crossed back to his desk and sank into his chair, his shoulders slumping as if all the fight had just drained out of them. "Yes, it's true, Ratski is gay."

"Not only gay, but the two of you are involved, aren't you?" I said.

Schwimmer looked at me in surprise for moment but didn't bother to deny it. Instead he nodded slowly. "We have been for a few years now. But if there's one thing that America can't forgive a sports hero for being it's a homosexual. Take all the drugs you want, train dogs to maul each other, heck, even beat your girlfriend. But heaven forbid you should fall in love with a man."

The bitter sarcasm was thick in Schwimmer's voice, and I couldn't say I blamed him. "How did Lacey find out?" I asked.

Schwimmer laughed, a hollow thing that held zero humor. "Look, in order to keep up his ruse John has this thing where he flirts with every woman he can find. He thinks it somehow insulates him from any question about his sexuality. Lacey was no exception. As soon as Bucky started dating her, Ratski went through the motions of hitting on her, just like he has all the other players' wives, girlfriends, even their mothers, if you can believe it." Schwimmer rolled his eyes toward the ceiling.

"If he hit on her, what tipped Lacey off that it was faked?"

"Look, Lacey was a gold digger, pure and simple. Bucky's the Stars' golden boy at the moment, so she sought him out. But it didn't take long before Lacey realized Bucky wasn't pulling in any real money. He had the fame but not the fortune she was looking for. That's when she set her sights on Ratski. He flirted with her a bit, and she thought maybe she had a chance of becoming his mistress and getting her hands on some hush-hush bling, at the very least."

The picture was becoming clearer in my head, puzzle pieces falling into place. "So Lacey tried to take the flirtation to the next level," I said.

Schwimmer nodded. "Truth is, John is a horrible flirt," he said, the laughter in his voice real this time, a note of affection coloring it. "It's a rare occasion when any of his lines actually works on a woman. So when Lacey tried to take it to the next level, John got flustered. He didn't know what to do, and, well, let's just say there was no Oscar-worthy performance on his part. For all of her questionable morals, Lacey was a smart little thing. She figured it out."

"And that's when she started blackmailing him."

Schwimmer bit his lip, pausing before he confirmed, probably more out of habit than any real hope of denying it at this point. "Yes. She said she would go to his wife, to the press, to anyone who would listen to the story, unless he paid her."

"Ten thousand a week," I said, quoting the amount Ramirez had found mysteriously deposited into her bank account.

Schwimmer raised an eyebrow. "Actually, no. It was five."

I felt a frown pull between my eyebrows. "Are you sure?"

Schwimmer nodded. "That's what John said. It was an exorbitant amount, and I told him not to pay it. Look, three years ago, it might've been death to his career. But with people like Jason Collins and Michael Sam paving the way, it's only a matter of time before more athletes come out."

"But Ratski didn't want to take that chance."

Schwimmer shook his head, confirming it. "No. If he was putting up numbers like Bucky's, maybe he would have. But

Ratski's not a rookie anymore. He's getting older. He felt that if something like this were to come out, he'd be the first expendable member of the team when his contract came up for renewal. He said he would figure out a way to deal with Lacey, but in the meantime he had to pay her off. "

My turn to raise an eyebrow. It was becoming more and more likely that his way to "deal with Lacey" was an amphetamine overdose into her tanning solution.

Schwimmer must have realized what he'd said as his eyes suddenly got big, and some of the fight returned to the set of his shoulders. "Look, John had nothing to do with what happened to Lacey. He was no fan of hers, but he would never hurt anyone like that. He's been beside himself since this whole thing happened. Trust me, whoever did that to Lacey, it had nothing to do with John."

While it was my gut instinct that Schwimmer believed everything he was saying, I wasn't inclined to share his favorable view of Ratski. Schwimmer might view Ratski as more of a lover than a fighter, but I also knew that desperate people took desperate measures when they were cornered. If Ratski really was worried about his contract coming up for renewal, chances were he didn't have an unlimited supply of cash to hand over to his blackmailer.

I was just about to grill Schwimmer on the shakiness of Ratski's alibi when a knock sounded at the door and the blonde receptionist poked her head in again.

"Excuse me, Mr. Schwimmer," she said in her evenly modulated voice. "But a client is here to see you."

"Who is it?" Schwimmer asked.

"John Ratski."

I felt myself freeze in place as if somehow the ballplayer's radar picked up the fact that I was there grilling his boyfriend. It took me a second before I realized how ridiculous that was. Clearly Ratski was just there because he was having a publicity crisis. Two days in a row he'd been featured on the *Informer* site.

"We were finished here anyway," I quickly said, ducking my head away from the door.

I heard another pair of footsteps approach. Fast ones. Big, baseball-sized ones, if I had to guess.

"Sorry for barging in, Theo," I heard Ratski, his voice at the door. "I was just going to see if you could—" Ratski stopped midsentence. Even though I had my back turned to him, I could feel his eyes shoot to me.

"You!"

Damn. Clearly the back of my head was as recognizable as the front. I slowly turned, doing my best toothy smile, blinking innocent eyelashes at Ratski. "Wow, what a small world."

While the bruises around Ratski's eyes were fading to a garish yellow, I noticed white tape across his nose where he'd taken the brunt of Ricky's blow. He looked like a boxer who wasn't very good at his job. "What the hell are you doing here?" he asked me.

By this time Schwimmer had stood up from his desk, his eyes were pinging between the two of us, his dark brows pulled into a frown. "You two know each other?"

"Uh…" I started.

"Oh, hell, yeah we do," Ratski said, his voice veering into dangerous territory. "This is the wife of that jerk cop who hit me."

"Hey, you started it," I protested.

Schwimmer turned to me, a sudden fire in his formerly soft eyes. "You told me you were a reporter."

"Well, technically, I said I was *with* the *Informer*. Which I sort of was. Earlier today…" I trailed off.

"Look, I don't know what sort of game you and your husband are playing," Ratski said, crossing the room in quick strides. The look in his eyes was pure anger, the clench of his hands menacing. No matter what Theodore Schwimmer said, in that split second I could easily see Ratski killing someone.

Unfortunately, at the moment that someone was me.

"Look, I don't want any trouble here…" I said, circling away from him, toward the open door.

"Well trouble is what you got, sister," Ratski informed me. His hand shot out, grabbing onto my arm.

In my defense what happened next was pure instinct. Maybe Ratski just meant to propel me toward the door. Maybe he was trying to keep me from getting any closer to Schwimmer. Or maybe he meant to strangle the life out of me. But as soon as his fingers clenched around my upper arm, I swung my purse with my right hand as hard as I could in the region of his face.

"Sonofa—" Ratski yelled, immediately letting go of me as both hands flew to his face. He staggered backward a few paces putting distance between us.

Distance I only increased by quickly backpedaling toward the door where the stunned receptionist was still standing, watching the entire scene unfold.

"Look what you did!" Ratski shouted. Blood gushed between his fingers, and as soon as he took his hands away from his face I could see that for the third time in as many days Ratski had a bloody nose.

"Ohmigod, ohmigod, ohmigod," Schwimmer chanted, rushing to his boyfriend's side. "Quick, grab some tissues. Call a doctor. Bring my car around."

The receptionist ran off to her desk to do one, two, or all three of the tasks being thrown at her.

With everyone's attention otherwise occupied, I took my opportunity to escape and quickly shot out the door. I took the stairs two at a time down to the ground floor and would have jogged to the end of the block if I hadn't been wearing heels. As it was, I power-walked quickly enough to put a mall-er-sizer to shame. I didn't feel safe again until I was inside my car with the doors locked. I felt my breath coming out in quick pants, my hands shaking at having been manhandled by a possible murderer.

I took a couple of deep breaths before I pulled out my cell and dialed my husband's number.

"Hey, babe," came his answer. I could hear the sound of children giggling in the background. It was comforting and immediately helped to slow my rapid heartbeat.

"I just hit somebody. Hard. In the face," I said, my words coming out in a barely coherent rush.

"What happened? Are you okay?" Ramirez asked. The urgency in his own voice suddenly had me feeling guilty. Truth was, I was fine. I might have a bruise on my arm later, but Ratski had taken the brunt of the encounter.

I took another deep breath and let it out slowly. "Yes, I'm fine. Now. I just…wanted to let you know that there might be some assault charges filed against me in the near future." I cringed, only halfway joking.

"Who did you hit?" Ramirez asked, his voice still tight and clipped with emotion.

I scrunched up my nose, wincing at the words. "John Ratski."

To my surprise I heard laughter on the other end of the phone. "Babe," he said. "Take a number. Who hasn't hit John Ratski this week?"

CHAPTER NINETEEN

———

As soon as I filled Ramirez in on all the gory details, he assured me he would call a buddy at the precinct to head off any assault charges filed against me. Then I hung up and dialed Dana's number. Three rings in I heard her breathless voice answer.

"Hello?" she panted.

"Uh...did I catch you at a bad time?"

"No. This is..." pant, pant "...fine. Why?"

"You sound just a little out of breath," I told her, squinting my eyes shut, so I didn't picture visions of her and Ricky doing something I so did not want to interrupt.

"Just at the gym," she said between puffs of breath. "No shooting today, so I thought I'd take the opportunity to get a workout in. Man, I'm out of shape."

Out of shape for Dana meant that she was only in *half* marathon mode. Prior to her acting career taking off, Dana had been an aerobics instructor, spending eight-plus hours a day leading spin classes, Pilates, kickboxing, and more. I would never say so to Ricky, but I had a feeling Dana could actually lift more than he could.

"I don't suppose you're in the mood for lunch?" I asked. I quickly filled her in on my run in with Ratski.

Dana did all the appropriate "ohmigods" and "no freaking ways" throughout the conversation, ending with a promise to meet me in twenty minutes at a place called Sprouts on Highland.

I'd never heard of the place, but with a name like Sprouts I was tempted to grab a drive-through burger on the way. However, I was also desperate to go over the latest development in our case with Dana, so I put my car in gear and headed toward the freeway.

Twenty-five minutes later I finally found parking on the street two blocks down from the restaurant. Which, as I approached it, looked just as healthy as I'd feared. The sign above the restaurant was fashioned like a large green alfalfa sprout scrolling through the letters. While the interior looked chic enough to be the new "It" lunch hotspot—dark wood floors, white walls, bright colorful geometric artwork, and sleek chrome tables and chairs scattered throughout the dining area—I wrinkled my nose at the scents coming out of the kitchen. None of them smelled greasy or bacony. I had a feeling this place was my penance for all the takeout I'd been eating lately.

I spotted Dana right away. She was at a table off to the side, near the far wall. She was still wearing her workout-wear of black spandex shorts, hot pink Nike running shoes, and a neon yellow sports top under a black asymmetrical collar sweatshirt. Though I noticed she had a ball cap and sunglasses on, presumably to fend off any further paparazzi pics ending up on the homepage of the *Informer*'s website.

"Hey," I said, sliding into the empty seat across from her. "Sorry, parking was a nightmare. Have you been waiting long?"

Dana shook her head. "No. But I ordered us both drinks."

I raised an eyebrow. Drinks might make this day better.

"Raspberry alfalfa kale shakes," Dana added, her eyes twinkling behind her semi-tinted glasses.

Then again, maybe not so much.

"So, tell me everything about Ratski's publicist," Dana insisted, leaning both elbows on the table.

I did, spilling everything Schwimmer had told me about Lacey blackmailing Ratski. "But he swears Ratski had nothing to do with her murder."

Dana scoffed. "Of course he does. What's he gonna do? Rat out not only his best client, but his boyfriend?"

I had to agree. Schwimmer was in no position to be objective.

"Okay, I have a question," Dana said, as our drinks arrived.

I gingerly sipped mine. Surprisingly, it wasn't too bad. Not an ice cream shake or anything, but palatable. "Shoot."

"If Ratski is gay, why has he been hanging out at the Glitter Galaxy?"

I blinked at her, my straw hovering halfway to my lips. "That, Dana, is a fantastic question."

And one I intended to find out.

* * *

As soon as we finished our lawn in a cup, Dana and I made tracks for the Glitter Galaxy. I texted ahead to make sure Ling was on shift, and as we entered the dark room full of pounding music and cigarette scented walls, I spotted her working the lunchtime crowd. A handful of guys in suits drinking their lunches made up the majority of the patrons. Ling was whispering something in the ear of a particularly pudgy, pink guy, who giggled in response like a middle school girl. She spotted us and held up her index finger, indicating she would just be a moment.

Dana and I sat at a table in the center of the room, and I watched as Ling leaned down, did some more whispering, and came back up with a couple of bills shoved in her bra strap. She blew the pudgy guy a kiss before sauntering our way.

"Did he just slip you a twenty?" I asked.

Ling made a "pfft" sound through teeth and shook her head. "Honey, that was a Benjamin. I don't make a guy giggle like that for just twenty."

I shook off a fleeting thought of becoming a stripper in my spare time, instead giving Ling the quick version of my encounter with Theodore Schwimmer.

"Wait a minute," Ling said, holding up a hand. "You trying to tell me that Ratski guy likes boys?" Her threaded brows rose in disbelief.

"That's exactly what I'm saying," I confirmed. "That's what Lacey had on him. Ratski was afraid that if word got out, it would be the end of his baseball career. And Lacey took advantage of it."

Ling shook her head. "That explains a lot about that guy."

"What do you mean?" Dana jumped in.

"He always tip a lot, but he never grabbed my ass," Ling said.

"Which begs the question," I continued, "what was Ratski doing here in the first place?"

Ling's eyebrows pulled down into a frown this time. "You know, that a really good question, blondie. We don't have any male dancers here. Our clientele is real specific."

"Is it possible he just wanted to be seen at a strip club to keep up his ruse?" Dana asked. "You know, kind of like he didn't mind being seen out with me the other night."

I pursed my lips together, running over that thought. While it was clear now that Dana was right—Ratski had purposely chosen a restaurant to meet her where he knew they would both be recognized and quite likely filmed—the Ratski I'd seen slinking into the Glitter Galaxy with his ball cap pulled low hadn't looked like he'd been trying to be seen. In fact, no offense to Ling and her many Benjamins, but the Galaxy wasn't exactly the flashiest place to see nude dancers in town. There were plenty of places Ratski could've gone in Hollywood where he'd be much more visible. So, why drive out of his way to Industry, in dark sunglasses and a ball cap no less, to watch nude girls dance?

"Ling, do you know if Ratski got private dances from any other particular girls?" I grasped.

Ling pursed her lips together, her eyes going to the ceiling, as if searching there for the info. "Well, I told you I dance for him sometimes. But, honestly, I think Janel is his favorite. He has a thing for redheads." She paused. "Though I guess maybe his thing is not the thing I thought it was, huh?"

"Which one is Janel?" I asked.

Ling's eyes searched the dimly lit club before she pointed out a girl with a tray full of drinks in hand. She was wearing a green thong, thigh-high platform go-go boots, and a pair of alien antennae atop a long, red wig.

"That's her," Ling said.

"Oh, Ling, Ling," the pudgy businessmen in the corner yelled out sing-song style across the club.

Ling gave him a playful wave then turned to us and rolled her eyes. "I gotta go. Duty calls."

I nodded my thanks to her, and Dana and I waited until the redhead had emptied her tray before hailing her to our table.

"Can I help you ladies with something?" she asked, eyeing us as if trying to size up our pleasure.

"Actually, we were wondering if we could talk to you about John Ratski?"

Janel looked from me to Dana, then back to me again, biting her lip nervously.

"We won't take much of your time, but I just wanted to ask you a couple of questions."

Her eyes narrowed. "What kind of questions?"

"What was Ratski here for?" Dana asked, getting right to the point.

The redhead's eyes ping-ponged between us again, and I could see her trying to figure out where we fit in. "Did Ratski send you here?" she asked. "Because he's late this week, you know."

Dana and I shared a glance. "Yep," I lied through my teeth. "Ratski sent us all right."

I could see the tension release from her shoulders. "Oh, good. You know I kinda thought maybe he wasn't coming this week. Which would totally screw me over since I already fronted for it, you know?"

I totally didn't know. But I was certainly hoping she could shed some light on it. "Well, we're here for him," I said, hoping I wasn't committing to anything too terrible.

She leaned in and whispered, "I'll be right back. It's in my locker." With that she got up and, as quickly as her six-inch heels would allow, crossed the club to a doorway behind the dark curtain next to the stage.

"What you think she's going to get?" Dana asked, whispering to me.

I shrugged. I hadn't the foggiest.

I didn't have much time to contemplate it as Janel quickly darted back out from behind the curtain and toward our table. She did a quick glance over her shoulder before she leaned down and extracted something from her tall go-go boot. She slid the item across the table to us, covering it with her palm.

I reached out and took it, pulling it closer to myself. I looked down. I was holding a bright green condom in a clear cellophane wrapper. I looked back up at her.

"Okay, I give up. What is this?" I asked the girl.

Janel's eyes darted back and forth. "It's a Jolly Green Giant," she said. "Ratski's weekly usual."

I looked down at the condom in my hand. I had a hard time believing he drove all the way to Industry just to get colorful protection.

Dana took it from me, turning it over in her hands.

"Wait, is this what I think it is?" Dana asked. She gave Janel a pointed look.

Janel did a quick nod.

"What?" I probed.

"I've heard of this on the *Lady Justice* set," she quickly whispered to me. "One of our interns got busted for carrying something similar a few weeks ago. It's the latest way to distribute designer drugs."

"Drugs?!" I asked, looking over both shoulders. Had I just taken part in a drug deal?

"Shhh!" Janel said.

"It's pretty clever, really," Dana continued, turning the wrapper over. "I mean, who's going to go through the condom packets in your pocket, right? Dealers stuff the drugs in the condoms, then stick them in these clear cellophane packages, and distribute them as party favors all over town."

Clearly I was going to all the wrong kind of parties. The only favors I was getting were pony poop.

"So, what's a Jolly Green Giant?" I asked Janel, hoping like anything she said it was some sort of amphetamine.

Janel bit her lip. "Look, a few of the girls here take them before a set. It just gives you a little extra pep."

I raised an eyebrow. Or a little pep to get through a baseball inning. Or, in massive doses, enough pep to induce a heart attack in a tanning booth.

"So, uh…" Janel cleared her throat. "Payment?"

Uh-oh. "How much?" I asked.

"Two-fifty," she said, rising from the table.

I blinked at her. Then I looked in my purse. I had exactly $12.50. I looked to Dana.

"Uh, you take credit?" she asked.

Janel paused. "You're kidding, right?"

Dana shrugged. "I'm a little short right now. Ratski didn't exactly tell us how much to bring."

"How short?" Janel said, putting her hands on her bare hips, her eyes narrowing. I could see a bouncer near the door tensing as her mood shifted.

"Um…" Dana dug into her shoulder bag. "I can swing maybe…fifty bucks?"

Janel rolled her eyes in disgust, snatching the condom back from us. "You tell Ratski to come here himself if he wants this," she said, wagging a finger at us. Then she shoved the wrapper back into her boot and stalked off.

"Come on," I said, glancing at the bouncer, who was narrowing his eyes in our direction now. "Let's get out of here."

* * *

I dropped Dana back off at her car and was just pulling my minivan into my own drive to tell Ramirez what we'd found when my cell rang. I grabbed it, seeing a number I didn't recognize with a 626 area code. Curiosity won over, and I swiped my finger across the screen.

"Hello?" I asked

"Maddie?" A vaguely familiar female voice came across the line.

"Yes?"

"Oh, good. This is Beth. Beth Ratski," my caller said.

I raised my eyebrow at the phone. After what had transpired in his publicist's office, Ratski's wife was probably the last person I expected to hear from.

But before I could question her motives Beth continued on, "Look, my husband told me what happened in Schwimmer's office earlier today."

"Oh?" I asked, highly suspect that Ratski had told her *everything* that had transpired in his publicist office.

"Yes," she said. "He told me that his temper got the best of him, and, Maddie, I just want to tell you how sorry I am. John knows he overreacted at seeing you there. He's just been under so much stress lately with all of these tabloid rumors swirling around. Of course I told him he shouldn't worry, since none of them have a shred of truth to them, but he just got so nervous when he saw you talking to his publicist, that he sort of lost it."

Well it was an interesting story, I'd say that for Ratski. Of course I guess he had to tell his wife something when he came home with newly-blackened eyes. "No need to apologize, Beth," I told her, feeling suddenly somehow like Ratski's slimy accomplice in lying to his wife about their sham of a marriage.

"Maddie, you are too kind," Beth said. "But really, John and I both wanted to make it up to you."

"Make it up to me?" I wondered just how worried Ratski was about the conversation I'd had with Schwimmer. While I know I had no intention of either going to the press or blackmailing him, clearly Ratski wasn't confident in that fact. Schwimmer must've told him that he'd spilled the beans to me. I suddenly felt slightly uncomfortable. The last woman who had learned Ratski's secret ended up dead.

"Really, Beth, that's not necessary," I assured her.

"Please, Maddie, I insist. At least please take our box at the Stars game this evening?"

It was on the tip of my tongue to reject her offer once again. But while Janel might not be star-witness material to Ratski's illegal dealings, the truth was Ratski had to be hiding his stash of Jolly Green Giants somewhere. Chances were good that somewhere was at the stadium, and if I could find it, that would be proof that even Laurel and Hardy couldn't overlook.

However going into the shark tank alone didn't seem like it was the smartest idea.

"Would you mind if I bring a plus-one?" I asked. "My husband is the biggest Stars fan ever."

CHAPTER TWENTY

————

"I have died and gone to heaven. This is frickin' amazing." Ramirez stared down through the large glass window at tiers of seating beneath us in the Stars Stadium.

As if there'd been any question in my mind, Ramirez had jumped at the chance to attend tonight's game, especially from a player's private box. We dropped the kids off at Mama's house and arrived at the stadium just before the game started. I had to admit the box was impressive. Plush recliner style seats looked out of the glass window with a perfect bird's eye view of the action. From our angle, we could not only see the players on the field, but we also had a pretty good view of the dugout, the bull-pen, and the stands as well. The Jumbotron was right across from our box, almost as if it was our own private big-screen television. I had a feeling that when Ramirez said he was in heaven, he wasn't exaggerating much.

"That's it, you need to hang out with Beth Ratski more often."

I rolled my eyes. "You do realize that she's possibly married to a murderer, right?"

Ramirez waved me off. "Hey, nobody's perfect."

I gave him a punch in the arm.

One of the stadium wait staff came into the box, looking for an order of food and drinks. Which, after they assured us it would be comped by the Stars Stadium, we put in for a couple of beers and a plate of wings.

The staff left, and an announcer called out the name of a former *American Idol* contestant who took the field to sing the national anthem. Some cities might have high school students sing, but former *American Idol* contestants were Hollywood's version of amateurs. After a heartfelt, if slightly pitchy rendition, the first honorary pitch was thrown and the away team, the San Francisco Giants, took their turn at bat. My husband leaned forward in his seat, intent on the action below me.

Me? I was a little more intent on snooping.

I walked over to the far right wall which was lined with shelves and cabinetry. The shelves mostly displayed sports paraphernalia and mementos from the franchise's long history. Signed photos of retired players', game balls behind glass, plaques commending various players for various things. While they were all interesting, none screamed "killer."

I moved on to the cabinets, pulling them open one by one as the third Giant struck out and our guys came up to the plate. I was vaguely aware of a couple of our guys coming up to bat, getting base hits.

"Bucky's up next," Ramirez called over his shoulder. "It's his first at-bat since the murder."

I had to admit to a little curiosity. I moved to watch over Ramirez's shoulder as Bucky assumed his batting stance. The pitcher spit, wiggled his hips, and stared Bucky down before drilling a ball toward him. Bucky swung and missed, and the sound of the entire crowd letting out a disappointed breath reverberated through the sound system speakers.

"Damn," Ramirez muttered under his breath. "He's gotta do better than that if he wants MVP this season."

I took the seat next to Ramirez as our server came back with the drinks and wings. Three sips later, Bucky had struck out.

"Poor guy," I said honestly. "I'm surprised he was playing at all."

"It's the sports equivalent of the show must go on," Ramirez said around a healthy bite of chicken wing.

I went back to my rifling through the cabinets as another player came up to the plate. I opened the first cupboard and found a variety of different liquor bottles. Most of my alcoholic knowledge came in the variety of wine and flavored martinis, but I noticed Scotch, Gin, and Brandy all in fancy crystal bottles. All probably old and very expensive. I closed the cabinet back up.

I opened the second one as I heard Ramirez cheering on the player who apparently had hit a double. I glanced at the Jumbotron and saw him slide into second base, then stand up with a large mud streak down the front of his uniform. The crowd cheered, and another player came up to bat taking his turn to face the grim pitcher.

I looked through another cupboard. This one held baseball caps with the Stars insignia on them. Probably promotional freebies for the Ratskis to give out to their guests. Promotional T-shirts sat in another, and schedules of the game and menus like the one our server had brought in the cupboard next to that. I was beginning to feel like there was nothing here. This might be Ratski's private box, but there was nothing personal about it. Clearly this was just a place for business deals to go down.

"Here comes Ratski," Ramirez said, leaning forward in his chair.

I walked up behind him to peek at the guy swinging for the ball, but he wasn't wearing Ratski's number.

"Where?" I asked.

"Over there," Ramirez said, pointing off to the right. Just to the side of the foul line, I noticed Ratski jogging toward the field, not from the dugout, but from up a long narrow stairway that looked like it lead somewhere down below the action.

"What's down there?" I asked, craning to see.

"Batting cages. It's where the guys can warm up before they take the plate," Ramirez told me.

"Does everyone do that?" I asked.

Ramirez shrugged. "Not every player. Some guys need more warm-up time than others."

"Like Ratski," I mumbled, sinking into the club chair beside my husband. I sipped at the cold beer as I watched Ratski walk up to the plate. We had one guy at second. I glanced up at the scoreboard. Two outs.

Ratski spit on the ground, shuffled his feet around a little, and nodded toward the pitcher.

The catcher did some complicated hand signals down by his knees, and the pitcher nodded, squinting his eyes. He threw his first pitch, and Ratski swung hard enough that his bat cracked in half. Unfortunately, the ball went foul, flying up into the stands.

Ramirez moved a little bit farther forward on his seat. Much more and he'd be kissing the glass.

Ratski got a new bat, some guys came out to talk to the pitcher on the mound, and the action generally slowed. I felt myself getting antsy. I knew I was right in the middle of the hornet's nest, but I couldn't figure out how to poke it.

Ratski came back up to the plate and swung at the next pitch. This time his bat connected perfectly, and it sailed far enough into the air that the crowd was on its feet in anticipation of a home run.

Unfortunately, it bounced off the far wall, instead, landing on the dirt.

But Ratski had taken off like a shot, running faster than I would've thought a guy with a beer gut like his could. He quickly rounded first and second base to make a slide right into third.

The crowd cheered, the roar deafening. My husband cheered right along with them. "A sweet RBI! That's what I'm talking about, Ratski!" Ramirez said clapping. Apparently, personal feelings had no place in baseball. If Ratski was bringing the team to a win, Ramirez was happy.

Then it hit me. I looked over at that narrow staircase to the right of the foul line again. I blinked as I watched another player come jogging up, bat in hand.

The batting cage the last stop before a batter hit the field. It was the perfect place to hide a little pre-game pick-me-up.

I knew it. I knew that the drugs were down there, and if I could find them, I bet that Ratski's prints would be all over them.

I looked over at Ramirez. He was completely engrossed in the game as our new player came up to bat, hoping to at least get a single to get Ratski in for a two run lead.

"I'm gonna go walk around," I told him.

He nodded as he stared down at the action below. "Uh-huh."

I made my way out of the box, and took the escalators down through the Stadium back to the main floor. The place was buzzing with sports fans in line at the beer stands, eating hot dogs with relish, onions, ketchup, and mustard, and purchasing hats, banners and foam fingers at stands scattered all through the causeway. I tried to get my bearings. The other times Dana and I had crashed into the private areas of the stadium, we'd gone through the players' entrance. I knew there must be a way to get there from the main public floors. I just wasn't sure what it was.

I walked toward the right side of the stadium, which is where I had seen the batting cage. I got to about the point in the main causeway where I thought the batting cages should be. But how to get down below was a whole other question. I looked out onto the field. I noticed our guys were there, tossing baseballs to each other. The inning must have ended. I looked up to one of the many scoreboards mounted near the ceiling and saw that Ratski had indeed scored us a run.

A vendor wearing a tray for delivering frozen lemonade walked past me. Most of his slots were empty, just a couple of melted drinks sloshing around in the middle. The guy veered left and went to a spot along the wall painted with a mural of film strips and palm trees. He pushed on a panel of film strip, and the wall opened, allowing him to slip inside. Had I not seen him do it, I never would have noticed the slight door-shaped crack in the mural.

I did a quick over-both-shoulders to see if anyone was watching me, but clearly everyone in the vicinity was engrossed in their own snack runs before the action started up again on the field. I made my way over to the door and gave it a shove. It opened as quickly as it had for the lemonade guy, and I walked through, letting it shut behind me.

I found myself in some sort of utility hallway. People in the staff uniforms of jeans and Stars T-shirts passed me in both directions, none of them paying much attention to me, even though in my sporty pink capris, long sleeved wrap top, and strappy slingbacks I feared I stood out like a sore thumb. I wished I had grabbed one of the T-shirts and ball caps from the private suite before heading down here. So much for my powers of disguise.

Then I remembered the press pass. It was still in my purse. I quickly rummaged through and grabbed the little laminated square identifying me as a member of the *Informer* staff and slipped it around my neck. I might be a little bit out of place in the service hallway, but at least I looked like I belonged in the private areas.

My heels click-clacked on the cement floor as I walked through the throngs of stadium employees. I had no idea which way the batting cages were, but I hoped I was close. I turned down a hallway that led to the left, went right a couple more times, then left again and found myself in what looked like offices. Wrong turn. I turned around, backed up, and went left, left, right, right, left…,and pretty soon I had no idea where I was. I could have been close to the batting cage or I could've been all the way back to the point I'd started at.

I was about to give up and ask one of the guys walking by carrying peanuts or cotton candy where the players' area was, when I spotted one of our mascots—the huge Charlie Chaplin— wobbling his way down the hall to the right. If he was going to the field, that must be the direction I wanted to go as well. I trailed him, trying to look like I *wasn't* trailing him, and, wonder of wonders, came to a stairway that opened up to the locker rooms at one side and a corridor that led to the field down the other.

I took the corridor to the field, and on the right side, after two more turns, I hit pay-dirt. A small nondescript doorway opened up on to a squat, cement batting cage. It wasn't much to look at. A rectangular room below ground, covered in mesh netting above and Astroturf below. I gingerly stepped inside, it was empty. With our team on the field, none of our players should be warming up at the moment.

But I knew my time was limited.

If I was going to find Ratski's stash, I had to find it now. I quickly scanned the batting cage. Honestly, there weren't many places to hide something. There was a rack of bats to one side, a couple bins of balls on the other, a small TV monitor mounted in the corner displaying the current action on the field, and the pitching machine itself at the far end.

Ratski had to put the drugs somewhere that only he would be able to find them. He wouldn't want every other player who came in to stumble upon them. I quickly scanned through the balls and the bats and dismissed those. There was nothing out of the ordinary, and they were way too public.

Behind the pitching machine there was a row of metal lockers, much like the ones that graced the walls of my high school. Only these were dingier and more rusted. Utilitarian but not very pretty. Then again, I didn't think anyone was giving out Good Housekeeping awards for a nice batting cage.

I gingerly stepped over discarded gloves, balls, bats, and what I could've sworn was a jockstrap (but I wasn't going to look at that closely. Ew!). Luckily for me, none of the lockers seem to be locked. I opened the first and found more of the random paraphernalia like on the floor. The next one had rolls of ace bandages and some white powdery stuff that looked a lot like the resin I'd seen gymnasts use on television.

I moved onto a large cabinet next to the lockers. It held helmets of all different shapes and sizes. I quickly picked one up and noticed a name written with a Sharpie on the inside. "Davis." Each player had his own! I dropped the helmet, quickly scanning through the others until I finally found one with the name "Ratski" on it.

I picked it up and turned it over in my hands. It was thick plastic on the outside and foam padding on the inside. I ran my fingers over the padding. I was starting to feel desperation bubble up to my chest as I glanced at the television monitor. Our guys were still on the field, but I noticed that the other team had two outs, and their current at-bat player was tipping foul balls. I didn't know a lot about baseball, but I'd learned enough in the last few days to know that my seconds were numbered before one of the Stars players came in here to start warming up.

I quickly moved my fingers over every slightly sweaty inch of the helmet…until they encountered a small bump just along the back rim.

I felt my heart rate pick up, my stomach fluttering with hope. I gingerly lifted the edge of the foam, peeling it back just enough to reveal a small, green, condom wrapper, just like the one Janel had tried to sell me.

I pulled it out with my nails, so as not to erase any fingerprints that might be lingering on the wrapper. I held the package up to the light. I'd bet my favorites Via Spigas this was exactly the same stuff that Janel had given us at the Glitter Galaxy.

I heard the crack of the bat above me as the Giants player finally connected with the ball.

The collective groan of the crowd was so loud that I almost didn't hear the person walking into the cages behind me.

Almost.

The hairs on the back of my neck stood at attention, and I spun around, ready to hold my press pass in front of me to anyone who accused me of trespassing.

As it turned out my press pass was not going to save me.

"Maddie, you just have such a hard time staying where you're told to, don't you?" Beth Ratski said.

It might have been a flippant conversational question… had it not been for the gun in her hand, pointed straight at me.

CHAPTER TWENTY-ONE

"Beth?" I asked, hearing the note of surprise in my own voice. "What are you doing here?"

Beth took a step forward, the gun never wavering.

"It doesn't matter what I'm doing here, Maddie," Beth said, her eyes cutting to the green package in my hands. "It's all about what you're doing here."

"I don't understand," I stammered, taking a quick step away from her. Though, the truth was there wasn't anywhere for me to go in the small cage. It was a cinder block rectangle, hemmed in on all sides except for the exits that Beth and her shiny little gun were blocking.

But Beth shook her head. "Maddie, the time for playing dumb has passed."

I paused, and I realized she was right. Someone here had been playing dumb. Her. And I'd totally fallen for it.

"Okay, then, no more playing dumb." I held up the green package in my hands, still careful to not smudge any fingerprints. "This is your husband's."

Beth nodded. "It's not his fault. Everybody does this stuff."

"But not everybody kills somebody with it."

"And John didn't either," Beth said with conviction behind her voice.

As I looked down at the gun in her hands, puzzle pieces fell into place, and I believe she was being honest with me.

"Because you did," I said.

Beth didn't answer. She just stared at me. "Maddie, I think it's time for us to go now."

I took an involuntary step backwards, coming up against the dingy lockers. "Go where?" I asked. I heard the crowd groaning behind me again. Damn, would this inning never end? The Giants seemed to be getting men on base one after another. For how anxious I'd been when they'd gotten down to the last out, that last out was now taking forever.

At least it felt that way with a gun trained on me.

"I'm sorry, Maddie, really I am," Beth said. And again, I had the feeling she was being honest. "But I can't let you walk out of here with that. If the police start questioning my husband about his drug use—"

"—he'll realize how much of his drugs are missing," I finished for her. "Because you took them to kill Lacey."

This time Beth nodded. "She was going to ruin everything, Maddie. I couldn't have that. After all John and I have worked for, after everything he sacrificed, everything he's done to be a Stars player. And this little nobody from the wrong side of town came in and thought she deserved it all? She wanted a starring role on our show, she wanted John's money, she wanted everything. Well, she couldn't have it."

"Including John?" I said, seeing it all come together now. It hadn't been about the money, it had been about jealousy.

To my surprise Beth threw her head back and laughed. I took the opportunity to take a step closer to the lockers, putting my hand out behind me. I felt around for anything I could use as a weapon. Baseball glove, cream, resin. Then I finally felt a little lift of hope as my hand clutched onto the top of a wooden baseball bat.

Only I didn't have a chance to use it as Beth's eyes snapped back to me, the gun going straight-armed in front of her as a new look took over her features. It wasn't the scared, apologetic one I'd seen her wearing around the other Baseball Wives. It wasn't the concerned one she'd worn around her husband. It wasn't even the regret I'd seen a moment ago, when I honestly believed she hadn't wanted to harm me. This was a hard, flat look of a woman who wasn't going to let a little thing like emotion get in the way of her success.

"How stupid do you think I am, Maddie?" she asked. "You really think I didn't know that my husband is gay?"

Okay, yeah, that was exactly what I had thought. So sue me. Playing dumb had worked for her reality TV character, and I was a bit naive that I was just now realizing what a *character* she had been playing.

"Of course I knew," she spat back at me. "You, Kendra, Liz…you all think I'm some idiot. Oblivious to my husband's flirting. You couldn't be farther from the truth. I'm the one who *tells* him to flirt with women. I'm the one who told him to go out with Dana in the first place, hoping maybe it would throw you off the scent."

"Wait, you set that date up with your husband and Dana?"

She shrugged. "How was I to know that Dana's boyfriend would go off hotheaded and hit John in the face? Some people can't control their emotions."

"But you can," I said, keeping her talking as I kept one eye on the gun. Unfortunately, her grip wasn't loosening any. There was no way I'd be able to swing the baseball bat at her before her finger could move the half inch it took to pull that trigger. However, if I kept her talking, maybe I could distract her for just the second…

"Of course I can," Beth said. "It's what I do best. It's my full-time job, truth be told."

"A full-time beard."

A slow smile crept across her face. "What can I say? It pays well. John needed someone to divert suspicion from him, and who better than an unsuspecting wife? Of course, there are certain financial perks to being his wife."

"And then there was *Baseball Wives*."

She nodded. "Another financial perk."

"There seem to be an awful lot of perks with this job," I said.

"Until Lacey came along." Her face fell.

"Lacey wasn't stupid either," I pressed, tightening my grip on the baseball bat. "She figured out John's game."

That creepy smile came back to Beth's face, but her eyes were still as dead as ever. "I wouldn't exactly call that tramp smart. She thought I was her friend. She felt sorry for me, thinking I had no idea that my husband was into men."

"But then the blackmail started."

Beth frowned, shaking her head. "It wasn't about the money. The amount she wanted was nothing. The problem was she was getting on the show."

"And?" I asked, not exactly following

"And what do you think *Baseball Wives* is all about? Secrets. Telling each other's secrets. When the ratings got low, it was Kendra who let it be known that Liz was sleeping around on her husband. In return, Liz needed more screen time after she and Tony started going to therapy, so of course she let it be known that Kendra had been attending shopaholics anonymous meetings. I'm not stupid. The amount my husband was paying Lacey was nothing compared to the hundreds of thousands of dollars that go along with being a celebrity reality TV star. As soon as Lacey realized she could grab the spotlight and the ratings if she let my husband's secret out, she'd sing like an opera star."

"And John wouldn't need you anymore," I finished for her.

I watched Beth's nostrils flare, realizing what her true motive was.

Schwimmer had been right. Ten years ago, professional sports would never have forgiven a gay player. But times were different. If it came out publicly that Ratski was gay, I'm sure he'd be on every tabloid news website and blowing up Twitter for days or weeks…but it would eventually blow over. And when it did, Ratski would have no need for a fake wife. There went Beth's moment in the sun, her position on *Baseball Wives*, and her cash cow of a husband.

"So Ratski knew nothing. He had no idea you killed Lacey?" Was I a terrible person that I was a little bit disappointed?

"Of course he didn't," Beth said. "You think John would hurt somebody?" She shook her head. "He is the kindest, sweetest, most generous man I've ever known."

And in that moment I realized not only would Beth be losing her cash cow, she would actually be losing the man she loved.

"That's why I had to protect him."

I could hear the crowd groaning again as the Giants took another base.

But I knew I was on borrowed time. Any minute now somebody was going to come in here. Beth knew it too. I couldn't string this conversation out much longer.

As if reading my thoughts, Beth took one large stride toward me, gun first. "We have to go now, Maddie. We're out of time. The inning will end any second, and Blanco will come in here to warm up. It's time to go."

Her voice was the same one I used with the twins when it was naptime. The I'm-in-charge-here voice.

However, just like my twins, I wasn't that compliant.

My hand clenched around the bat, and I swung with all I had toward the arm holding the gun. There was a crack of wood on metal, and then a much louder crack of a bullet flying from the gun and embedding itself in the wall.

However, if anyone above us heard, they must have thought it was just another batter warming up.

Beth screamed in pain, dropping the gun. I dove around her for the door, but I only got two steps before I felt my feet flying out from under me, Beth's hands going around my ankles as she dragged me down from behind.

My knees scraped on the plastic Astroturf as I fell, the drug-filled condom flying from my hands. I kicked backward with my slingbacks, connecting with something soft, and I heard Beth grunt in response.

She let go of my ankles, and I scrambled to my feet and spun around just in time to see her grab another unused bat and swing in my direction. I dropped to the floor again, ducking under the whoosh of the bat. I scrambled to the right and grabbed another discarded bat. I stood, holding it out in front of me like a sword.

Beth paused, then let out a warrior scream as she came toward me, bat held high above her head like a club. She swung downward. Instinctively I brought my bat up to shield her blow. The force of it vibrated through my arms.

She bounced off of me, and I swung blindly toward her, connecting with her bat as she blocked my attack.

We must've looked like two overgrown children playing with light sabers in the dugout if anyone had been watching. Unfortunately, as I heard the crowd yelling, I knew no one was watching our action. Everybody's eyes were glued to the field.

Beth swung again, and I blocked her just in time to keep her bat from smacking me in the head. Unfortunately it glanced off my shoulder, and pain jumped up my right side. I gritted my teeth, trying not to lose my grip, and swung toward Beth again, just barely missing her as she jumped out of the way.

Then came the most welcome thing I'd heard all day. The crowd cheering in delight, followed by the announcer signaling it was the end of the inning.

Beth must've heard it too, as she paused.

In that same moment, both of our eyes cut to the gun.

I thought about making a lunge for it, but there was no way I could get it without being hit in the back of the head by her bat first. She must have deduced the same thing, as we both stood there, poised in fighting position.

Until the door swung open.

"What the hell?" Blanco said, his eyes, cutting from Beth to me, and back again.

It was all the distraction Beth needed.

In one motion, she dropped the bat, grabbed the drugs from the floor where I'd dropped them, and took off like a shot through the field entrance.

On instinct I dropped my bat and ran after her. I'd gone this far; I wasn't going to let Lacey's killer get away now.

I raced through the entrance, which was an upward ramp going from our underground bunker to the level of the playing field. The players were still in the process of switching sides, the Giants' players tossing baseballs between each other, and the big-headed Charlie Chaplin and Marilyn Monroe shooting free T-shirts into the crowd with a giant cannon. Beth paid no attention to any of them, barreling onto the field, running blindly, with me a quick heel step behind her.

At first no one tried to stop us, two crazy women running onto the field, our heels sinking into the soft grass like clumsy cleats. However, it didn't take long before the players stopped throwing the ball and turned our way. I was vaguely aware of the announcer shouting something into the loudspeakers, security spilling onto the field from different directions. Out of the corner of my eye I saw Beth and me flashing up on the Jumbotron as the cameras turned our way. In fact, the only people in the stadium who seemed unaware of what was going on were Charlie Chaplin and Marilyn Monroe.

As I well knew, they had zero peripheral vision inside those huge heads. Which is probably why instead of getting out of Beth's way, Charlie Chaplin weeble-wobbled right into her path. She tired to veer off, but it was too late. She rammed into him, taking them both down, and knocking his head off…which rolled across the field like a victim of battle.

Beth scrambled to her feet, but Marilyn Monroe, now aware of the danger, turned around, aimed her shirt gun right at Beth, and shot at close range.

Beth flew backwards, taking an extra-large to the belly, and landed on her butt in the grass just as security arrived and grabbed her under both armpits.

"I'm Beth Ratski! I'm a Baseball Wife! I belong here!" she screamed as they dragged her off.

I heard the crowd cheering as if a home run had just sailed over the wall and turned around to see my disheveled appearance on the Jumbotron, ten times larger than life. My hair was flying in all directions, my adorable Capri pants marred with grass stains, and I think one of my shoes was missing a heel. I did a feeble smile to the crowd. Then turned to the Ratski's box where I could just make out the shape of a man standing at the window, pounding at it with both hands.

I waved in his direction. "Hi, honey."

CHAPTER TWENTY-TWO

The game was delayed, which was just as well for the Stars, since we were behind six-to-two. It was late by the time I had finally given my statement to the Stars security, several uniformed police officers, and finally the stunned Laurel and Hardy, who had wisely declared that there would be no comments and no press conferences today. Ramirez stood by my side, silently smirking the entire time. Though I couldn't tell if he was impressed I'd thwarted the escape of a murderer on my own or angry I'd gone after evidence on my own. In hindsight, I probably should have clued him in. A sentiment I shared with him as the officers finally cleared me to leave.

"I probably should have told you what I was up to, huh?"

"You probably should have," he agreed. He paused. "Though I probably should have known you were up to something."

I grinned. "Yeah, you probably should have."

* * *

"Ohmigod, Maddie, I can't believe you actually ran onto the field!" Marco said the next day at Fernando's salon. Turns out almost being killed by a psycho Baseball Wife is as hard on a manicure as getting hit by a foul ball. I was getting my nails repaired, and I was happy to report that three out of four of the chairs beside me were filled as well. News of Beth's arrest had been shot across the gossip universe at light speed, along side news that it was the stepdaughter of Fernando's salon owner who had caught the killer. While I wasn't sure I should take sole credit for bringing Beth to justice, Ramirez was just happy someone other than Laurel and Hardy was in the spotlight.

"The truth is, my fingernails fared better than my shoes," I told Marco. "I think I left a heel at second base."

Marco tsked, clicking his tongue. "Sacrificed in the name of justice." Then he bowed his head in a solemn moment of silence for my shoe.

"So what now?" he asked. "Is it true that Beth confessed everything?"

I nodded, repeating what Ramirez had told me that morning after coming back from the station. (After being reinstated, by the way. It turns out that all the charges Ratski was levying against my husband magically disappeared the moment his wife was arrested for murder.) "Beth's claiming temporary insanity, saying that living a lie all these years took a mental toll on her."

"So how did she do it?" Marco asked. "How did she actually administer the poison?"

It was a good question and one the police had asked Beth, too.

"Turns out that Beth had been planning this for some time and was just waiting for the right day. She found out Lacey's salon schedule right from the source. Then she picked a day when she knew Lacey would be here tanning and the Baseball Wives would be on set. Beth actually deliberately loosened wires around Kendra's car battery the night before, so that she'd be late to the set. Beth made a big deal of pointing out that she was missing. So, while everyone was looking for Kendra, Beth slipped away to Fernando's."

"Where she slipped in the back door and added the lethal dose of amphetamines to the tanning solution in Lacey's booth," Marco finished for me, then did a shudder. "I'm never tanning again."

"That makes two of us," I agreed. "Actually, I heard Mom and Ralph talking this morning, and he said he's thinking about discontinuing spray tans. Just too creepy to send another client into that booth."

"Amen to that," Marco agreed. He paused, moving the LED to my other hand. "I just have one question?"

"Shoot," I told him, inspecting my shiny nails.

"If Schwimmer admitted that Ratski was paying Lacey five-thousand a week in hush money, where was the other five-thousand she deposited each week coming from?"

I grinned at him. "You didn't think Ratski was the *only* person Lacey was blackmailing, now, did you?"

"Get out!" He smacked me on my arm.

I laughed. "Okay, I'll admit, I didn't figure that part out either."

"Who was it?" Marco asked, leaning in close. "Kendra? Liz?"

"Actually, kind of both of them."

Marco sucked in a breath. "I've died and gone to gossip heaven. Do tell."

"Well, it turns out Beth wasn't lying when she said something was off about Liz's finances. But it wasn't about *missing* money, so much as *extra* money."

Marco raised an eyebrow. "Go on."

"Ling was right about the quality of bags Liz was selling. Liz would order bags from the designers, but then she'd order knockoffs of the same bags from overseas. She'd sell the knockoffs in her store, then sell the original bags to another boutique."

"She was double dipping!"

I nodded. "That's where Kendra came in. She admitted that she has a friend who owns a boutique in New York. They were shipping the real designer items to her, acting as a distributor, then selling the fakes at Liz's boutique. That's what I'd overheard Kendra talking about on the phone at the studio. And that loan that Beth said she overhead Liz asking for from Kendra? It wasn't actually a loan at all, but capital for their venture to purchase the fake bags."

"She admitted all of this?" Marco asked.

"According to Ramirez, as soon as the police started questioning the wives, Kendra sang like a canary."

"Talk about fodder for a great *Baseball Wives* episode."

I nodded. "If the two of them can stay out of jail, they'll be sweeping the ratings for sure."

* * *

After my nails were Passion Pink and my toes had been soaked, scrubbed, and hot stone massaged, I made a quick stop at the *Informer*'s offices to drop off my press pass and apologize for dragging their good name through the mud. Almost literally. There was still grass and mud stuck in the lanyard.

Then I pointed my minivan toward home. I'd had enough of being the detective in the family, and I was looking forward to an afternoon of just being Mrs. Mom.

I pulled my van into the driveway and got out, listening at the door for the telltale signs of crying in stereo. Only there was nothing but quiet. Of course it was quiet. The kids were with Super Dad.

I stuck my key in the hole and pushed the door open.

"I'm home," I called out.

I stood in the doorway and blinked at the chaos in front of me.

The twins were on the floor finger painting with chocolate pudding (Oh, God, please let that be chocolate pudding!) on the newly cleaned rug. Livvie only had one sock on, and Max was missing a shirt. Both of them had their hair sticking up at odd angles, and I thought I detected a Cheerio stuck to the side of Max's face. Toys were scattered in every direction, and there was a loud noise coming from the laundry room.

"Jack?" I asked, stepping in a little farther into the house, looking for Mr. Mom himself.

He emerged from the laundry room, the sleeves of his black shirt rolled up to his elbows, arms covered in soapsuds, the front of his jeans smeared with something yellow, and I thought I saw a Cheerio in his hair as well.

I took a step forward, unable to suppress the grin taking over my face. "How's everything, honey?"

Ramirez blinked at me, giving a stunned look that quickly faded into defeat.

"You caught me. We haven't had a chance to clean up yet. I didn't expect you to be home so quickly."

"Dana canceled lunch. Her shoot went long." I paused, pulling the Cheerio from his hair. "Rough morning?" I asked.

A lopsided grin tugged at one corner of his mouth, "Babe, it's always a rough morning around here."

"Really?" I quirked an eyebrow at him. "And here I was thinking you were Mr. Mom."

"Mr. Mom?"

"Well, every time I came back from investigating something, you had the house immaculate, the laundry done, the kids looking like tidy, sleeping angels. I give up. How did you do it?"

The grin turned sheepish and Ramirez averted his eyes. "Busted," he finally said.

"Busted?" I quirked the other eyebrow.

He threw his hands up in the air tossing little bits of soapsuds onto the carpet. "All right. The truth is, the first day you left us alone, I overloaded the washing machine, I put the wrong soap in the dishwasher, Livvie swallowed a dime—which by the way, was a *ton* of fun when it came out the other end, and Max got a rubber eraser stuck up his nose—narrowly avoiding a trip to the emergency room."

I blinked, trying not to laugh.

"That's when I broke down and called in Mama," he admitted. "She and The Aunts have been here helping every day since."

"Every day?" I asked. The sneaky little rat had called in the big guns: Grandma.

"Okay, not every day," he conceded. "One day she was busy. So I called your mom."

I couldn't suppress the laugh any longer. "That's parenting cheating, and you know it!"

"Oh, yeah. I cheated big time. I'm man enough to admit it." He grinned at me. "Babe, I don't know how you do this every day. It's the hardest job ever."

I came in for a hug, ignoring the soapsuds. "It is also my favorite one," I told him.

"Honestly? Mine, too," he whispered into my hair. Then he leaned down and gave me a long, lingering kiss that made all thoughts of kids, party planners, and murderous baseball wives disappear.

When we came up for air, I looked over my shoulder at the twins, who were still gleefully finger-painting.

"Would it be wrong to call your aunts to come watch them for just *one* more day?" I asked suggestively.

Ramirez's face broke into a wicked grin. "If that's wrong, I don't ever want to be right."

ABOUT THE AUTHOR

Gemma Halliday is the *New York Times, USA Today* & #1 Kindle bestselling author of the High Heels Mysteries, the Hollywood Headlines Mysteries, the Jamie Bond Mysteries, the Tahoe Tessie Mysteries, the Marty Hudson Mysteries, and several other works. Gemma's books have received numerous awards, including a Golden Heart, two National Reader's Choice awards, a RONE Award, and three RITA nominations. She currently lives in the San Francisco Bay Area with her boyfriend, Jackson Stein, who writes vampire thrillers, and their four children, who are adorably distracting on a daily basis.

To learn more about Gemma, visit her online at http://www.gemmahalliday.com

Series in print now from Gemma Halliday...

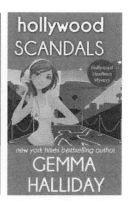

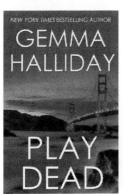
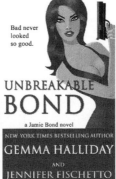

Want to get an email alert when the next High Heels Mystery is available? Sign up for my newsletter today and as a bonus receive a FREE ebook!

www.GemmaHalliday.com

Made in the USA
Columbia, SC
08 July 2019